Searching For Leah

By

John W. Huffman

OTHER NOVELS

A Wayward Wind

Tiger Woman

The Baron of Clayhill

Above All

Cold Hearts Burning

America's Diplomats, The Road To Attleboro

ISBN-13: 978-1466201392
ISBN-10: 1466201398

This book is a work of fiction. People, places, and situations are the product of the author's imagination. Any resemblance to actual persons, living or dead, are purely coincidental.

ACKNOWLEDGMENTS

My heartfelt thanks to Susan Scoggins, Sigrid Schroter Spangenberg, Gina Plant Roberts, Whitney Brock, and Kay Fuller for their invaluable input, advice, and recommendations in the early drafts of this book.

I give special recognition to Whitney Brock for the unique cover design, and to Fay Sprouse for the meticulous proof reading.

To each, I extended my deepest gratitude and appreciation.

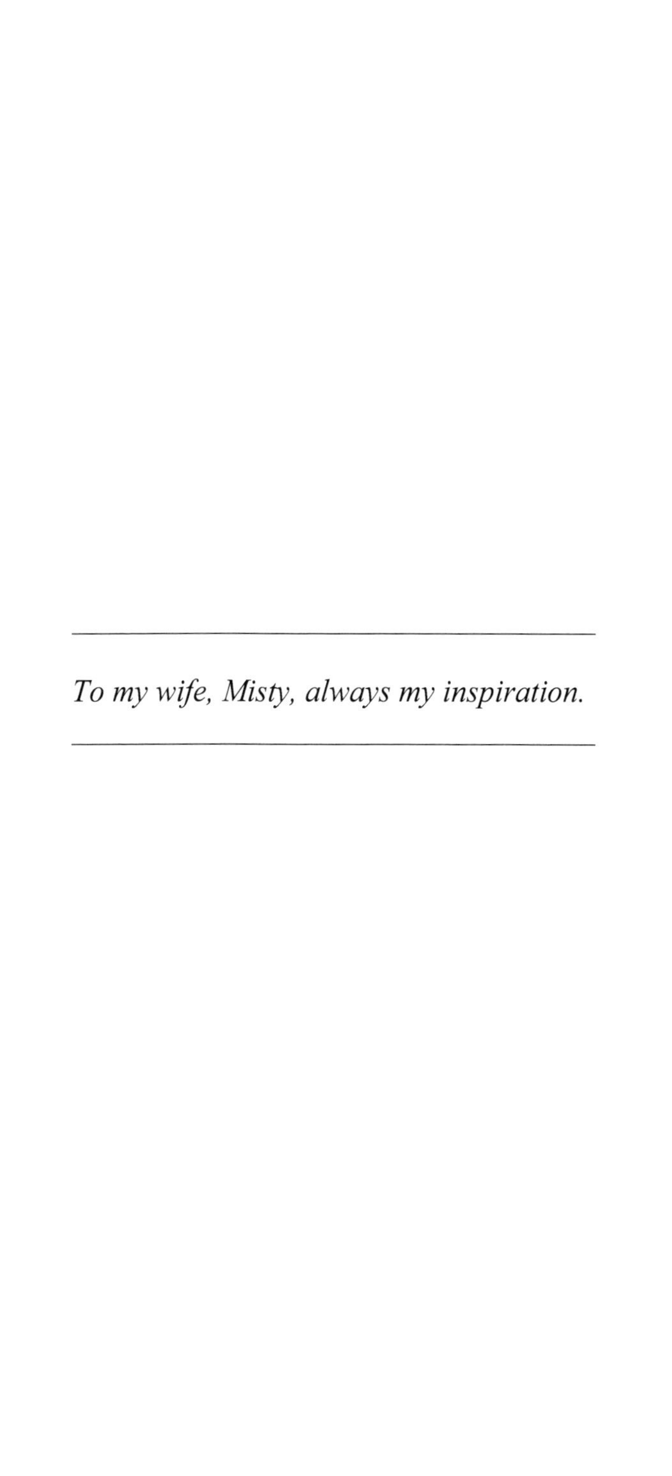

To my wife, Misty, always my inspiration.

Chapter One

So this is how the bottom feels Clint moped despondently as he shifted his cumbersome cast on his fractured left ankle, sucking in his breath when his three cracked ribs protested sharply. He glumly returned his sluggish, medicated thoughts to the last race of the series three days previously, which ended in a resounding crash into the outer wall on the last lap while scuffling for the third place position. Even more disparaging news followed the next day while still in the hospital—his primary sponsor was going with a new team for the upcoming season. He suspected his associate sponsor was in danger of leaving as well. Even if Raisin Bread stayed, he would only have enough funding to get through the first few races of the twenty-two scheduled events, assuming he didn't tear up anything in the process. If he couldn't land a new sponsor in the few short months between now and then, he'd be forced to hang around the pits like a dozen other wannabes hoping to fill in for a driver with a permanent ride who was sick or injured, a grim prospect indeed.

He started the season on a high note, which quickly spiraled downward into sour disappointment at midseason. Though running on a weak budget from the outset, he was fourth in the point standings at the time, a most coveted position in his rookie year, when the twenty-six team with their premier sponsor hired his very capable crew chief out from under him for twice the salary he could afford to pay. Afterwards, he hadn't finished in the top ten in a single race and dropped to the middle of the pack by season's end. Now he was in the uncomfortable position of having to search for a new benefactor and crew chief, and the middle of the point's standings was not a coveted position from which to attract either. The future indeed looked bleak.

"Hungry?" Skip asked, glancing at him in the rearview mirror as he steered the van into the parking lot of a building advertising *Rebecca's Seafood Restaurant* in weathered script.

"Where are we?" Clint asked, disorientated from having slept through most of the ten hours of their long trek north from the bottom of Florida.

Skip shut the engine off and swung his diminutive frame around. "On the outskirts of Charleston. This is supposed to be one of the best seafood joints in these parts."

"Hell, I know *I'm* starved," Ron groused from the bench seat behind Clint as he sat up yawning and stretching his thickset beer-barrel body.

"Count me in," Bobby agreed from the last bench seat in the rear as he sat up and rubbed his eyes.

Clint gingerly slid over to the door. "You guys are bottomless pits."

"Here, let me get that for you." Skip hurried around to open the sliding door.

"I can't afford to feed myself," Bobby grumbled as he worked his way forward in the narrow aisle, pointedly reminding them of his lowly position as a volunteer working for food and pit passes in order to gain enough experience to become a full-fledged paid team member.

Skip grabbed Clint's arm as he attempted to navigate the step down to the ground. "Here, let me help you."

"*Ouch*! *Damn*—you trying to finish me off?" Clint gasped as he stumbled down into a tentative half stoop.

"You're doing a pretty good job of that on your own," Skip retorted. "I could let you fall on your face and be done with it."

"You shouldn't even be moving around," Ron cajoled as he exited behind Clint. "You're supposed to be in bed."

"Doctors don't know nothing," Clint swore as he gingerly put weight on his left foot.

"They know you've got a bruised sternum, busted ribs, and a broke ankle," Ron quipped. "Checking yourself out of the hospital early wasn't one of your brightest moves. Here's your crutches."

"Put the damn things back. I can't stand up straight enough to get them under my arms!" Clint protested as he leaned against the side of the van seeking relief from the pain, his attention drawn to a red Corvette with two attractive blondes in shorts and halter-tops parking near them.

"Drivers are a dime a dozen and every damned one of them contrary as hell," Skip allowed, secure with his three years on Clint's team in offering his unflattering opinion.

"Losing our best car is the worst part," Bobby complained as he stepped out of the van, referring to the wreckage that had gone ahead of them in their primary hauler back to the shop.

"It'll never be competitive again, that's for sure," Ron allowed. "We'll have to make it a show car now."

"Best damned chassis we had," Bobby swore. "That damned twenty-six team! First they steal our crew chief, and then destroy our best car, the bastards."

Clint forced his body into some semblance of an erect posture and flashed a brilliant smile as the two women strolled by appraising the van with the number thirteen painted on the side followed by *Clint Long* written in script above AMERICAN RACING ASSOCIATION in block letters. He shifted awkwardly in a vain attempt to hide the *Sponsored by:* with the noticeable blank space formerly occupied by his primary sponsor before Skip peeled the letters off in a fit of rage, *and Spring Fresh Raisin Bread.* When they passed, he slouched and reluctantly refocused on the more pressing issue of breathing through the liquid fire in his lungs and walking on his own accord as he hobbled into the moderately filled restaurant and settled into a chair at the nearest table.

"I assume you'll be handing out pink slips over the next few days," Skip observed after placing his order for the Captain's Platter without consulting the menu.

Clint met his eyes. "Is that your subtle way of serving notice?"

Skip shrugged. "Nothing personal, my wife's just a little worried about our financial security …"

"Who made you an offer?" Clint challenged.

"Well … actually, Chuck did speak to me about a position with the twenty-six team …"

Clint nodded. "Maybe you should take it."

Skip shrugged. "Maybe, but I'd prefer to stay with you if you're going to be running next year."

Ron nodded, absorbed by his menu. "Same here. The forty-three team approached me as soon as they heard we lost our sponsor, but I've got two years invested in you and would prefer to stay here if possible."

Bobby sighed. "I signed on as a volunteer until somebody offers me a paying position, so I reckon I'll hang around till then."

Clint nodded grimly. "You're all good men. I appreciate your patience with my situation."

"You just need a break," Skip encouraged. "Hell, it don't pay much, but you still won rookie of the year, even as shitty as we ran after Chuck bailed on us. That ought to help you some in finding a new sponsor."

"That bastard!" Ron swore. "I didn't like him from the get-go. I can't believe you let him out of his contract."

"I didn't have a choice," Clint replied. "He had a clause that required me to match his best competitive offer during the season."

Skip scowled. "Nobody else wanted him when you hired him on."

Clint shrugged. "The only reason I got him so cheap to begin with was because his team ran so bad last year, but you have to admit he didn't have much of a driver to work with. He's a good crew chief and I was fortunate to have him for the time I did."

"Maybe so, but he also used you as stepping stone to get his own net worth jacked up."

"I agree," Ron added. "He didn't have much going for him until you came along and made him look good."

"Excuse me," a soft voice interrupted. "Is one of you a racecar driver?"

Bobby turned to the two women from the Corvette as they paused at the table, his gaze sweeping up their long, tanned legs. "You betcha, darling! This here's Clint Long, the best damned driver in the ARA."

Her brown eyes held Clint's. "Hi, I'm Carol. Can I have your autograph?"

"My pleasure, Carol."

The other one smiled engagingly. "Hi, I'm Sherry. Can I get my picture taken with you?"

Clint stood with difficulty, balancing his weight on his right foot. "With someone as pretty as you, it'd be my pleasure, Sherry."

Sherry hurried out to the car to get her camera as Carol produced a pen from her purse and pulled back her halter top to expose a generous portion of her left breast. "My boyfriend will kill me, but I don't care."

Clint signed the top of her breast and then posed with her and Sherry while Skip took their picture with Carol prominently displaying her new autograph.

"What happened to you?" Sherry asked as Clint eased painfully back into his chair.

"He rammed a cement retaining wall at a hundred and fifty miles an hour," Skip allowed dryly. "I've warned him about that time and again."

A young boy elbowed his way between Sherry and Carol. "Excuse me, can I have your autograph too, Mr. Long?"

Clint took the extended pen and paper. "Sure thing, young man, what's your name?"

"Harry. And can I get one for my sister, Mary? She's not here, but she would sure appreciate one too."

"You bet. Where are you from?"

"Moncks Corner," the boy replied, eyes shining in anticipation.

"Who's your favorite driver?"

"Dale, Jr. and before that I liked his old man in the three car, too."

"They're two of the best, partner," Clint agreed.

"I'm going to pull for you now, too."

Clint ruffled his hair. "I sure appreciate that, Harry. I'll try real hard to win one for you."

"Thank you, Clint," Sherry cooed. "You look me up if you're ever back down here in these parts, honey. I'm in the book under *S. Tanner*."

"I'll do that," Clint assured her with a flirtatious wink.

"Bye now, Clint," Carol echoed. "I'll be rooting for you next season."

"You do that, sweetheart. I need all the support I can get."

A woman approached holding a little girl by the hand. "Would it be an imposition to get an autograph for my daughter?"

"Not at all, Ma'am." Clint smiled at the child. "What's your name, sweetie?"

She shrank back shyly. "Melissa."

"Well, Melissa, you're sure a pretty little thing," he teased as several others formed a line behind them. "Do you have a boyfriend?"

"Hi, I'm the manager here," a slim brunette wearing an apron offered as she stepped up. "I'll comp your meals if you and your crew will pose with me in front of your racing van with my restaurant in the background."

"I'd consider that an honor, Ma'am …"

***

"That was fun," Skip allowed as they crawled into the van.

Ron slid into the driver's compartment. "Damned good seafood, too."

"You have a lot of patience," Bobby praised.

"Fans are what it's all about," Clint replied. "Without them none of us would have a job."

"Say, do any of you believe in them things?" Ron asked as he turned onto a side road leading back to the Interstate.

"Believe in what things?" Skip asked lazily from the backseat.

Ron pointed at a small, hand-lettered sign advertising *Readings by Miss Bessie* tacked onto a fencepost. "Them fortune-telling people."

"Hell no!" Skip scoffed. "Bunch of charlatans, is all they are."

"Whoa now, buddy," Ron argued. "Some of them are for real. My aunt's been seeing one for years and swears by her."

"Yeah?" Skip offered. "Then your aunt's as full of crap as you are."

"I'm serious," Ron insisted. "She ain't no flake either. She's got more money stashed away than any of us will ever see in our lifetime, I guarantee you that."

"I bet *you* ain't in her will no where's though," Skip chortled.

"If she's all that foolish, she'll probably leave her dough to her cat," Bobby agreed.

"Or more likely to that crazy fortune teller she goes to," Skip added.

Ron scowled at them in the rearview mirror. "Maybe so, but I—"

"*Stop*!" Clint ordered as an irresistible impulse coursed through him.

"*What tha hell*?" Ron swore as he slammed on the breaks, throwing everyone forward in their seats.

Clint clenched his teeth as he eased back onto his seat. "*Damn*, that was worse than hitting the wall!"

"Well, hell's bells, I thought I was running over something the way you yelled like that all of a sudden," Ron complained.

Clint pointed at the weathered clapboard hovel that looked near collapsing. "Pull in there."

"Are you kidding?" Ron demanded. "I said my *aunt* believes in them weirdo's, not *me*."

"I ain't going near that place," Bobby swore.

"Oh, hell, boys, let's have us some fun," Skip urged. "I'm about bored out of my wits from driving all day listening to you three snoring in the back."

"Are you serious?" Ron demanded.

"Pull in, damn it," Clint ordered. "And take it easy, for Christ sakes. I'm half dead as it is without you scrambling my insides any more than you already have."

"I ain't going in no she-devil's shack to let her put a hex on me and steal my soul," Bobby swore.

"You're probably going to hell anyway, so there's not much use in her bothering to steal your sorry old lost soul," Skip taunted.

"You got no call to talk like that, Skip," Bobby argued. "I live as right as the next man."

"Do you say your prayers like a good little boy every night before you go to bed like your mommy taught you?" Skip teased.

"I try to live decent enough like my mother taught me, and I ain't ashamed none to admit it," Bobby argued. "But it's hard to do around godless sinners like you."

"Lucky your mother wasn't standing there when the twenty-six car put Clint in the wall," Skip allowed. "She wouldn't have heard much Christian fellowship coming out of your foul mouth then."

"That's different," Bobby insisted. "Even the Lord could understand me being upset about that."

"I bet the Lord wouldn't have used your exact words in describing Glen Johnson afterwards," Skip chided. "Are you coming with us or not?"

"I'm staying right here," Bobby declared.

Ron opened his door. "I'll come in, but I ain't gonna get my fortune told. There's some things a man don't have a right knowing."

"Maybe she can tell me where to find a new sponsor," Clint teased as he limped up onto the porch and paused to knock amid the heady aroma of burning incense wafting out through the screen door.

"Come in, children," a frail voice beckoned.

Clint eased into the murky interior as Ron and Skip dogged his heels, his attention drawn to a single thick candle on a small table in the back corner of the room illuminating an old black woman sitting impassively, her face creased in folds and white patches of scalp showing through thin wisps of stringy gray hair. Her eyes stared straight ahead in unseeing milky orbs as she tugged at a black smock draped over her wizened, hunched frame and pointed a spindly finger at Clint.

"Sit down, youngster," she cackled. "You intrigue me. You come to me in pain, yet I sense you do not seek solace for your bodily injuries."

Clint eased into the chair across from her. "What do you charge for a reading, Ma'am?"

"Recompense comes from the heart based upon the merit you find in my assistance," she replied. "Place your hands on the table before me, youngster."

She clasped his hands with a strong grip, and then shuddered as if jolted by electricity as she swung her head about wildly, her unseeing eyes rolling back in her skull as she emitted a low, shuddering wail.

Ron shrank back. "She's having a stroke or something!"

"Ma'am?" Clint gasped, attempting to extract his hands from her vise grip.

"She's putting a spell on you, Clint!" Ron yelped. "Turn her loose!"

Clint jerked the old woman halfway across the table as he lurched up. "*She's holding on too tight*!"

Ron lunged for the door. "I'm to hell outta here!"

"Help me pry Clint loose!" Skip yelled.

"Are you *crazy*?" Ron demanded. "I ain't touching her!"

Clint lurched back, wincing from the pain stabbing at his ribs as the old black woman released him and collapsed back into her chair panting.

"*You … you're the one*!" she gasped. "*I-It's a miracle*!"

"I'm outta here!" Ron swore. "This shit's getting crazy!"

"Come on, Clint!" Skip urged, tugging at his arm.

Clint backed away unsteadily. "Are you okay, Ma'am?"

"Please," the old woman gasped. "I need to talk with you, youngster!"

"Sorry, Ma'am, we're on a tight schedule," Clint advised as he limped to the door. "Are you okay now? Do we need to call someone for you?"

"Please, youngster, you must wait," the old woman wailed as they stumbled out the door in a cluster. "I must speak with you! This is truly a miracle!"

Skip helped Clint into the back of the van and slammed the door shut behind them as Ron fired up the engine and backed rapidly down the lane.

"*Ouch*! *Easy*!" Clint groaned as the vehicle jostled across the ruts in the dirt driveway.

"What happened back there?" Bobby demanded, wide-eyed.

"Damned if I know," Skip panted. "Some old hag started having a satanic fit or something when she took Clint's hands, yelling he was the one and that it was a miracle, or some shit like that. It was weird, man."

"S-she s-scared the l-living s-shit out of me," Ron stuttered as he fought the wheel around and shifted into a forward gear."

"I knew you shouldn't have gone in there!" Bobby admonished. "She didn't steal your souls or anything, did she?"

Clint turned to him with bared teeth. "*Ohooooo*! *Fresh blood*! *Let's drink our fill*!"

"*Arraaaahhhhhh*!" Bobby yelped as he lunged over the backseat clawing at the rear door.

Skip, convulsed in laughter as Ron hit the gas and surged forward dumping Bobby on his head, grabbed his wildly kicking legs and tugged him back into his seat. "Easy, Partner, Clint was only joshing you."

"*You're all a bunch of degenerates*!" Bobby bellowed through their peals of laughter. "*I swear to hell I'm joining up with Glen Johnson and the twenty-six team as soon as we get back to Charlotte*! *I swear I am*!"

Chapter Two

The four men and eight women mutely entered the old barn, each carrying a black velvet pouch. They stripped off their clothes and meticulously hung them on a peg on the wall before drawing robes of various colors over their bare skin. When cloaked, they filed clockwise to the center of the barn to pause behind twelve wooden chairs forming a nine-foot circle facing a small round table where a strong maiden, young in years with flowing golden hair robed in white with gold trim, waited with arms crossed reverently over her chest. The strong maiden uncrossed her arms, picked up the single black candle burning on the table, and walked clockwise around the circle using the tip to light each of the two white candles situated between the four larger unlit ones standing to the north, east, south, and west of the circle. She replaced the candle on the table, picked up a small bell, rang it three times, and again crossed her arms over her breasts. Twelve robed members from each of the twelve tribes entered in a long line circling clockwise to align themselves behind their individual tribal leaders in the inner circle and sank down on the floor cross-legged one behind the other in the outer fringes of the iridescent candle light. The strong maiden lifted the black candle, touched the flame to a small silver censer, and waited for the flash to die into embers.

"I consecrate this circle to ward off all evil that may dwell here," she intoned as she walked clockwise around the circle start to end, swinging the censer to and fro, filling the air with a pleasing fragrance to mix with the fresh sweetness of new-bound hay.

"Blessed be!" each inner circle member intoned as she passed, sweeping their palms through the trailing smoke to pull the scent around themselves.

The strong maiden replaced the censer on the table, picked up a small athame, passed the short blade over the flame of the flickering black candle, and used the point of the ceremonial dagger to etch a pentagram in a base of smooth sea salt spread in the center of the table. She then dipped the point into the center of the pentagram and tipped the pinch of sea salt into a bowl of fresh spring water beside it, picked up the bowl, and walked the circle clockwise, pausing before each council member.

"I cleanse thee for purity of thought and deed," she blessed as she placed her finger in the water and touched it to their forehead, left thigh, right shoulder, left shoulder, right thigh, and back to their forehead.

"Blessed be," each member replied before removing a clear crystal skull from the velvet pouch and placing it on a pedestal on the back of their chair.

When the strong maiden completed the circle, she returned the bowl to the table and crossed her arms over her breasts.

Merle, at one hundred years the second eldest member of council, shuffled forward with his Book of Shadows clutched against his sleek silver robe, placed it on the table, and picked up the black candle. In his stooped posture, he walked to the large unlit blue candle in the eastern quadrant standing on a pedestal and lifted the black candle high.

"Oh mighty essence of hallowed air, from darkness I give you light and beg of you to share in our rite so that we may honor your life sustaining oxygen. I bid you hail and welcome!"

"*Hail and welcome*!" all chanted as he touched the tip of the black candle to the larger blue one.

He circled to the large red candle in the south and raised the black candle above it. "Oh mighty essence of hallowed fire, from darkness I give you light and beg you to share in our rite so that we may honor your life sustaining warmth. I bid you hail and welcome!"

"*Hail and welcome*!" all chanted as he touched the flame to the wick.

He continued clockwise to the large green candle in the western quadrant and lifted his candle. "Oh mighty essence of hallowed water, from darkness I give you light and beg you to share in our rite so that we may honor your life sustaining moisture. I bid you hail and welcome!"

"*Hail and welcome*!" all chanted as he touched tips to share the flame.

He made his way to the yellow candle in the north and raised the candle above it. "Oh mighty essence of hallowed earth, from darkness I give you light and beg you to share in our rite so that we may honor your life sustaining harvests. I bid you hail and welcome!"

"*Hail and welcome*!" all chanted as he touched flame to bring forth flame.

He shuffled back to the center of the circle and spread his arms skyward with black candle extended. "Oh Ultimate Deity, from darkness you gave us life and I beg you to share in our rite so that we may honor all you have created. I bid you hail and welcome!"

"Hail and welcome to the Ultimate Deity! *Hail and welcome to the Ultimate Deity*! *HAIL AND WELCOME TO THE ULTIMATE DEITY*!" they chanted in unison, each salutation rising in volume as the crystal skulls over their chairs pulsed in a kaleidoscope of colors and rose above their circle in a shimmering cone to merge into an apex of pure white in the center.

Merle leaned forward and briskly blew out the black candle. "So mote it be!" he ordered in the sudden silence.

"Blessed be!" the others chanted in unison before seating themselves in their chairs with their focus on Merle standing in the center of the circle.

"We gather as High Priests and Priestesses of the original twelve tribes the ancient ones placed here to populate this planet," he announced in a feeble voice. "For many thousands of years we were held in great esteem by kings and commoners alike, who sought us out for our magic, our cures and spells, and our visions.

"Though the oldest dogma on earth, for reasons we still cannot fathom, the emerging Christian religions in the Middle Ages labeled us as pagans and vilified our sacred Craft as an evil cult. We were horribly persecuted and burned at the stake or hung from the gallows until ultimately driven into the wilderness and banned from contact with our fellow man.

"Our hallowed ancestors slowly came together from the many far-flung continents to this single land of touted religious freedom in hopes of massing our collective strengths, only again to face persecution in Salem and points beyond.

"Thus for over five centuries we have been driven underground to become obscure and all but forgotten. In spite of all, we persevered into this modern era, where others rarely take us seriously. Indeed, they consider our Craft and even we as individuals slightly deranged. We no longer enjoy the liberty to be that which we are, but instead, pretend to be that which we are not. Over time, our natural powers have eroded and become weak. We are near extinction and daily drift further from the rhythms of nature and the all-encompassing vitality of the universe, whose elements are our essential life forces.

"Thus I have summoned you for a most important disclosure—a revelation that could reverse our ill fortunes and restore us to our former reverence." Merle pause as all leaned forward in anticipation. "I take great satisfaction in informing you that a member of Council has discovered the long-rumored eleventh genetic linkage!"

An immediate uproar ensued as members of Council lurched to their feet and others shrank back in shocked disbelief, while individuals within the tribes outside the circle whispered hurriedly amongst themselves amid mutterings of "*Blessed be*!"

Merle rapped on his Book of Shadows with his gnarled knuckles until the chaos subsided into awed silence. A tall, thin, balding man in his forties dressed in his ceremonial purple cloak stood in the renewed hush.

"Master Merle, you have been of Council longer that I have been born. You have given me the benefit of your wisdom throughout my life. I hesitate to challenge you, but are you suggesting that nature on its own accord has actually achieved what we and our hallowed ancestors could not accomplish in five thousand years?"

Merle turned to him. "Master Vaughn, you are a wise and widely respected banker in the other world, and have proven a credit to our society in this world. You have no need to hesitate to challenge me on this issue, for a matter of such gravity certainly warrants a high degree of skepticism. Let our member of Council address this matter directly."

He turned to the feeble black woman with her crop of erratic white hair contrasting against her ceremonial robe of pure black heightening the dark mass of wrinkled creases holding milky eyes. With the sudden focus of attention, a large ancient cat with scraggly white hair leapt up on the arm of her chair and surveyed the assembled group with hostile yellow eyes as it disdainfully flicked its tattered tail.

"Aunt Bessie, please address Council on this matter, if you please?" Merle directed as he seated himself in his chair.

"This one came to me quite by accident," she rasped, her unseeing eyes staring straight ahead as all leaned forward to catch her words. "He stopped by as a lark to have his palm read with some friends."

A heavyset woman in her thirties wearing a gold cloak with ringlets of brown hair cascading around her shoulders stood. "And through this reading you saw he possessed eleven of our genetic linkages?"

Aunt Bessie turned her head to the voice. "He wore a talisman of some sort, Lily, which allowed me only bewildering images upon direct contact with his persona. There was much information to absorb in such a short span by a mind as weak as mine, thus I mainly saw a confusing jumble of imagery. But I had a brief moment to clearly read this one's aura, and was quite startled when I recognized him as the rumored one."

A white haired man in his sixties stood and gathered his flowing yellow robe around him. "Aunt Bessie, with all this confusion, could you please elaborate on exactly what you saw in his aura?"

"Adrian, you will recall nearly a quarter of a century ago when a well-respected member of our world, who was a doctor in the other world, birthed the child of a couple in a crisis and recognized the lineage of the male child he delivered as holding eleven of the twelve crucial genetic links. When the doctor urged the parents to meet with Council to verify their child's lineage, the parents became alarmed at such a proposal and chose to flee before he could arrange for such to occur. I clearly recognized this one as that child."

A matronly Asian woman in her early sixties wearing a light brown robe stood. "Meaning no disrespect, Aunt Bessie, but due to your age and this blockage you speak of which produced confusing images resonating from his aura, I propose we obtain additional verification by another member of Council to authenticate this one's true lineage."

"I take no offense of this, Shoshanna," Aunt Bessie replied. "Some say I'm might-near a hundred and twenty years. I don't rightly know for sure. I quit counting when I was a young woman in my eighties. It doesn't matter really. I'm still here and functioning, though my body has journeyed far beyond its expected time and my eyes are filled with cataracts that rob me of sight. Fortunately, I am still blessed with wisdom and knowledge, the very things you often seek of me, and of which I always give freely, though my mind is oftentimes frail." She stroked Jasmine to settle her down on the arm of the chair.

A light green robed, slim, attractive woman in her early thirties with flowing blonde hair stood. "What did you tell this one, Aunt Bessie?"

Aunt Bessie turned her head in her direction. "I was unable to tell this one anything, Gretchen. In the short time I had before he became alarmed and withdrew his hand from mine, I saw only that he currently lives in Charlotte, North Carolina."

Hellene stood. "Is it to be Council's intent to lure this one to our Craft in order to foster a connection with the remaining twelfth linkage?"

Drew stood. "We are *not* going to *lure* this one *anywhere* within our Craft, Hellene. We must carefully watch ourselves on this matter."

Ginger stood. "I suggest we delay our debate on our actions concerning this one until we have confirmation of his lineage."

Lily stood. "I agree. Until we have corroboration, discussing further actions is pointless."

Merle looked around the circle. "Are there any objections to Shoshanna's proposal to get a second reading of this one by another member of Council?"

Herschel, a thin woman in her late thirties robed in light gray stood. "What about this one's blockage Aunt Bessie speaks of that gives confusing images?"

A plumpish, attractive woman in her early thirties with raven black hair and a dark pink robe stood. "Surely we must remove the impediment to get a clear reading?"

Drew stood in his splendid red robe. "A point well taken, but how would one go about performing this deed?"

A short, stout woman in her mid-forties wearing a hunter green satin robe stood. "Aunt Bessie has indicated this one is young in years. I propose we dispatch someone near his own age and attempt to forge a bond of trust with him."

A dark haired, attractive woman in her early twenties wearing a modern, lightweight, burnt-orange robe stood. "I would deem it an honor to attempt to verify this one's lineage, if that is Council's wish. But where do I find this one?"

Vaughn stood. "That is very noble of you, Lola. Aunt Bessie, what is this one's name?"

Aunt Bessie turned to him. "Clint Long."

Vaughn went to the table, picked up the athame, stood before the circle in the east, swiftly cut an opening in the cone of light, hurried to his gray double-breasted suit hanging on a peg on the wall, and extracted a cell phone. "Yes, Information? Charlotte, North Carolina, please. Yes, I need a listing for a Clint Long. Yes, and do you have an address?" Vaughn pulled a pad and pen from his suit pocket. "Thank you." He closed the cover, replaced the phone in a pocket, and smiled smugly as he reentered the circle, sliced a pentagram in the air to reseal the cone, and thrust the paper at Lola. “Onward to Charlotte for verification!”

Allay turned to Lola. “Since this is so significant to us, should not another accompany you to get double verification?”

“If Council feels the need, my friend Gretchen may accompany me, if she so wishes,” Lola offered.

A thin, waspish Hispanic woman in her seventies stood, her blue robe flawlessly arranged around her prim body. “Let the matter be settled before Council then. Lola and Gretchen will visit this one in Charlotte to attempt to verify his lineage.”

Merle nodded. “Thank you, Hellene. Does any other member of Council wish to address any other issue? Then let us give our blessings to our Deity and bid our wishes of goodwill to each and all.”

The strong maiden took a platter from the table and circled the council counterclockwise passing out cake and small goblets of wine to the council members. When she returned the platter to the table and crossed her arms, Merle broke off a piece of his cake and placed it on the ground at his feet, spilled a few drops of wine on it, and lifted his goblet high in toast.

“If it harm none, do as ye will!”

“Blessed be, so mote it be!” the others chanted before taking a bite of cake and a sip of their wine.

Merle set his goblet on the table, picked up the athame, and pointed it high in the center at the circle of white light. “We bid our Ultimate Deity thanks and farewell!”

“Thanks and farewell to our Ultimate Deity, blessed be!” the circle chanted as the multi-colors of light slowly dimmed and faded back into the crystal skulls.

Merle walked to the eastern large blue candle and poised the athame over the flame. "We bid our essence of air thanks and farewell!"

"Thanks and farewell," the circle chanted as he used the flat side to snuff out the flame.

Merle repeated the salutation counterclockwise around the circle to the essence of earth in the north, water in the west, and fire in the south before returning the athame to the table.

The strong maiden then picked up her tray and paraded counterclockwise around the circle pausing before each council member.

"Blessed be to thee!" she chanted as they placed their goblet on her tray.

"So mote it be," the members of Council intoned as they stood and placed the skulls in the velvet pouches.

The strong maiden placed the tray on the table, picked up the censer, and walked counterclockwise end to start around the circle. As she passed, the council members filed out of the circle counterclockwise to remove their robes and redress.

When the last member of Council departed through the barn door, the strong maiden rang her bell three times and the individual tribes stood in sequence and filed counterclockwise from the room in silence.

Chapter Three

Clint hobbled over, leaned his crutches against the side of the booth, and eased his sore body in across from Carl Peterson and Joe Miller.

Peterson shifted his heavyset, late fifties, leather skinned bulk topped with short gray-flecked hair and extended his hand as Joe Miller's, tall, lanky, mid-forties frame slouched beside him.

"Thanks for coming, Clint. Beer?" Peterson motioned for the waitress, who hurried from her station at the end of the bar to smile invitingly at them. "Beer for my *compadre* here, sweetie." Peterson eyed her shapely legs below her short cocktail skirt as she turned to fill the order, and then shifted his attention to a petite brunette and a curvaceous blonde who entered together, giving them his full attention as they strolled past to sit at the bar before smacking his lips suggestively. "I'll take either one of those babes for the main course and the other for dessert."

"So what's on your mind, Mr. Peterson?" Clint asked, looking him in the eye.

Peterson smiled, continuing to stare at the two women. “Straight to the point, Clint, just like you drive. I like that. Sorry about Florida. You healing up okay?”

“I’m fine, thanks,” Clint lied, unwilling to admit his left ankle was giving him constant pain. “I’ll be better in a couple of weeks when I get this cast off.”

“The twenty-six car leaned on you pretty hard there at the end, didn’t he?”

“We were both leaning on each other hard, seeing as it was the last lap,” Clint replied, following the unwritten code amongst racers of not commenting on an ongoing feud with another driver because rumors could run wild to exaggerate the smallest thing said. “I just got the short end of it. That’s racing.”

Peterson grinned knowingly. “Uh huh, I suspect a little payback is in store somewhere down the road.” When Clint didn’t change expression, Peterson’s crafty smile waned and his gaze refocused on the two women at the bar. “To be frank, Clint, I’m interested in discussing you running my thirty-three car this coming season.”

Clint hesitated, subtly aware that the thirty-three team, sponsored by a grocery chain headquartered in Charlotte, was sorely under-funded. “Thanks for the consideration, Mr. Peterson, but I have my own car to run,” he replied as the waitress sat his beer in front of him.

“Set those two lovelies at the bar up with a round on me, darling,” Peterson ordered, and again watched her shapely derrière departing. “They didn’t make ‘um like that in my day,” he remarked before refocusing on Clint. “The word on the street is you don’t have a sponsor. I’m not making a formal offer to you for the ride, you understand, I'm just thinking out loud, so there's no reason to play hardball at this point."

Clint masked his irritation at the reminder of only having the partial sponsorship from Raisin Bread, which was barely enough to start the season, and ruefully reminded himself that his meeting with two other potential sponsors the previous week had produced nothing close to a commitment. Though he had appointments with several other prospects, he gauged the chances of picking up a major sponsor this late in the season virtually slim to none. At this stage, he should seriously consider running for another team, but Peterson's outfit would never be a consideration, at least not at the moment—desperation tended to make *never* a short time span.

"I'm honored you would consider me driving for you, Mr. Peterson," Clint replied evenly. "You've got a good team and a very capable crew chief in Joe here, but I'm committed at present to running my own team next season. If things don't work out for me in the next few months sponsor wise, I might be forced to reconsider."

Joe Miller pulled his attention from the two women at the bar and scowled. "We intend to narrow our short list down by the end of the week, so we don't have time for indecision. No hard feelings, but if you need time to think about it, I can make better use of my time by moseying on over there and laying a load of charm on those two whores who can't seem to take their eyes off us. Excuse me." He slid out of the booth and ambled over to the women, leering.

Peterson frowned. "Look, Joe didn't mean to come across that way, Clint. Hell, he's just a little abrupt at times. I know you two have had some differences in the past, but that's part of racing. He's a good crew chief. Nobody can argue that fact. I think you two could work some magic together if you ever got on the same wavelength."

Clint nodded. "I'll think on it, Mr. Peterson, and again, I appreciate your consideration."

Peterson's jaw hardened. "Like I said, this wasn't an official offer or anything, just an exploratory discussion. If you'll excuse me, I'm going on over there to help Joe out with those two little cutie pies. They look lonely. Enjoy your beer." He slid out of the booth and strolled over to the two women sitting at the bar.

Clint sat back, picked up his beer, and sipped. Had he made a mistake? Most likely, but Carl Peterson's race team was not where he wanted to be. For one thing, Peterson was a known drunk with a bad temper who had hired and fired no less than four drivers the past season, mostly without justification. For another, Miller was a good crew chief, but he'd never gotten along with Joe and probably never would since their dispositions were too dissimilar for a good working relationship, an essential ingredient for a winning team. Lastly was the poor quality of the sponsorship for Peterson's team. Unfortunately, the almighty dollar sign was the symbol for speed in today's racing venue. Still, he hadn't burnt any bridges. If bad came to worse, he'd be willing to race a dump truck for the County Sanitation Department in order to compete in the ARA.

"Hi, handsome, I'm Lola. Can I buy you a drink?"

Clint glanced up at the attractive brunette from the bar standing beside his table, taking in her promising smile below almond eyes with long lashes in a pretty face and slender, enticing body in a clinging white curve enhancing dress.

"Hi yourself, darling, I'm Clint Long. Have a seat," he offered, glancing over at the blonde watching Lola with interest, as Peterson and Joe sat on each side of her staring at him with envious hostility.

Chapter Four

"What are your findings for Council concerning this one?" Merle asked of Lola without preamble as the council settled into their seats around the circle after completing the opening ceremony.

Lola stood. "This persona does in fact have eleven genetic linkages, as Aunt Bessie initially reported."

Merle waited for the clamor from the assembled tribes to quite. "Give your verification to Council."

"Gretchen and I arrived at this one's address just as he was leaving and followed him to a local pub, where he had a business meeting of some sort with two other men. When the meeting ended, I decided to meet with this one in the casual setting and offered to buy him a drink. I found him to be very outgoing and attractive. He was pleased I had a room close by and eagerly joined me there. Afterwards, I had much time to analyze the sequence of his lineage as he slept. I have documented this in my Book of Shadows for your review." She handed her journal to Shoshanna to study and pass around the circle. "As you can see, this one's lineage began in 1454 when a High Priestess from the tribe Dana passed her seed to a son. She was burned at the stake in Spain shortly afterwards, and the father, from the tribe Zaire, took their infant son and fled the country to protect him. The father became ill during the journey and placed a protective Tiger's Eye talisman around his neck before passing on to the other side, thus never exposing his son to our Craft.

"The child was taken in by a Christian family and grew into a man to begat a firstborn daughter with a maiden from the tribe Tarawa. The daughter grew into a woman and begat a firstborn daughter with a member of the tribe Kato. That daughter grew and begat a firstborn son with a member of the tribe Demy, and so on firstborns through the Ilk, Fen-din, Aikido, Be-zed, Mimeo, and Liana tribes, all quite by accident and all without ever knowing of any genetic connections to council members up to the present time. Through these generations, the chain remained unbroken with the talisman handed down as a family heirloom to the firstborn, thus producing a blockage for each persona in the line through the many centuries past.

Gretchen stood. "I too verify this as true. Lola spent two engaging nights with this one as I listened from an adjoining room while their tryst took place, each time with his protective Tiger's Eye talisman removed when she complained it was cold against her skin. With Lola's assistance, I even slipped into the room while he slept on the second night and laid my palm against his chest to read his aura myself."

Merle's eyes swept the group. "That would make the only missing genetic connection my own tribe, Jacopo. Does anyone wish to challenge this report to Council, or desire further proof?"

Adrian stood with a concerned countenance. "I trust you did not find this task on Council's behalf too taxing, Lola?"

Lola smiled as she stood. "Not at all, Master Adrian, in spite of his injuries, I found this one to be a consummate lover and am predisposed to spending more time with him of my own accord."

Gretchen stood. "I would enjoy spending time with this one myself. Two nights of listening has left me wanting for his touch. He is very handsome and masculine."

Hellene stood, sharply impatient. "Could we please channel this discussion back into a more constructive format? Was there any indication of this one's beliefs?"

Lola stood. "I teased this one a bit to feel him out about our Craft. He thinks we are something of a joke and slightly off center. His beliefs are jumbled and confused. He does believe in a higher Deity, but can't bring it to focus in a specific realm."

Merle stood in his stooped fashion. "It is good that this one is not fixated on the Christian form of their God. We may be able to work him around to our Craft in time."

Vaughn stood abruptly. "We cannot cross the line here! Our Craft must be of one's own choosing. We must only make this one aware and not lead him where he does not choose to go. We must be eternally vigilant in this matter."

Ginger stood. "But what if this one does not choose of his own free will to join our Craft? His sacred lineage could be lost to us."

"I suggest we consider gathering his seed without his knowledge to complete the final genetic link," Aunt Bessie spoke quietly from her chair.

In the stunned silence, Drew stood and adjusted his disheveled scarlet robe. "Aunt Bessie, surely you are aware that taking his seed without his consent would be a wrong fostered upon him?"

"This one is obviously not of our world, therefore giving his seed freely is not something we could expect him to consent to," Aunt Bessie replied. "But by gathering his seed to complete the lineage through his firstborn, does not all mankind benefit?"

Lola stood hesitantly. "I am the youngest of Council and offer my thoughts with great care. I caution Council that this one is young and promiscuous, and as such, is subject to pass his seed accidentally to a female at any time. When I was with him he showed no concern for preventing such from occurring, leaving that responsibility to the female he couples with, as most males do in this age. Would it wrong him to take his seed deliberately under such circumstances?"

Hellene stood. "I agree with Lola that in view of his promiscuous tendencies, no harm occurs under that situation. I suggest we charge Merle to find a maiden of his tribe Jacopo willing to serve as his vessel and gather his sacred seed as soon as possible."

Lily stood. "I think this suggestion is highly unusual and fraught with hazard of violating our Rede!"

"I offer my insight on this issue," Aunt Bessie replied from her seated position. "Under normal circumstances, I would be prone to agree, but these are not normal circumstances. I have considered this issue carefully and taken it upon myself to exchange thoughts with my friend Hazel from Merle's tribe Jacopo, as I am the Godmother to her daughter, Leah. After great deliberation, Hazel assures me Leah is willing to serve as this one's vessel and pledges her purity until we can make the essential arrangements for this one to cleave with her."

Drew stood. "What essential arrangements do you foresee Council having to contend with in this endeavor, Aunt Bessie?"

"Hazel … insists this event must occur at her home on the outskirts of New Orleans. She will not agree to transport Leah to this one and insists he must come to Leah. The problem is Louisiana is a considerable distance from North Carolina. We will need to conceive of a plan to lure this one to Leah there."

Hellene stood. "Hazel and Leah are Solitaries, are they not? Should we not select another maiden from the tribe Jacopo with a more accommodating tribal disposition instead of sending this one to someone who practices alone?"

"Hellene, the fact that Hazel and Leah are Solitaries has no bearing on this issue," Aunt Bessie admonished. "Gathering this one's seed is our first priority. In the regard of using another, we could spend valuable time looking for what we already have, an attractive eighteen-year-old female who is pure and willing to serve as this one's vessel for his sacred seed. Is this not the most essential consideration?"

Hellene stood. "What are the merits of this Leah for such an honor other than her purity? How advanced is she in our Craft? Are there not better candidates that Council need consider before we proceed?"

"Leah is pure, of course, which is important in serving as a vessel for this one's seed," Aunt Bessie replied. "Beyond that, she is highly advanced in contact visions, in fact, skilled beyond most with vastly more training than she has thus far received, as she seems to come by this talent naturally. She is true to our Craft, though a Solitary due to the influence of her mother. She is progressing well in her cures and shows promising aptitude to be a great healer, spiritually as well as physically, though she is still very young and has much to learn. She is adequate in her spells, though mostly uninterested in this area of magic. Her major weaknesses are telepathy and immaturity."

Adrian stood. "Could you please elaborate on these weaknesses, Aunt Bessie?"

Aunt Bessie turned to him. "Being a Solitary, she does not regularly meet with others or exchange thoughts, therefore has virtually no psychic telecommunication skills other than to read others directly by touch. We can overcome this by channeling our communications through Hazel. Leah's greater weakness is in knowing virtually nothing of those in the other world due to Hazel keeping her in such a sheltered environment."

Vaughn stood. "I do not feel these deficiencies disqualify Leah from serving as this one's vessel. I propose we proceed with the task of gathering his sacred seed in Leah, and then we can determine a proper approach to him concerning our Craft."

Lily stood and smoothed her gold cloak. "Aunt Bessie, please explain to Council how you and Hazel intend to prepare Leah to receive this one's seed. If Leah is as primitive and innocent as you say, surely her preparation is of great importance, otherwise she could fail to entice this one to cleave to her and all of our efforts would be for naught."

Allay stood with a secretive smirk. "It has always been my experience that naïve and inexperienced young females draw out the basic beast lurking in the male persona."

Adrian stood indignantly. "There is no cause for crudeness, Allay! All males are not beasts who prey on innocent, naïve young females!"

Merle rapped his knuckles on his Book of Shadows to calm the uproar. "We will observe a modem of order! Please, Aunt Bessie, address Council on this issue."

Aunt Bessie nodded. "I have every confidence Hazel will adequately prepare Leah in receiving this one's seed when the time approaches."

Adrian stood. "Is that wise, Aunt Bessie? Would not a more modern female better serve to coach Leah through this significant phase of her lifecycle? If Hazel has thus far failed to teach her the basic principles of coping with the other world, as you have advised, how can we be sure she is capable of teaching her the basics of attracting and coupling with a male from that world? Hazel is an old woman. She may well have forgotten what a female is expected to know on that topic and be incapable of properly coaching her. I feel this matter is far too important for us to leave to chance. We cannot afford to have her fail to appeal to this one in this instance."

Aunt Bessie fixed her unseeing eyes on Adrian. "You see before you an old, weathered crone, nearly bald and near blind as well. I am what you see. But I wasn't always so. Once I too was a beautiful, naïve young girl with flowing hair and a zest for life. I have not forgotten those days, nor lost my knowledge of the carnal pleasures derived from coupling. Does any member of Council seriously question Hazel's ability in this endeavor after bringing a child of her own into this world?"

Drew stood. "I still feel the essential central question here is what if this one does not desire to cleave with Leah when we lure him to Hazel's?"

Aunt Bessie sat quietly for a moment. "I propose in that eventuality, we cast a spell to ensure he does couple with Leah. Gathering his sacred seed is paramount, is it not?"

Vaughn stood with a pained expression. "Aunt Bessie, what you are proposing is not within our Rede! To cast a spell to have this one cleave to Leah, whose main qualification is the fact that she is a virgin, in order to conceive his firstborn child is highly improper, it would seem. An attempt to inflict our will upon him without his consent is subject to the three-fold law. What goes around comes around and we open ourselves to three times the bad karma to be inflicted back down upon us, as you well know."

Aunt Bessie nodded. "You are right, Master Vaughn, if it so happens they cleave together without this one's free choice and it in fact turns out to be a wrong inflicted upon him. As I have stated, my first thought is to gather his seed. I ask for full advice of Council in this matter and thus will be properly guided, I trust."

Lily stood. "If we successfully lure this one to Leah and he does not find her desirable enough to couple with, what spell are we to cast on him in order to coerce him into copulating with her that will not be going against our Rede?"

Drew stood. "If our objective here is simply to gather his seed, we can cast a primitive spell of lust. After they have coupled and Leah has received his seed, he need never know what transpired. It would be no different than if he planted his seed in some female he met casually in a bar, such as with Lola."

Herschel stood. "I agree with Drew. If we permit a lust spell, it is of no wrong to this one since he is a young man with promiscuous tendencies to begin with. Since Leah is willing to serve as the vessel, she is not wronged either. Therefore, we will not be subjected to three-fold bad karma for our actions."

Drew stood. "And it harm none, do as ye will."

Shoshanna stood. "For the good of all is the only reason one should cast a spell. This ensures the three-fold law of good karma in return. Is it not truly for the good of all to have the Council of Thirteen finally formed after five-thousand years to serve all?"

Ginger stood and smoothed back her black cloak. "I do not wish to further cast disparaging doubts upon Hazel's competence in this regard per se, but due to the importance of this occurrence, I think it imperative that Council directly confirm the passing of this one's seed to Leah in view of the significance of the event."

Drew stood. "How do you propose Council verify this, Ginger? Surely you do not suggest a member of Council observe their union firsthand?"

Hellene stood. "It is an important consideration Ginger has surfaced. We may only get one chance to pass this one's seed. I agree it is important that Council ensure the seed is passed before we allow their union to dissolve."

Merle stood. "In view of Leah's innocence and naivety, and this one's lack of knowledge as to our objective, it will be impractical for a member of Council to observe the coupling. We are expecting too much from the circumstances given. I see no reason we cannot place our trust in Hazel in this matter as well."

"It is not a matter of trust, it is a matter of confirmation," Hellene insisted as she rose to her feet. "Regardless of what Lola experienced, what if this one should impulsively use some form of protection, as many young men are inclined to do these days, and the seed does not take? We must ensure their union is free of these unfavorable possibilities."

Gretchen stood. "But how is this to be done? Short of actually observing the mating and watching for these potential problems, how will we know for certain they have not occurred?"

Allay stood. "It is not totally inconceivable that another party cannot be present. If this one is so promiscuous, we could possibly have another female accomplice."

Adrian stood in exasperation. "With one as pure as Leah? A threesome? Surely you are not serious in this line of reasoning?"

"If it pleases all, I will dispatch Jasmine to observe their union," Aunt Bessie offered as all eyes turned to the scruffy old cat licking her paw on the arm of her chair. "Since this one is a nonbeliever, he will take no notice of my familiar, and Leah will be spared the discomfiture of prying eyes as she experiences her first coupling."

Vaughn stood. "An excellent proposal! Jasmine is the solution to this enigma we face."

Hellene stood. "I suggest a strong casting of the lust spell as well. In view of the fact that we cannot afford to fail in passing this one's seed while we have the opportunity, two or more couplings would be better than one to ensure success."

Shoshanna stood. "What is your opinion on this proposal, Lola? Would this be an undue hardship placed upon this one?"

Lola stood, smiling. "In my experience, this would not be a hardship on this one at all. Actually, I'm not sure casting a lust spell is even necessary. This one is quite virile and lustful of his own accord when with the right woman."

Allay popped up with an inscrutable smirk. "Do I denote a touch of boasting, Lola?"

Lola stood. "I do not mean to boast, Allay, only to provide an observation based on personal experience."

Hellene stood. "In any case, I think we can all agree that an ounce of preparation on the front end might be worth a pound of toil on the back end. There is always the chance this one might not find Leah as appealing as he apparently found Lola."

Aunt Bessie spoke from her chair. "If all agree, I will instruct Jasmine to cast a strong spell of lust to further ensure the success of their union. Getting the two of them together would seem to be our next priority." She turned her unseeing eyes to her left. "Lola, if you are so inclined to spend time with this one on your own accord, perhaps, when he has his talisman off, you could implant a visit to Hazel's home into his psyche as an inducement to get him to Leah."

Lola stood. “I’m not sure this one will follow my telepathic suggestions. He is very strong minded. I think it may take many suggestions over an extended period to convince him to visit with Hazel, but with Council approval, I will invest as much effort into the task as necessary.”

Allay stood and smirked at Lola. “Keep in mind, Lola, we don’t want this one so sated when he arrives at Hazel’s that his lustful edge is worn off.”

Hellene stood. “In that regard, it would appear that since this one does have a somewhat lustful edge, I feel we need to tone down his yearnings until we actually have him in place with Leah to ensure his seed is not passed to another by accident and lost to us.”

Adrian stood. “Rarely do I have the opportunity to agree with Hellene, so I do not want to miss this opportunity to endear myself to her. I agree with her in this instance. Perhaps we should sanction an indefinite stay for Lola with this one to keep his edge off, since Lola is so inclined, until we can maneuver him to Leah. Thus, Lola can insure this one’s seed is not passed to another by accident.”

Gretchen stood. “Perhaps the both of us should return to service this one’s needs so he does not tire of one woman, as young males his age are inclined to do. I am agreeable to serving Council in this manner.”

Lola stood, her face flushed. “I hardly think that necessary, Gretchen. I did not feel this one was bored in the least, and I assure you I was not tiring of him.”

Gretchen stood quickly. “I apologize for such an inference, Lola. That was inconsiderate of me, but there is also the very real danger that with someone as charming as you, he may become overly enamored as well, and therefore have no desire to couple with Leah."

Merle rapped his knuckles on his book to still the growing disorder. "It is good to see such enthusiasm on Council's behalf. In view of these issues, I propose you both return until we get the details worked out concerning this one's union with Leah. I recommend you use alternating nights to help maintain his interest and to further dissuade emotional attachment to either. Master Vaughn, you are located in New Orleans. Hazel lives very near there. Can you contrive of any arrangement to lure this one there to get him in the vicinity of Leah, since the closer he is the stronger will be Lola's power of suggestion to visit Hazel?"

Vaughn stood, immersed in thought. "Lola, did you pick up on any financial needs this one may have while you visited with him?"

Lola stood. "All this one thinks about is money for his race team. He lost his sponsor last year and apparently doesn't have the funds to race this year. He is currently looking for a new sponsor everywhere."

Allay stood. "This one is a racecar driver? How exciting! How does this sponsor thing work?"

Lola stood. "I'm not sure exactly, but basically someone gives him a million dollars to run his racecar."

Drew stood in shocked repugnance. "A million dollars? Do they really spend that kind of money on that silly sport?"

Vaughn stood. "Actually, they spend more at the higher levels, but in any case, that is the insight I need. I can pose my bank as a potential sponsor. It should not be a problem to get this one to agree to meet with me in New Orleans if he is as anxious as you suggest."

Merle stood. “Then we will end the Circle and reconvene when appropriate. And if it harm none, do as ye will.”

The strong maiden passed around the cakes and wine. After their toasts and farewells to the Deity, they chanted their well wishes to each other and filed out.

“Come on, Lola,” Gretchen urged as she hurried past. “Let’s get going before this one finds someone else. I get the first night with him since you’ve already had two nights of your own. That’s only fair!”

Lola quickened her pace. “That doesn’t count, Gretchen! This is a whole new assignment from Council and should stand on its own merit as such!”

“You two be gentle and caring with this one!” Vaughn called after them anxiously.

Allay scowled. “Fat chance of that happening! Those two vixens will have this one so worn out he’ll be of no use to us when we do get him to Leah!”

Chapter Five

Clint downshifted and swept into the sharp curve as the Firebird swayed hard on its right side clinging to the narrow ribbon of pitted asphalt that defined the borders of the old farm to market road. He pressed the throttle to the floor as he swung out of the turn and power shifted to a higher gear, the surge settling him back into his contoured bucket seat. The car followed his every whim behind the modified three hundred and fifty horsepower engine mounted on a cut and balanced frame molded to the specifications of a road racer over racing shocks and springs. It wasn't street legal, but only an expert would know it, and only after a thorough diagnosis. The velocity soothed his agitation as he charged through the enveloping countryside paying scant attention to the draping trees forming an arch over him blotting out the sun, or to the sloping shoulders leading down to the brackish swamp around him.

He drove with the finely honed artistry of a professional driver, keeping well within the bounds of his proven skills, though a passenger would have been alarmed with the seeming wanton recklessness of his roaring excursion. He felt only impatience to reach the

Interstate, giving no thought to the thundering machine under him, his mind preoccupied with the upcoming racing season starting in just two short months and his failure to lock in the New Orleans banker as a sponsor earlier that morning. After driving fifteen hours to meet with the man, the conference had lasted less than half an hour, and after the first ten minutes, he had known it was a waste of his time.

As his mind churned, he instinctively locked his brakes and downshifted as an old, scraggly white cat strolled out into his path, fighting the wheel to keep the Firebird on the narrow lane of asphalt and out of the bog on each side of the road as his tires squalled in protest. He grimaced from the pain lancing up his left leg from his ankle recently removed from its cast and cursed under his breath as he glared at the feline standing in the middle of the road staring at him in the wafting tire smoke. The cat wandered across the road and down an almost invisible path past a weathered white sign reading *Cottonmouth Pointe* with *Readings by Hazel* scrawled in crooked black letters under it.

A vague stir sifted through him as he stared at the rickety old sign and studied the thin pathway with grass growing between the two ruts, trying to bring the elusive thought to focus, but the essence escaped him. For some inexorable reason his mind flashed back to the old black woman who attempted to read his palm in the Low Country of South Carolina some weeks back. It had excited him at the time when he saw the similar sign with *Readings by Miss Bessie*, but he had been careful not to show the growing intrigue he felt to his friends when he suggested they stop. Once inside the old crone's house he had lost his nerve and gotten out of there fast before she could forecast his future.

He stared hard at Hazel's sign, feeling the same puzzling attraction. *Why not? Where's the harm? No one is around to razz me about it afterwards. It might even be entertaining enough to take the edge off this disappointing trip.* He eased the car onto the trail through the clutching branches, grimacing as they scraped against the sleek black velvet paint job and lacquered satin finish.

After a quarter of a mile the trail disappeared and forced him to stop. He slammed his palm against the steering wheel in frustration, regretting his whim to let off a bit of steam on the side road, which led to his hasty decision to visit a stupid fortune teller, which in turn had him stuck on this dense goat trail with no place to turn around.

He got out and limped around surveying the tangled growth as he inhaled the pungent stench of rotting vegetation from the slush less than a foot on either side of the rutted lane filled with decaying flora and Cyprus stumps. He looked ruefully back down the rutted lane behind him, realizing he would have to back up all the way to the asphalt, and paused as the old white cat appeared at the edge of the tangled brush in front of his hood, its unkempt fur and yellow eyes peering at him inquisitively. Momentarily mesmerized, he irritably shook off the effect as the cat turned and strolled down an almost indiscernible path in the dense wall of shrubbery. He impulsively shrugged his way into the brambles behind the creature. A hundred yards along, he drew up before a small, decrepit old shack perched on a tiny peninsula on the edge of the vast marsh surrounding it. The cat had vanished.

He appraised the miniature, unpainted house with rough-cut board siding warped and faded from age with its rusty tin roof sagging in places and seemingly on the verge of collapsing. A small front porch held two rocking chairs and a cluster of coffee cans with ferns growing in them. A ragged wooden pier jutted a few feet into the sluggish water at the rear with a decaying, flat-bottomed boat tied to the wobbly pilings. A line strung between two trees in a minute patch of sunlight in the heavy gloom of the interior held white sheets suspended by clothespins. Further to the left there appeared to be a single grave under a moss covered tree with a board sticking out of the ground serving as a headstone. Though rough, the place had a certain charm to it with its neatly arranged clusters of flowers blooming in patches of bright color providing a sense of balance in a welcoming ambience of homely affability.

"Hello," a soft female voice greeted from his rear.

He spun to find a young, bronze-skinned woman holding the white cat in her arms with a large, ugly black dog by her side, and sheepishly tried to mask the fact that she had startled him. He judged her eighteen and drop-dead gorgeous as he took in her long, unruly blonde hair falling in ringlets around her pretty, makeup free face, and thick, un-plucked eyebrows above the bluest eyes he had ever seen, noting her long fingernails were unpolished and her feet bare below a pair of cutoff jeans with the jagged edges trailing strings down her shapely legs. A faded red shirt tied at the waist revealed a smooth, flat stomach.

"Who're you?"

She took in his lean, six-foot frame, broad shoulders, silky blond hair, and blue eyes curiously. *So this is the one, come at last*. "I'm Leah," she replied as her heart pounded.

She had known the time was growing perilously near when Aunt Bessie's familiar appeared the day before. Her mother had informed her that this one did not know the purpose of his visit. She was to receive his seed as quickly as possible and allow him to depart. When her mother first broached the subject of her serving as the vessel for his child some weeks back, she was intrigued that Council chose her above all others for such an honor. Up to that point, she had been merely an ordinary soul living a solitary life on the edge of a vast swamp with no acquaintances outside of her mother and no social life beyond the frugal existence they scraped out by plying the locals with their skills, though she secretly longed for friends to talk to and dreamed of traveling the bewildering other world waiting just outside the narrow confines of this trepid patch of hated marshland. Now that he was here and the moment at hand, she was terrified. She had been in a tizzy since the moment she saw Jasmine sitting on her front porch staring at her through the screen door, as if questioning her worthiness for such a high privilege.

Clint tore his eyes from her uncapped breasts bulging from the top of the tied-off blouse. "Are you Hazel?"

Her cheeks flushed at his brazen appraisal. "No."

"Is she here?"

You're not here for my mother. You're here for me, even if you don't know it yet. "Come to the porch and I'll get you a glass of tea."

She brushed past him on the narrow pathway, the tantalizing musk of her un-perfumed body intriguing to his senses, the contact with her sending tremors of pleasure racing through him, leaving him stunned by the sudden, powerful attraction he felt for her. No female had ever affected him like this at first sight, he marveled as he shifted his focus down to her pleasing, heart-shaped posterior swinging along in front of him and limped along behind her.

She led him up onto the ramshackle porch and indicated one of the ancient rockers, unsure of what she should do beyond serving him a glass of tea. She knew very little about the physical act of coupling, and had only a vague understanding of the physical differences between the male and female anatomies, which she gleaned from pictures in the magazines she pulled out of the trash dump just down the road. When she questioned what was required of her, her mother simply told her to be compliant to his wishes. Beyond that, she was clueless. As with all other knowledgeable things of the outside world, she would need to rely upon herself.

"I'm in a bit of a hurry," he offered, feeling the need to break the silence, but thinking he wasn't in *that* much of a hurry now that he had met her. "Will Hazel return soon?"

"You never said your name," she evaded as she sat the white cat down on the edge of the porch.

"Sorry, I'm Clint Long." He sank down in a chair to get the weight off his throbbing ankle, eyeing the cat as it twitched its tail and rubbed against her well-formed ankles. Her ugly mutt of a dog wandered over and nudged his hand as it wagged its tail. "What's this big fellow's name?" he asked as he scratched the dog's ears.

Leah opened the screen door and entered the shack. "That's Old Blue."

"What's the cat's name?" he called after her as she disappeared into the house.

"Jasmine," she called back.

"Hello, Jasmine," he cooed as he stretched out his other hand to the animal. The cat backed away hissing in scorn. "You're not a very friendly little puss, are you?" he chastised as the cat moved to the corner of the porch and lay down, curling and uncurling its tail.

Leah returned and handed him a glass. "I keep the jug in the spring to keep it cool."

"Thanks." He took a sip. "So when will Hazel be back?"

"I guess you're really here to see me." She locked eyes with him and held her breath.

His pulse quickened as he imagined them joined in the fiery throes of passion. "Do you read palms and tell fortunes and such too?"

"Yes," she replied, finding his frank appraisal of her unsettling.

She had tried to communicate with Aunt Bessie the day before upon the arrival of Jasmine and again this morning, to beg her to prepare her for this one's arrival since she knew nothing about mating, but her almost nonexistent telecommunication skills failed her. She tried to give herself a quick lesson in basic coupling from the articles in a stained copy of a Playboy magazine she found in the dump, which only confused her. She had thought she was ready, but now she was losing confidence. She steeled her jumbled emotions and attempted to regain her poise.

"Where are you from?"

"Charlotte, North Carolina. Do you live here?" he asked, feeling silly as his imagination ran wild with erotic images of her.

"I'm Hazel's daughter."

"Oh …"

He seems surprised. What if he doesn't find me appealing enough to plant his seed in me? Should I do something to entice him? I've read in the magazines that women do that sort of thing, but I'm not sure what I should do to attract him. She lowered her eyes in misery. "I hope you're not disappointed in me."

"Why would you think that?" he asked uneasily.

She looked out across the swamp. "I know I'm not much to look at and all."

"Actually, I think you're very pretty."

She glanced at him covertly. "Mother always said I was pretty, but I guess that doesn't count for much. I think you're very pretty too."

He laughed as his eyes met hers, again bringing out the tiny, thrilling pulses in his stomach and the wild images in his mind. "You're making fun of me, right?"

She lowered her eyes. "You make me feel all flustered. I meant to say you're handsome."

He grinned. "Well thank you, coming from such a beautiful girl, I'm flattered."

Her stomach fluttered. "You don't have to say such if you don't mean it."

He sensed she was pleased from the deep blush rising in her cheeks. "Oh, but I *do* mean it." He also sensed she was unaccustomed to personal compliments from men. He stood, wrenching as his ankle took his weight. “Should I come back another time to see Hazel?”

Why wasn’t the spell Jasmine cast on him working? *What should I do to keep him here until he does what he is supposed to do*? “It wouldn’t do you any good.”

“Why not?”

“That’s her out there under that old tree.” She indicated the wood headstone off to the side of the house with a forlorn look. “She passed on to the other side a week ago.”

He looked at the grave cautiously. “I’m very sorry to hear that. Why did you put her there?”

“Christian folks would never allow me put her in their graveyard.”

“Why not?”

“Because they claim she was a witch.”

He stared at the crude, makeshift tombstone uneasily. “They sound like narrow minded Christians.”

“That’s kind of you to say.”

He looked at the squalor around them. “Do you live here alone now?”

“Just me and Old Blue.”

He indicated the cat staring at him as it flipped its tail to and fro. “What about Jasmine?”

She reached down to pet the cat. “She’s just visiting.”

“Don’t you have any family you can turn to now?”

“Momma didn’t talk much about kinfolks to me.”

“Don’t you get lonely out here all by yourself?”

“Sometimes.”

“Aren’t you concerned about being out here all alone?”

"The common folks don't come around here much, but most are afraid of me."

"Why are they afraid of you?"

"Because they think I'm a witch, too."

"What a bunch of morons to think some damn fool thing like that!" he exclaimed. "Look, I guess I better get going."

"Don't you want your fortune read?" she asked anxiously, thinking it would be interesting to read his aura and that maybe it would even give her some indication of what she could do to make herself attractive to him.

"I don't really believe in that fortune telling stuff."

"Most common folks don't believe at first. I got the vision from Momma. It was her gift to me. I'm real good at it, Momma said better than most. But it scares people, I guess. I don't know why. Does it scare you?"

"No, it doesn't scare me, I just don't believe in such," he replied. "Do you think you're a witch?"

She tensed. "That's just a silly name used by those who don't know any better."

"Good, because I think witches and fortunetellers are pure nonsense."

Her cheeks flushed as she fought to control her temper. "I am what I am, you can believe or disbelieve as you wish." *This isn't going the way it is supposed to. Why doesn't he just do what he came here for and leave? Jasmine has already cast the lust spell on him, so why doesn't he just get it over with? What can I do to attract him? This is getting more frustrating by the moment.* A wave of shameful remorse washed over her at the thought of failing in her efforts to gather his seed for Council due to her ignorance.

When a tear trickled down her cheek, Clint pulled her to him and placed his arms around her in a protective gesture, angry with himself for having hurt her with his callousness.

She stiffened in his arms, awkwardly keeping her arms at her sides as her heart hammered. *Finally he's going to do what he came here for.* Tremors of fear swept through her, leaving her nauseous.

He held her tenderly as a searing longing consumed him. "I'm sorry, Leah. If you say you can read fortunes, then I'm sure you believe you can. I'm a wise-ass myself, in case you haven't noticed."

Now surely he'll do what he's supposed to do. He's holding me in his arms. That has to be the first step. Her heart thundered in her chest as his hands caressed her back and she waited for him to go to the next phase, which would probably mean him taking her clothes off. She blushed at the thought of being nude with him. *What if he doesn't like my body?*

"I've never been held by a man before," she whispered.

"I've never held a witch before, either," he teased, and tipped her chin up with the tip of his finger to look into her captivating eyes. When she closed them shyly, he lowered his lips to hers in a sudden, irresistible impulse, tasting the sweet softness of her flavored by the salt of her tears. Instantly deep, soothing warmth flowed through him, filling an inner vacuum that had always existed within him.

Her eyes flew open and she drew away from him, her heart pounding so hard she thought it might burst. *I didn't expect him to put his mouth on mine. I read where boys like to kiss girls, but I didn't anticipate him wanting to do it to me. I thought he would just undress me and do what he came here for.*

Clint grinned, his lips tingling with the taste of her, longing to hold her again, to explore the softness of her body, to recapture the rapture her lips. "I didn't mean to offend you. You're not going to put a hex on me or anything, are you?"

She lowered her head, still trembling. "It just surprised me, is all."

The white cat strolled over and rubbed against her leg, giving her comfort. She dried her eyes with her fingertips and stiffened her resolve, fearful she had offended him. "Tell me what you want me to do and I'll do it."

"Well … you can read my palm, I guess, if you still want to, or tell my fortune, or whatever you do," he replied hesitantly.

She stared at him helplessly. *You were sent here for me to gather your seed, but I don't know how I'm supposed to do it and you're not helping matters. The lust spell should have worked by now.* She looked down at Jasmine, silently imploring her to do something to help the situation, but Jasmine seemed content to rub against her leg as if nothing was wrong. Not knowing what else to do, she looked up at him warily.

"I guess I can do that," she advised, relieved to be back on familiar ground.

"Great, what do you charge?" he asked, reaching for his wallet.

"I probably shouldn't charge you anything."

"Why wouldn't you charge me?" he asked.

She frowned indecisively. Business had been slow since her mother passed on and she had been living off catfish stew and cornbread because she had no money to buy staples. She needed the cash from a reading, even if it was from him. "I'm not sure it would be right."

"Right by whom? That's what you do, isn't it?"

She sighed, unable to think of a taboo against it, and needing the money. "I'm not generally so dopey when people come around. I normally charge five dollars for cures, ten dollars for potions, and fifteen for readings."

"I sort of like you dopey," he teased as he peeled out a twenty and a ten and handed them to her, relieved that she seemed to be getting herself back together after he had frightened her so badly. "I've only been to one of these fortune telling things before when I was just fooling around, so I guess I'll take the whole works."

"Everything?" she asked, startled.

He shrugged. "Sure, let's do it all. What's to lose? Especially the cure part, since I've got some pain in my left ankle that the doctors can't seem to properly diagnose or treat."

She slid the money into the back pocket of her jeans, the gesture sending sensuous images to him as her palm conformed to the pleasing curve of her backside, and opened the screen door expectantly.

"Well, come on then."

Chapter Six

Clint limped inside the dark, single room and sat as directed at a small table with two chairs just inside the door. Leah lit a large candle on the table, which cast a wavering light to reveal a sagging double bed against the rear wall, a wood burning cooking stove on the left wall with a small cupboard on one side and a battered pantry on the other, and a worn sofa perched against the right wall. Though Spartan, the place was exceptionally clean and neat, with everything openly in its place and there for a purpose, with no knickknacks cluttering or wasting space.

Leah placed a cigar box next to the candle, poured hot water from a kettle simmering on the stove into a cup, and sat down across from him. "First tell me what you seek," she commanded as she opened the cigar box.

He saw the box held several colorful candles, a deck of tarot cards, three small bottles tinted brown, green, and blue, a palm-sized rose crystal heart, a small carving knife with a white bone handle, a longer dagger with a black bone handle inscribed with strange markings, and several plastic bags containing roots and leaves. "I really don't know if I'm *seeking* anything, other than relief from pain."

"Tell me of your pain," she instructed.

"Well, my ribs hurt a bit, but my left ankle has been giving me fits since they took the cast off."

She came around and knelt at his feet, placed her hands on his ankle, and gently probed.

"The doctor says I've got nerve damage," he advised. "He doesn't seem to know what to do to about it. Putting weight on it is like driving a nail into my flesh."

"I will attend to this later," she assessed, rising to place her hands on his ribs and exploring gently, her touch sending ripples of desire coursing through him. "This will take care of itself in time." She went back around the table and sat down. "Is there anything you would like to know?"

He shrugged. "Well, yeah, I'd like to know if I'm going to get a sponsor this season or not. Time is running out on me."

She shoved a small plastic bag of green leaves and the cup of hot water at him. "Sprinkle a pinch of tea leaves in the cup," she directed as she began shuffling the tarot cards. "What is a sponsor?"

"It's someone who gives you money to … look, this really isn't necessary." He indicated the cards and teacup. "I feel ridiculous. Like I said, I don't believe in this fortune telling stuff."

She dug in her back pocket and reluctantly slid the bills on the table between them. "You can have your money back then."

He hesitated, sensing that she obviously needed the money. "You can keep the money if you'll let me sit and talk for a while."

"What do you want to talk about?"

"You said you and your mother had 'the vision' thing and it scared people. What's scary about it?"

She shifted in annoyance. "You said you don't believe in such, so why do you want to talk about it?"

"I'm just curious, I guess."

She fought against her rising irritation. "If you don't believe, why did you stop to see Hazel today?"

"I don't really know why. I was in this neck of the woods by accident. I drove down to meet with a potential sponsor in New Orleans, a banker. I should have known better. Bankers are too tight with their purse strings. It was a wasted trip. I drove around on the back roads to let off a little steam and almost ran over your cat in the middle of the road. When I stopped, I saw Hazel's sign and here I am."

She crossed her arms and stared at him. He seemed so lost and troubled. "Before my mother's passing, she got a message you were coming here." She stared out the screen door at Jasmine sitting on the porch. "I was beginning to think you weren't coming after so much time. Now that you're here, it scares me half to death."

He leaned forward, intrigued. "Who sent your mother a message I was coming?"

"Aunt Bessie."

"That crazy old black woman back in South Carolina? How could she have known I would come here? She said something about me being the one and that it was a miracle. What does that mean?"

She turned back to him. There had never been a reason for her to lie, or even to deceive anyone, in her whole life, but she couldn't be completely truthful with him on this matter either. "You'll have to wait for someone else to tell you."

"Why can't you tell me?"

"I'm not qualified."

He sighed and kicked back in his chair. "So who *can* tell me what it means?"

"They will come to you in time."

"*They*? So why am I here with you then?"

"You'll come to know that in time as well, if it is meant to be. I don't know what I'm supposed to do next. Nobody ever told me."

"What you're supposed to do next? Do about what? This is all too damn mysterious for me."

Perhaps Council made a mistake in sending him here for me to collect his seed. She experienced a tug of guilt for questioning the wisdom of the Council. "No one prepared me for you asking so many questions."

"Can you at least explain the vision thing to me?"

"It is an image of events in one's life. It can be good or bad. It gives one the power to alter their future if it's used wisely. It can also be very dangerous to those who use it foolishly."

He glanced at her bleak surroundings. "So why don't you use it to alter your own future?"

"It doesn't tell me of events in my life, only of others. It's a reading of their aura. I can't read my own aura."

He grinned. "That sounds kind of hokey."

She tensed, reminding herself that he was not intentionally being offensive to her and her Craft, that he was simply stating his opinion as a nonbeliever. "It's for each person to say for themselves. It depends on how they interpret the events given through their aura and how they use the information afterwards."

"I can see how people might think you're a witch. Okay, tell me something about my life."

"This is not a game," she warned sharply. "Once you have the information revealed by the vision, you will also have the power to alter it."

He found her direct stare compelling with the intensity mirrored in her eyes, as she paused for emphasis.

"You must be very careful about changing your future," she continued. "Once you alter the sequence of events it cannot be undone. Each event leads to another event and from there to another. It is very dangerous to alter the path that binds those events together."

He chuckled. "Kind of like a cue ball fired into a rack of pool balls, right?"

She frowned. "I don't know what that means."

He shrugged. "Okay, hit me with your best vision thing. Tell me something that's going to happen to me today."

She hesitantly took his hands, closed her eyes, leaned her head back, and breathed deeply. She opened her eyes and looked at him in puzzlement. "I can't read your aura. I'm not sure what that means." She examined his hands and frowned, finding his fingers bare. She examined the watch on his arm and discounted it with a shake of her head. "Do you have any symbols on your person?"

He reached inside his shirt and pulled out the gold chain hanging around his neck with the lucky charm hanging on it. "Only this. My mother gave it to me just before she died. It's been in our family for generations and is supposed to protect me from evil."

"You'll have to remove it for me to read your aura. It blocks my powers."

He grinned slyly. "Protecting me from you reading my thoughts might be a good thing."

She stared at him directly. "You must decide this."

When he removed the chain and placed it on the table, she again took his hands and leaned her head back, seeming to enter a trance-like state, rocking her head from side to side. Her eyes flew open and she quickly dropped his hands as she flushed.

"What did you see?" he asked anxiously.

She turned from him with her cheeks glowing deep red. "I can't tell you!"

"That's not fair!" he argued. "You said it was *my* vision. You've got to tell me! I've already paid you in advance remember? A deal's a deal." He slipped his chain back around his neck as a shiver worked its way down his spine. "Is it a bad vision or something? If it's something bad, I need to know about it. You said I'd have the power to change it."

Her cheeks reddened. *I should never have offered to give him a reading.* "I don't know if it's good or bad. Only you can decide that. But it's very humiliating to me. Please don't make me tell you."

"I want to know, Leah! I'm sorry if it makes you uncomfortable, but you've got to tell me what you saw. That's only fair."

She lowered her head, her voice a mere quiver and so soft he had to lean forward to hear her. "I saw you lying down with me …"

He stared at her as his heart beat rapidly. “I thought you couldn’t tell your own future.”

She cut her eyes away. “That’s not my future. It’s an event I saw in yours. You now have the power to alter it.” She sat in extreme degradation before him with her eyes on the floor.

He rose to his feet, his heart pounding. “Do you want me to alter it?”

“That’s not for me to say,” she whispered. “Only you can make that choice.”

“Don’t you have a say in it?”

“I must not interfere. It is forbidden.”

He pulled her up and placed his hands on her shoulders, sensing the panic rising in her as a pulsating vein in her neck beat rapidly, reminding him of a baby rabbit he once caught in a trap as a child. He pulled her stiff body against his as desire welled up within him.

“Forbidden by whom, Leah?”

She tried to control her breathing, knowing the moment was finally at hand, tried to make herself relax, but her body refused to respond. “I am not allowed to alter your future. You must control that. Others must advise you on this. I am not qualified.”

“What others? Aunt Bessie, who supposedly sent me here to what, *seduce* you? That doesn’t make sense. I don’t even know you, and I’ve only met her once. This is crazy. How do you feel about all this?”

“That is not for me to say.”

He felt his control slipping. “You’re so pure and honest.”

“My thoughts are not always pure, but I’m always honest.”

"You are truly a phenomenon," he mused. "Since it involves your future as well as mine, I insist you help me decide if I am to alter my … *our* futures." He kissed her as she trembled, forcing her lips open with his tongue and finding hers in her moist mouth before sliding down her neck as she stiffened. "You can say stop anytime you want to, Leah. It's your future too." He nibbled at the base of her neck as tremors shot through her rigid body.

"I don't know how to do this," she whispered, fearful she was going to faint. "I know you've been with other girls. Will you tell me what to do?"

His mind flashed back over the multitude of women he had known, mostly one night stands and casual short term affairs, his thoughts centering on the last few weeks and the dizzy cycle he had gotten into with the dark, lithesome Lola, and the blonde, oversexed older woman called Gretchen. Between the two they had engaged him virtually every night. They worked for the same company, were off on alternating nights, and had made it clear from the outset they did not mind sharing him. For a time it had been entertainingly erotic to have two women in his life, but eventually it began to wear a bit thin. He had been thankful to get away for a few days in New Orleans.

"Just relax and do whatever feels natural," he murmured against her lips.

As his lips searched her throat in teasing nibbles, she stared past him out the screen door so terrified she thought her heart would explode, and fixed her gaze on Jasmine on the porch watching them. *Please help me, Jasmine*! she urged silently. *Please, I'm so scared*! The sudden, burning intensity of the animal's stare startled her. A warm, comfortable glow spread through her cold, rigid body. An ache rose in her stomach, confusing her, chasing the panic away, filling her with tenderness and a deep longing for this man who held her in his arms.

He tugged at the knot holding her blouse and pulled back to admire her taut breasts as it parted. She caught her breath as he stroked each in turn, bringing her nipples to hardened points of pleasure. He lowered his lips to first one and then the other as she arched her back and clutched his head, moaning as she pulled his eager lips against her bosom, gasping through ripples of delicious desire at his touch, never having imagined coupling could be this way, wanting him to never stop. Taking his seed was the last thing on her mind as he stoked her body into molten embers, her only thoughts of allowing him to please her as he was doing now.

His head spun as his emotions fought between the raw desire engulfing him and the appalling guilt lurking in the back of his mind, sensing what he was doing was wrong. The fact that a man had never touched her flashed through his mind, but apparently this Aunt Bessie creature sent him here on this mysterious quest, he reminded himself. Even Leah herself had confirmed this event with her own vision thing. He vaguely analyzed this strange sequence as his hunger within, fueled by the sensuous vibrations of her body responding hungrily to his touch, overrode the guilt.

He slipped his hand down and unfastened her jeans, kissing her breasts and working his way back up her neck to her lips, enjoying the shivers running through her body. He slipped his hand down inside the back of her jeans and cupped her, squeezing softly, surprised that she wore no panties as he edged the jeans downward to drop at her ankles and guided her as she stepped out of them. He peeled her blouse off and pulled his own shirt over his head.

She closed her eyes as he openly admired her nude body before him quaking with anticipation as he kicked his shoes and trousers off. He pulled her to him with her breasts massaging his chest and kissed her amid her pulsating ripples of hunger. Her quaking legs gave way and she allowed him to guide her to the floor, his tongue working in delicious swirls against her own as he rubbed and probed her body freely. She pushed against him eagerly wanting more, her breath turning into sharp gasps as she twisted and dug her nails into his shoulders pulling at him. He opened her legs as she moaned in intolerable pleasure, arching her hips forward to receive him, desperate to have him enter her, pulling him down on her, urgently needing him to quell the fire burning out of control in her stomach.

He filled her completely as she cried out in pain and pleasure. She clutched at him as her hips worked hungrily building her desire and felt him increasing his cadence to match hers. She thrust at him with increasing desperation until a searing explosion rifled through her. She cried out and sagged under him as gratifying shock waves coursed through her, and closed her eyes as tears coursed down her cheeks, breathing in ragged pants as intense currents of pleasure pulsed through her depleted body held tightly against him.

After a time, she stirred and wrapped her arms around him. "Thank you for helping me."

"Is this what being 'the one' meant?" he gasped.

"Partly," she whispered.

"Are you sorry I didn't alter our futures?"

"No. Are you?"

He lifted up on his elbows and grinned down at her. "I think I'm officially bewitched now." He kissed her and dipped his head down to her breasts as the fire began to rekindle deep within him. "I think I'm developing a thing for witches."

She moaned in delight as he took her slowly and more sensuously than before, his manipulations driving her higher and further, leaving her writhing in ecstasy and pleading for him to end the torture of waiting for fulfillment.

When he could endure it no longer he thrust deep inside her in a crushing release that exploded through him with such intensity he thought his head would burst. He collapsed over her as she lay quivering under him, too weak to move.

After a time, he rolled onto the floor beside her and pulled her to him. He closed his eyes and drifted in a state of bliss with her cradled in his arms, the last twenty-four hours without sleep and the contentment of the moment a strong sedative to his senses.

When he awoke the sun was setting. She sat at the table fully dressed, bathed in the weak glow of the candle, watching him intently as she clutched the rose crystal heart in her palms.

Chapter Seven

Merle turned in the hush after the final evocation to the Deity. "Aunt Bessie, please address Council on the matter of Leah."

Aunt Bessie stared straight ahead with unseeing eyes in the quiet. "I am pleased to report this one mated with Leah this afternoon." She waited for the excited buzz to subside. "Though it took many weeks to get him there, I duly had Jasmine cast a strong lust spell upon him, as instructed by Council, and he passed his seed to Leah almost immediately."

Drew stood. "And was Leah comfortable throughout this ordeal?"

Aunt Bessie hesitated. "There were some awkward moments, I'm sorry to say. As I informed Council, Leah has led a very sheltered life, but all ended well and Jasmine left them sleeping in each other's arms."

Shoshanna stood. "Aunt Bessie, please elaborate on these *awkward moments* you speak of."

Aunt Bessie clutched her Book of Shadows in her lap. "This one was filled with lust due to the strong spell Jasmine cast upon him. Leah, though willing, was initially unsure of herself. Due to her sudden illness,

Hazel apparently was unable to prepare her to receive a male before she passed on to the other side. Leah, due to her poor psychic communication skills, could not summon me to help when the time came and had no one else to turn to. I did not realize this until the last moment as the event was evolving."

Shoshanna looked around the Council cautiously. "Has any transgression against our Rede been committed in this endeavor, or has anything occurred outside the sanction of Council that we need to be made aware of?"

Aunt Bessie gathered her thoughts. "I was unable to communicate with Leah to prepare her for what was to come. She was terrified of the corporeal act of surrendering her body to this one and did not know how to proceed. In haste … I directed Jasmine to cast a spell on her as well, to help ease her through the ordeal. She then found her way."

Herschel stood, eyes narrowed. "Exactly what *spell* did you have Jasmine cast on Leah, Aunt Bessie? Are we to assume it was merely one of lust as well?"

Aunt Bessie composed herself. "Leah was near panic. I was desperate to help her and the time at hand was short. I had Jasmine … cast a love spell."

"You cast a *love* spell?" Herschel gasped. "Mercy be! I *suggested* a more contemporary member of our Craft for this enterprise, but you reassured Council Hazel could properly prepare Leah to receive this one's seed. There should have been no reason to act in haste and thus avoid such an error."

Hellene stood. "Are you saying Leah did not expressly *request* your assistance in receiving this one's seed since you could not communicate with her, and that you specifically cast a love spell without her *knowledge*? This is a *serious* breach of our Rede!"

Aunt Bessie sat rigid. "She did request Jasmine's assistance, but was unknowing of the love spell cast upon her. In her state, I felt compelled to help her. I can only hope she will be appreciative of my assistance, under the circumstances."

Adrian stood. "Aunt Bessie, the love spell would overcome her natural decision making processes. It would take away her ability to make a clear choice of her own free will to proceed or not to proceed. She may understandably have decided against consummating the act given that she was so uncomfortable, thus you altered her fate. I fear this is indeed a serious violation of our Rede. If she in fact regrets her actions, you could suffer the threefold bad karma for having imposed your will upon another."

Lola stood. "Aunt Bessie was only trying to help Leah through a trying time! Leah had already freely chosen to serve as the vessel for this one's seed, but simply did not know how to consummate the physical act of taking his seed. This was plainly an act of kindness on Aunt Bessie's part. In any case, Leah has now taken his seed, so no harm should come from loving the one for whom she now bears a child."

Vaughn stood. "Ultimately, this is not for us to judge. If it is indeed a violation of our Rede, the forces that be will extract their measure of justice on the perpetrator. The act is done and now must be judged against the outcome."

Merle stood. "Now that we have collected this one's seed to ensure the future of his sacred lineage, we must consider our next move."

Gretchen stood. “Lola and I have discussed this issue at length. He is clearly a strong persona who does not take to coercion easily. I suggest Lola and I return to begin a tutoring process to guide him to our world.”

Allay stood. “It’s always you and Lola, why not another member of Council? I am senior on Council to both of you. Do you dispute my qualifications to entice this one to our world?”

Lola stood. “It’s not a matter of seniority, Allay, it’s simply that Gretchen and I have spent a great deal of time winning this one’s trust. It would seem we are in the better position to lead him to our world.”

Vaughn stood in near outrage. “*Guide*? *Entice*? *Lead*? What am I *hearing* here? We can do *none* of these things! Are we not *thinking* clearly? Listen to what you are saying here! Our Rede allows *none* of this! It is outright *recruiting*! This one *must* of his *own free will* seek these things of us, not be *coerced* into it!”

Shoshanna stood. “I say we proceed with extreme caution. I recommend Lola and Gretchen return yet again, since they have established a relationship with this one, to gather more insight and report back to Council so that we might collectively make a more informed decision after carefully evaluating the matter.”

Gretchen stood. “I agree.”

Lola stood. “I agree this is a sound course for Council to take.”

Allay stood. “I object!”

Merle rapped his knuckles on his Book of Shadows to regain order. “Does any member of Council, other than Allay, object to this course of action?” Silence prevailed. “So be it then, and be it so ordered by

Council. Let us enjoy our cake and wine as we wish each other well. If it harm none, do as ye will."

The strong maiden served the wine and cake, and when the ceremony was finished, they filed out counterclockwise with the individual tribes following their departure.

Chapter Eight

Leah placed the rose crystal heart back in her cigar box, removed a simmering pot from the stove, and placed it on the table. Clint stretched and slipped on his pants before sitting down to sniff at the delicious aroma rising from the pot as she placed a plate of cornbread before them and sat down across from him, her eyes downcast.

"Are you okay?" he asked, guilt tugging at him.

"I'm just sad," she replied. Looking at him across the table, bare-chested, with his hair ruffled, filled her with such tender longing it made her queasy. *Now that I have taken his seed, the thought of him leaving is unbearable.*

"Because of what happened?" he asked.

A thrill riffled through her sorrow. "No. I liked that after I got over being scared. I'm sad because you will leave now."

He looked inside the pot, his emotions ajar. *Of course I'll leave now, or in the morning at the latest—what do you expect me to do*? He cleared his throat. "This looks good. What is it?"

"Catfish stew." She picked up his bowl and ladled, self-conscious of such a meager offering. "It's better if you crumble your cornbread and make a mush."

"It smells great," he praised, wondering how she existed in such a Spartan environment with no friends or family.

She held her breath. "You were … very good …"

He stopped crumbling his cornbread to stare at her. "What do you mean?"

"I read that in a magazine … that a woman is supposed to tell a man that for his ego after coupling." She flushed when he burst out laughing. "Did I say it wrong?"

He stifled his laughter. "You are truly a treasure." He reached across the table and clasped her hand. "You were very good yourself."

His direct stare sent pleasing ripples through her. "As good as other girls you've been with?"

"Better," he assured her grandly as he scooped up a spoonful of the catfish mush.

She smiled as she tore her cornbread into chunks over her bowl. "Are you going to do it to me again before you leave then?"

"That's up to you," he replied in amusement as he spooned the mush into his mouth amid stirrings of desire seeping through him.

She scowled, realizing she wasn't saying things right, but not knowing what she was expected to say afterwards anymore than she had known what she was supposed to do beforehand. "I don't know what that means, but you're laughing, so it must mean you're making fun of me."

He met her intriguing, angry eyes. "I'm not making fun of you, Leah. I find you enchanting and the most natural woman I've ever met."

Her stomach clutched. *I just can't let him leave and never see him again. I read somewhere that one had to seize the moment—this is my moment*!

"I know I'm not sophisticated. Momma home schooled me, and she wasn't real book smart herself. Most of what I know about the other world comes from the magazines I get out of the trash dump. I haven't been around many people other than the ones who came to her with their troubles. I know I lack the social graces of other women, but I'm a real quick learner."

He shifted in discomfort. "Why are you telling me this?"

She took a deep breath to gather her courage. "I don't want to spend the rest of my life here in this old swamp like my momma. I want to be like the women in those magazines and have fancy store bought clothes and go to beauty parlors and have my hair done up real nice and all and see beautiful places. I want you to know I'm a fast learner in case you want to … take me with you when you leave …"

He inhaled a chunk of cornbread and convulsed coughing as he beating at his chest with his fist.

"I said the wrong thing, didn't I?"

"You definitely took me by surprise," he wheezed.

She steeled herself. "It just slipped out before I could catch it, but I can do a lot for you, like cook and clean for you, and be there when you want my body and all, if you'll give me a chance." She fought against the humiliating tears threatening to spill down her cheeks.

He tried to gather his wits. “Leah, I realize I’m the first man you’ve ever, uh, *been with*, and it’s only natural for a woman to cling to the first man—what I’m trying to say is, you’re a beautiful woman who can do anything you want in life and there are a lot of men out there who can give you everything you want—but I’m not that man.”

Panic clogged her throat. “I-I can do things to help you in your world if you’ll tell me what you need.”

Time to head this craziness off. “Leah, I know you think you’re a witch, but that’s all hokey crap your mother and others around here have led you to believe. There’s no such thing in real life. It’s all just a myth.”

The opportunity to escape this place is slipping away. “I really do have strong powers in my world, Clint, strong enough to help you do whatever you want in your world, if you’ll let me help you.”

He stared at her uneasily. “I’m not sure what you mean about having strong powers or your world and my world …”

“I know you don’t know of these things, but you could teach me your world and I’ll teach you mine.”

“Leah, I live in *my* world, and there’s no such thing as *witches* there.”

“You just don’t know the things I can do for you.”

“Prove it, Leah, show me some witchcraft.”

“I don’t like that word, but you’ve already seen I have the vision. What else do you want me to do?”

He squelched his annoyance. “If you’re referring to our *being together,* I think that was more intuition than fortune telling. We were both attracted to each other from the moment we met. What else can you do that’s magical?”

"I can make potions to heal, read people's auras, cast spells—"

"*Doctors* can heal, Leah, and so can a lot of other people who know about herbs and that sort of thing. I'm not even sure what a potion is, to be honest, but I assume it's some form of chemical mixing of different ingredients, like making aspirin or cough syrup, and therefore more science than supernatural. As for the vision thing, some people claim to be psychic, or clairvoyant, or whatever, but it's never been proven to be a fact. I flat out don't believe in spells and curses, good, bad, *or* evil. That's just pure superstition. None of it is black magic."

She hung her head. "You're saying no aren't you?"

"What you're asking of me is impossible." He studied her bowed head. *She's so innocent and childlike. What was I thinking when I took her so lustfully*? He slurped his mush as he brooded, keeping his eyes on his bowl as heavy remorse washed over him. *I should never have touched her. She is far too naïve and unsophisticated for me to have taken advantage of, no matter how appealing.*

A gloomy silence settled between them as she took their bowls, washed them in a pan on the pantry, and put them on a shelf before placing the remainder of the stew and cornbread into a dish for Old Blue, who seemed subdued now as well.

"Leah, how do you bathe around here?" he asked, looking around the sparse room.

She turned to a shelf for towels. "I'll show you."

He slipped on his shoes and limped after her, still bare-chested, some thirty yards along a narrow trail until they came to a stream of spring water flowing into a small pool formed around scattered boulders before it disappeared into the large marsh beyond. Leah hung the towels on a limb, modestly peeled off her clothes, and slipped into the cool water. He shucked his pants and shoes and joined her, where they splashed around for a few minutes, the silence heavy between them as the full moon lit the area around them in a silver haze.

"Are you still upset with me?" he asked.

She climbed up on a rock and sat with her knees pulled up under her chin, her arms laced around her legs. "I'm just disappointed that you won't take me to your world."

Backlit by the moon and bathed in the silvery light, she was a nude, enchanting goddess with wet hair slicked down and hanging over one shoulder. He couldn't help himself—he wanted her again. He pushed the insidious thought aside, determined to put a definitive end to this nonsense

"Leah, you need to understand something about me. I'm a drifter, a vagabond, and a loner. I tend to be selfish and self-centered. I'm a race junkie who doesn't even have a secure ride for next season. My only goal in life is to make it to Cup racing, and I'll do whatever it takes to get there at whatever the cost. I don't even have a real home. I live in the back of my race shop on an old cot when I don't have anywhere else to go." *Like when I can't find a friend to mooch off of or a girl to shack up with.* "I spend most of my life in different motel rooms in different cities every week when I'm racing. I'm almost always broke because I manage my money poorly, and besides that, when I've had a bad race, which is most of the time these days, I get a really crappy attitude and I'm not much fun to be around. You can do better than me, trust me."

"We can change all of that," she insisted. "We can help each other."

"I don't *want* to change it, Leah. It's my way of life, and I really don't think you would like my world if you got to know it." *What an incredibly naive, backwoods country girl*!

He treaded water before her, dolefully finding her desperation to escape her wretched environment heartrending. But hell, he was struggling too. He had no idea where his future lay, or even where his next meal was coming from, or where he would sleep tomorrow, assuming he stayed here tonight, which appeared to be in some doubt at the moment. He was twenty-four years old and had $26,000 in his personal bank account left over from his winnings last season, which was dwindling fast. Outside of driving a racecar, he had no formal training, education, or marketable skills. Hell, some people even doubted his ability to drive a racecar. In that endeavor, he had a $100,000 commitment from an associate sponsor and needed $900,000 more to run the full season, with not a clue as to where it was coming from. He had absolutely nothing to offer her in the way of security or long-term commitment. And face it, she might be a raving beauty, but she also had a couple of screws loose and rattling around up there somewhere because her elevator didn't quite go all the way to the top if she thought she was a witch.

"I promise I won't tie you down," she pleaded.

"You're moving too fast for me, Leah." *Christ, how do I get myself into these fixes? With a plethora of beautiful, sophisticated women throwing themselves at me on a daily basis, I just had to have this pure little country dumpling as an added dessert, damn it, and now she's getting heavier by the minute.*

"I've been waiting my whole life to get out of this old place. The last week has been the hardest for me after Momma passed on to the other side. I don't know how to get out of here on my own or how to survive in your world."

Damn, this isn't getting any better. Maybe it'd be best to play along with her until I can figure out a good escape plan. Thank goodness, I put my lucky charm back on so she can't read my thoughts. Damn again! *She's almost got me believing that crap now. I'm going Looney Tunes hanging around here*. He smiled up at her. "Leah, we just met. Let's get to know each other a little better before we think about doing anything rash, okay?"

She slid off the rock into his arms as a spark of hope fluttered. "Oh, thank you, Clint!"

"That was only a *maybe*," he cautioned as her curvaceous body conformed to his, warming him in spite of the chilly water.

"I'll take a maybe over you just driving off and leaving me," she whispered, her lips searching his as her legs wrapped around his hips.

In spite of the cold water, he was fully aroused again and waded out of the pool into the warm night air with her still clinging to him.

"Are you going to do it to me again now?"

He eased her to the ground and reached for his towel. "It's called *making love*, Leah, and let's at least use the bed this time."

“Making love? That’s exactly how I felt when you were doing it to me.”

He sighed in dismay. *Nice move, dumb ass!*

As they dressed, she whirled around and stared off into the darkness.

Startled by her demeanor, he listened intently, hearing only the frogs croaking out in the swamp.

“Somebody’s at your car,” she whispered.

Cold shivers raced down his spine as he stared at her in disbelief, thinking *this is one spooky chick*. “How do you know that?” he demanded in the sudden quiet, realizing that even the frogs had stopped their croaking.

“There’s three of them.”

“You can’t be serious!” He jumped in surprise when his horn began blaring in loud, pulsating bleeps and turned for the trail. “Damn! That’s my alarm!”

She grabbed his arm and pointed in another direction. “This way is closer!”

He ran after her and emerged onto the rutted lane a hundred yards behind his car with its flashing lights outlining three figures running towards them.

“Hey! What’s going on here?” Clint shouted.

“*Holy shit*! *It’s the witch*!” a young boy yelled as they rushed by.

“*Yiiieeeeeee*!” a girl shrieked.

“*She’s got a warlock with her*!” a second male voice yelped as they disappeared down the rutted trail in a blur.

“It's just kids,” Leah soothed, clutching Clint’s arm as he started after them. “They come out here at night to prove their courage. They don’t mean any harm, they just don’t know any better.”

"Damn them!" he swore as he trotted to his car, dug for his keys, and hit the deactivate button. He took his flashlight from the glove compartment and worked his way around the car checking it carefully. "I think the alarm scared them off before they could do any damage," he appraised as a car engine fired up in the distance and tires squealed on asphalt.

He reset the alarm. "How did you know someone was fooling with my car?"

She shrugged. "I guess I'm in harmony with you now, even if I can't read you because of that thing around your neck."

"How did you know it was three people? That's eerie. *Now* you're scaring me."

She wrapped her arms around his neck and stood on tiptoe to kiss him. "Are we still going to bed so you can do it to me again?"

He grinned. "*Make love to you*, Leah, and it's something we do *together*."

She grabbed his hand. "Make love together, that's what I mean. Come on!"

Later he lay in near exhaustion in the tangled sheets, with Leah curled under his arm playing with the hair on his chest in contentment, as he stared up at the ceiling. "Leah, about this *thing*, you know, your curses and spells and such? If I don't take you with me you wouldn't, you know, turn me into a frog or something, would you?"

She giggled. "Of course not."

He sighed. "I guess that sounded kind of silly."

"Frogs are too complicated." She traced his lips with her fingertip. "Toads are *so* much easier."

His heart lurched. "*Leah*!"

She tugged playfully at the hairs on his chest. “I’m just teasing you.”

“Oh, good,” he sighed.

“Who would want to curl up like this with an old toad?” she continued. “I’d much rather have a cat.”

“*Good night, Leah*!”

“Clint?” she whispered after a short silence. “Can we do it again in the morning, if I’m not too sore?”

“If you promise you won’t turn me into a cat.”

She snuggled in next to him. “I’ll have to think about that.”

“Where’s that white cat I saw earlier? Why doesn’t it sleep with you?”

“That was Aunt Bessie’s familiar. She’s gone on back home now.”

“What’s a *familiar*?”

“Don’t you know *anything* about my world?”

“Apparently not … do you have a familiar?”

“What do you think Old Blue is, silly?”

At the mention of his name, Old Blue reared up on the side of the bed with his tail wagging furiously and licked him copiously in the face.

He sighed. “Sorry I asked. Goodnight, Leah.”

Chapter Nine

Clint awoke to a radiantly beautiful woman smiling down at him wrapped in a faded, torn blue robe and holding two steaming cups of coffee, one of which she handed to him as she sat down on the side of the bed. He propped back against the headboard and sipped in gratification as he met her sparkling blue eyes, thinking that in the light of morning she wasn't nearly as daunting as in the darkness.

She leaned down and kissed him, her heart bursting with affection for the new meaning her life had taken on since meeting him on the trail. "I like waking up next to you."

He smiled. "You're one gorgeous girl-witch in the morning."

"I'm awfully sore, but I still want to do it again, if it's okay with you," she murmured as she kissed him again. "I like this kissing thing a lot, too."

He chuckled. "You're wearing me out."

"I never knew doing it could be so pleasurable. Momma said it was a woman's burden to endure. Momma was wrong."

"Your momma was wrong about a lot of things. Let's go bathe and I'll show you something special."

They had a short splash in the frigid spring waters and then lay on a flat rock to dry in the morning sun.

She snuggled in under his arm and laid her head on his chest. "What are you going to show me special?"

"Close your eyes. This is just for you." He kissed her lips, moved down to work on her breasts, and then continued down across her stomach as she quivered.

She moaned as the heat rose within her in delectable currents of pulsating delight as he pinned her to the rock, lashing her into escalating spasms of throbbing rapture. A searing eruption left her shaking violently in waves of sensuous ecstasy with her head spinning wildly.

"I almost fainted," she gasped.

"That was just a warm up."

She whimpered as he started on her again, slowly building a rising tide of wanton craving within her. "Oh, my goodness," she whispered, shivering in delight, having never imagined anything could be so deliciously enthralling, and experienced an even greater explosion of searing fulfillment. She lay quaking in a near trance, knowing she could not survive without this man in her life, that her love for him was boundless, that life before him had been meaningless, and now that she had experienced him, unable to imagine living without him.

"You're going to kill me," she moaned. "No one could ever make me feel the way you do, and I don't care if you do think it's only because it's my first time with a man."

"That kind of praise will get you in trouble every time." He started on her breasts yet again, working his way down her body, and then back up, tasting, kissing, nibbling, rubbing, probing, systematically turning her into a rippling state of gasping desire.

"Please, Clint!" she begged. "I'll probably die if you make me do it again."

He paused. "Promise to never turn me into a cat?"

"Promise to take me with you when you leave?" she countered.

He chuckled evilly as he settled his lips back down on her. "Silly girl, you never negotiate from a position of weakness!"

"Oh, my goodness ..." she moaned, squirming helplessly as he worked on her methodically until the next, even more violent explosion reduced her to an ebbing, shuddering, molten heap. When she could finally breathe and think clearly again, she surveyed him with half-lidded eyes as he swam around in the pool at her feet.

"Come on in," he invited.

"I'm so weak I'd drown," she complained. "Come lay with me in the sun." She draped herself across his chest when he crawled up beside her. "You're cold!"

"Your hot water doesn't seem to be working."

"Do I please you like you please me?"

He pulled her close. "Totally."

"I can't move," she whispered weakly. "I want to hold you like this forever."

He awoke with her on top of him kissing him in teasing twirls with her tongue. She reached down, slid him inside her, and sank down on him.

"I thought you were sore," he teased as her warmth consumed him.

"You worked the soreness out of me."

"I like waking up like this," he murmured.

"This is just for you," she murmured back.

Later they slipped back into the pool and frolicked together, splashing each other in glee. Afterwards they dressed and he limped back down the trail to her shack in contentment with her clutching his hand.

"When are you going to try to leave me, Clint?"

He reached to ensure his pendulant was still around his neck. "Try?"

"*Here, kitty, kitty, kitty,*" she teased.

He scowled. "That's not funny, Leah!"

"When, Clint?" she demanded.

"I've … got to leave tomorrow at the latest."

"Why do you have to go so soon?"

"I've got a million things to do and I'm running out of time."

"What kind of things?"

"For starters, I've got to meet with some potential sponsors for next season, find a new crew chief, and put together a team. I've also got to meet with my chassis man and my engine builder, and a dozen other people to get ready for the new season. I'll come back soon."

Her heart skipped a beat. "If you take me with you now you won't have to come back."

He paused, choosing honesty over deception. "I don't have any way to take care of you right now, Leah. My life is so unstable half the time I don't know where my next meal is coming from or where I'll lay my head at night. I'm going to be on the road a lot meeting with people, and sometimes even sleeping in my car instead of at my race shop. That's no life for you. I'll be back in a few months when things settle down, I promise."

"A few months!" she cried. "I'll die if I have to wait that long, Clint! *Please* take me with you now!"

"Leah, it just wouldn't work out right now," he soothed. "There's so much to do I don't even have time to take care of my own self. You don't understand what my world is like. It's hard and cruel and filled with a lot of uncertainty."

"You don't have to take care of me, I'll take care of you! I won't be a burden to you. I can travel, sleep in the car, go without a meal, or whatever is called for the same as you can."

"What would you do all day while I'm running around doing my thing, Leah?"

"I can help you do your thing if you'll teach me how. I'm very resourceful."

"There's really nothing you can do to help. I'm the only one who can do what needs doing, and you'd be bored to death following me around watching me do it."

"No I wouldn't! I'd love it. Your life is so exciting with all the travel and people. *Please*, *please*, *please* take me with you!"

"Living on the road is no life for you. You'd be miserable. You need a home and some stability. Believe me, it's no picnic."

"Look at my life now in this old swamp, Clint! I live alone in a shack with Old Blue and survive by bringing in a few dollars every now and then using my powers to help people who won't even admit they know me to other people. I'd be much happier taking care of you in your world. Really I would!"

Her desperation filled him with unease. He had to admit that even living on the road or in the back of his race shop was probably better than what she had here. Still, what would he *do* with her? Maybe he should let her tag along, at least for a couple of weeks, and help her find a job and a better place to live, help her get started on her own somewhere out of this damned swamp she hated so much.

"Leah, if I *should* decide to let you come with me, you've got to promise to cool it with the witch thing. People will think you're crazy and I've got an image to maintain."

She held her breath. "Okay, I promise my powers will be our secret."

He pulled her around to look her in the eye. "You would be so easy for a man to love. But right now is not the right time for me. Do you understand what I'm saying?"

Painful hope surged in her. "Does that mean that maybe someday you could learn to love me when the time is right for you, Clint?"

His stomach sank. "Well, I … uh, love … takes time, Leah. It's not an instant kind of thing. We barely know each other."

She threw her arms around his neck. "You won't regret giving me a chance!"

"I honestly can't think of *one* good reason why I should do this," he fumed.

She smiled impishly up at him. "I can think of one good reason."

He scowled. "And what would that be?"

"It's better than being a cat."

He grinned. "Being a cat might not be so bad."

"It depends," she insisted.

"On what?"

"Old Blue."

"What does Old Blue have to do with it?"

"He ate the last cat I had."

"Very funny," he growled.

"Please, Clint, I ain't ever begged for anything in my whole life, but I'm begging now. I'll get down on my knees if you want me too." She dropped to her knees. "Please don't leave me behind."

"*Damn*!" he swore. "What do you need to pack?"

"I don't have very much stuff."

"What about your house?"

"It belongs to a farmer up the road apiece. He just let my momma live here because she helped him with his troubles sometimes."

"What about Old Blue?"

"He'll be less trouble than I am," she assured him.

"What if things don't work out between us?" he demanded.

"They will."

"But what if they *don't*?" he protested, taking her hands and pulling her to her feet.

Her eyes danced. "*Then* I'll turn you into a cat for Old Blue to snack on!"

"Leah, I'm trying to be serious here!"

"Let's just be positive, Clint. Take me to your world and you'll see. I'll learn to be a real lady for you and make you proud of me."

He sighed in resignation. "Sometimes I think you really are a witch! Okay, we'll try it for a few weeks and see how things work out, but we need a firm understanding." He took her by the shoulders. "Number one, no more talk of you being a fortuneteller or whatever that nonsense. Two, no more talk about your world and my world and that kind of crap. We're going to *my* world and leaving *yours* behind. Understand? *You've* got to adapt to *my* world, period."

She threw herself in his arms. "Thank you, Clint! We'll live in your world, I promise!"

"One last thing, tell me what 'being the one' is supposed to mean and why you think that old hack in South Carolina sent me here to seduce you?"

Her joy shifted to trepidation. "Clint, I promise I'll help you find someone to explain it to you, but it can't be me!"

He watched the vein in her neck throb as her fate hung in the balance. "Okay, I'll accept that for now."

She clung to him. "You won't regret this!"

He limped to his car for a change of clothes from his suitcase. She was waiting on the porch with the small blue bottle from her cigar box when he returned.

"It's time to work on your pains," she advised as she lifted his shirt.

"What's that?" he asked suspiciously.

"Something to help you heal," she replied as she placed a few drops of oil from the bottle in her palms and gently rubbed it into his sides around his rib cage. When finished, she pushed him down in the rocker and went inside to return with a pan of steaming water, a clear pint jar filled with a yellow crystal substance, and the small green bottle from her cigar box. She set the pan on the floor before him, opened the jar, shook some of the powder inside into the pan, and placed three drops of liquid from the green bottle in before swishing it around to dissolve.

"And what is that?" he demanded.

"Natural sea salt and a special mixture of essential oil I made up," she replied as she removed his shoe and placed his left foot in the hot water. "Let this soak."

He spent a restful hour sitting in the rocker with his foot soaking in the mixture mentally making a list of people to see and things to accomplish in the next few weeks. When the water began to cool, Leah returned with the small brown bottle from her box and began massaging the thick oil into his left foot and ankle.

"And what is *this* witches' brew?" he teased as her soothing hands worked the comforting balm into his skin.

"It's another special blend of essential oil I made up," she replied cryptically.

"And you think your secret concoction will fix what the doctors can't even diagnose?" he challenged.

"Rest now while I get my things together and fix us some supper," she instructed.

He dozed the afternoon away in contentment with Old Blue curled up at his feet. When she kissed him awake at dusk, he stood and looked down at his ankle in astonishment. "There's no pain!"

She smiled and led him inside for dinner, which he found surprisingly good after the initial shock of her serving crawfish, grits, and cornbread.

Afterwards, they went to bed early, kissed and explored each other for a time, then made passionate love before falling asleep in contented exhaustion.

* * *

"Wake up, sleepy-head," Leah insisted as she sat on the side of the bed and held a cup of coffee out to him. "I'm packed and waiting on you. Let's go bathe and get going!"

He sat up and stretched, noting she wore the same tattered blue robe with her hair piled on top of her head by an attachment, thinking that if it were possible, she was even more beautiful than the day before. "You mean you don't want to *do it* for a change?"

"Does it always keep getting better and better?"

"I'm beginning to feel like a boy-toy," he grumped as he took his coffee.

When they returned to the shack after bathing, Leah slipped on a worn red dress at least ten years out of style and two sizes too large for her, thrust her feet into a scuffed pair of brown men's loafers, grabbed two large paper bags, one of which held her cigar box on top, and looked at him expectantly.

"Aren't you going to wear panties and a bra?" he asked uneasily.

"I don't have any," she replied as Old Blue sat beside her with his tail thumping on the floor and his tongue hanging out.

He eyed the paper bags. "You don't have a suitcase for your things?"

"I've never needed one before."

"Leah, are you sure about this?"

"Hush, Clint, me and Old Blue are ready now. Let's go see your world."

He shrugged and opened the door for her. "I sure hope this isn't a mistake—"

"Wait! I almost forgot." She handed him the two bags and rushed back into the house to reemerge with a jar, ran to her mother's grave, scooped a handful of dirt into the container, and then walked backwards around the site thirteen times.

"Sorry, I had to say goodbye to Momma," she explained as she rushed back to him and placed the jar in one of the sacks, took them from his arms, and turned to the trail leading to the car without a backward glance, as Old Blue loped ahead of her barking in excitement.

He trudged after them. *Christ-almighty! What have I gotten myself into?*

Chapter Ten

Clint placed the sacks in the trunk, settled Old Blue down in the backseat, strapped Leah into the bucket seat on the passenger side, and slid in behind the wheel with a sinking sensation in his stomach. He fired up the Firebird with a throaty roar and began backing up the quarter mile to the blacktop with limbs slashing the sides of his car. *I should have done this three-damned days ago when I first got here*! *Just how in hell am I supposed to take care of a backward country girl who thinks she's a witch and her dumb mutt of a dog,* and *manage my floundering racing career*? *I was nuts to agree to this*!

Hating the trapped feeling building within him, growing fearful of the awesome new responsibility he had so carelessly taken on, and consumed with anger at the world in general for the injustice of it all, he spun the wheel around when he reached the asphalt and peeled rubber through the gears with smoke boiling from the tires. Old Blue whined in the backseat and lowered his head onto his paws as Leah clutched at the dash in white-knuckled terror as the powerful engine roared. He hit the first sloping curve at a steady ninety miles an hour and power shifted down in a controlled slide as gravel flew off to the side, picked up speed as he came out of the turn in a roar of thunder, and slammed through an S-turn with the car swaying as it clung to the blacktop. He flat-footed it down a short straightaway and downshifted hard into a ninety degree turn as the rear end jumped around, hit the accelerator to power out of the turn, and swept down a short stretch towards another hairpin turn at full throttle.

"*Clint, please*!" Leah shouted over the noise.

He worked the clutch and throttle, swept through the curve, and powered down another straightaway as Old Blue tumbled out of the backseat into the floorboard with a startled yelp.

"*Clint, please stop*!" she pleaded.

"Relax!" he shouted. "I'm just playing around! This is what I do for a living! I love speed! This is nothing! Wait till you see me race!" He slung the car into the next turn, working the gears, clutch, and throttle masterfully as the car fishtailed out of the turn.

"*Clint, you can take us back if you want to*!"

"What's that?" he shouted as he glanced at her hanging onto the door panel and the dash while staring out at the pavement zipping under them.

"*You can take us back*!"

He downshifted and worked the brake to bring the car to a shuddering halt in the middle of the road and turned to her. "What's it going to be, Leah? I've got no time for games. Either you want to come along or you don't. Make up your mind!"

She blinked back her tears. "I-I want to come with you, Clint. I just d-don't want you to be s-so mad at me for it. Y-You're scaring me and Old Blue to death."

"I know what I'm doing with a car, Leah. I drive for a living, remember?"

"I-I know that, Clint, but I've only rode in the back of a farmer's truck once who took momma and me to town. It smoked and rattled a lot, but went real slow…"

His heart ached as she sat shivering, staring straight ahead, so vulnerable and frightened. Feeling like a total jackass, he shifted into neutral, opened his door, walked around to her side, opened her door, reached in, unbuckled her seatbelt, pulled her out, and hugged her to him as she shook. "I'm sorry, Leah. I told you I could be a real jerk at times," he soothed as he rocked her in his arms. "You deserve so much more than me."

She clung to him. "I-I don't want m-more than you, Clint. I j-just want you to be happy with me, too."

Her heart pounded against his chest as he rocked her in his arms. When she stopped shaking, he helped her back in the car, buckled her up, got back under the wheel, and eased off, keeping the speedometer at the posted fifty-five miles an hour. *What a fool I am. This isn't her fault. She's desperate and I'm her only hope out of the wretched fate she's been unfairly dealt.*

Old Blue curled up on the backseat, lowered his head onto his paws as his frightened eyes stared up at him, and thumped his tail.

At ten 'o clock in the morning they hit Shreveport, Louisiana, and pulled into a motel that advertised *Pets Welcome*. He checked in, threw their bags in the room, settled Old Blue down with some hamburger patties from the Hardees next door, placed Leah back in the car, and drove to the nearest beauty salon. He asked for the manager, and a slim woman approached with a curious half-smile.

"Ma'am, I want you to take this little lady and give her the works. Fingers, toes, facial, hairdo, and anything else I don't know about women get done to themselves in places like this."

She surveyed Leah with care. "I can take her in about two hours. I'll need her for about three hours when she comes back."

Clint checked his watch. "I'll have her back at one o' clock on the dot. Do you have a young lady about her age I can borrow from you until then? I'll pay for her time."

She frowned. "A young lady you can borrow, Sir?"

"We've got to do some clothes shopping and other girly stuff. I need someone to help us with the newest fashions and women's under-things and such."

Leah blushed as the slim lady turned to a young girl standing behind the counter. "Debra, would you mind assisting this couple in shopping for a new wardrobe?"

Debra flashed a warm smile. "It would be a pleasure. There's a mall just down the street with some very good women's apparel shops."

Clint dropped Debra and Leah off two hours later with several bags holding a blue silk dress, matching shoes, panty hose, slip, panties, bra, and an assortment of fake pearls, earrings, and a small lady's gold watch. In the backseat were boxes and bags holding a red dress, a white one, and a black one, each with matching shoes and appropriate undergarments, four pantsuits, three skirt and blouse sets, two sets of jeans with cotton shirts, and a pair of tennis shoes, along with numerous belts, purses, and pieces of cosmetic jewelry. They also purchased three slinky night gowns, a bottle of high priced perfume, and a whole batch of bath salts, creams, lotions, eyeliners, lipsticks, and other whatnots women needed. Lastly, he bought two matching suitcases and an overnight bag.

He tipped Debra a hundred dollars, drove back to the motel, picked up Old Blue, and found a park. As he sat on a bench with Old Blue sitting quietly in front of him, he sighed. "Just what in hell am I supposed to do with you two?"

Old Blue thumped his tail on the ground and laid his head on Clint's knee as he stared up at him with mournful eyes.

"Just take care of you the best I can, I guess. I sure as hell haven't had much choice in the matter. I feel like I've been hijacked or something, but I'll try to make the best of a bad situation for us all," he said remorsefully.

Old Blue thumped his tail on the ground and licked Clint's hand. At four 'o clock sharp he and Old Blue pulled back up to the salon.

"You wait outside," he directed, and Old Blue sat down at the door as he went inside.

The slim lady greeted him with a smile. "Leah will be out in a few minutes. I think you'll approve of the results. Would you care to settle up now?"

"Yes, Ma'am. How much is it?"

"Six hundred and fifty dollars, Sir."

He grinned weakly. *That's twenty-eight hundred dollars spent today, counting Debra's tip—damn near the cost of four sets of racing tires*!

The staff paraded out and turned to face the rear. Leah glided out alone, taking precise steps as she balanced precariously atop the first set of high heels she had ever worn, finding it took more skill than she had ever imagined, so nervous she was afraid she was going to be sick. *What if Clint doesn't like my new look—I practically didn't recognize myself?*

Clint gaped at her newly trimmed, softened, swept up princess hairstyle with draped and dangling jewelry adding an elegant touch to complement subtle red manicured fingernails, toenails, and matching lipstick. He slowly took in the flawlessly applied makeup casting a golden hue below thinned, plucked, and shaped eyebrows and subtle eyeliner highlighting sparkling sapphire eyes above the matching blue silk dress. His gaze drifted down to the creamy pantyhose drawn over smoothly shaved legs in a tempting, glossy sheen, which disappeared alluringly up under the silk dress inviting him to guess lustfully as to what awaited there, judging she could easily make the cover of any women's fashion magazine in the world as she stood shyly watching him, her newly bound breasts' inviting twin peaks threatening to push through the thin fabric.

The slim woman turned to him. "Do you approve?"

"Great god of racing thunder!" he whispered. "I can't carry her to a racetrack looking like that! She's so beautiful I'd have to fight every man there!" *Hell, she's worth five sets of racing tires!*

Leah tottered to him and threw herself in his arms. The staff applauded as Old Blue reared up on the window outside howling with his tail wagging in a vicious cycle.

Clint helped Leah into the car and drove her back to the motel, teased by tantalizing whiffs of her new perfume, and unloaded all of her boxes and bags before turning to the door as waves of desire worked through him.

"You sort out all of your junk and get it packed in the suitcases. We'll be leaving at first light in the morning. I'll take Old Blue out to a butcher shop to get him some steak bones and then I'll be back to take you out to a fancy restaurant for dinner."

Leah wrapped her arms around his waist and laid her head on his chest. "I'm so grateful for everything you've done for me. I didn't expect all this."

He inhaled her sensuous aroma. "If you're going to be my girl, we've got to do it right. Like I said, I've got an image to maintain. God almighty, you're one beautiful woman, Leah."

Her throat constricted. "I like being your girl most of all, Clint."

He tilted her chin up and tenderly kissed her newly painted lips. "If I don't get out of here right now, I'm going to undo a whole day's work done on you."

She darted her tongue between his lips in a soft, teasing thrust as her half-lidded eyes dared him. "Promises, promises."

He pushed her back. "Damn! Witches sure learn fast! Come on, Blue, or I'll be eating hamburgers from next door and you'll be begging for the crusts if we don't get out here!" he swore as he and Old Blue bounded for the door a step ahead of the Jezebel's clutching grasp.

Chapter Eleven

"Do you have a reservation, Sir?" the hostess inquired as she hovered over her book expectantly.

Clint slipped her twenty dollars and watched her frown melt into a gracious smile as she picked up two menus. He didn't miss the appreciative stares from every male in the dining room as she led Leah, who was preoccupied with walking erect in her new high heels, to their table. The hostess placed menus before them with a flourish and the wine steward handed him the wine list in anticipation. He selected an inexpensive bottle of merlot and settled back to admire the beautiful, petrified woman across from him.

She leaned forward covertly. "Clint, there's too many utensils here. I don't know which ones to use!"

"Just use what I use."

She concentrated on her menu. "I don't know what half of this stuff is."

"Do you prefer steak or seafood?"

"I don't care. I'm too nervous to eat anyway."

"Let's try the surf and turf and sample both."

The steward appeared with the merlot, flashed the label for confirmation, popped the cork, presented it for inspection, poured a small portion into Clint's glass, received a nod after his sip, and filled their glasses. With the stewards' departure, Clint lifted his glass.

"To the most beautiful lady in the world!"

Leah smiled demurely as the couple next to them glanced their way. "You're embarrassing me!" She took a tentative sip of her wine and frowned. "It's bitter."

"It's an acquired taste. I can order you some tea if you prefer?"

"No, I want to learn everything." She took another thoughtful sip.

When their meal arrived, her eyes widened. "I'll never eat all this. What is it?"

"Filet and lobster. Try a little of both and we'll take the rest back to Old Blue. That little cup in front of you with the flame under it is melted butter."

"I've got so much to learn it scares me to death," she whispered, conscious of the couple at the next table watching them in wry amusement. "I feel so dumb."

"You are *not* dumb, You're just experiencing something for the first time."

"Which fork do I use?"

"The one with the longer tines, the shorter one is for salad. Use the knife with the wooden handle for your steak and lobster. The funny looking one there is a butter knife for the rolls, which you place on that little saucer there after you've spread butter on it." He passed her the breadbasket, split and buttered his roll as she watched and mimicked him. "Now you need to prepare your baked potato. I use butter and sour cream."

He demonstrated by slicing the potato down the middle and adding the condiments as she watched and followed suit. He then cut a bite of his steak and placed it in his mouth as she again followed his lead. He cut a bite of lobster, dipped it in the melted butter, placed it in his mouth, chewed, and took a sip of wine, with her following his every movement.

He smiled. "See, it's easy. How do you like it?"

"It's delicious. The lobster reminds me of crawfish, only better. I think the wine is making me dizzy. Am I doing okay, Clint?"

"You're doing fine. Slow down on the wine though. You're supposed to sip it, like this." He demonstrated a small sip for her. "Women usually drink a little water between sips. And, Leah, you really shouldn't prop your elbows on the table. It's considered bad etiquette in a restaurant."

She pulled her elbows back. "Oops, sorry!"

"Umm, I like this." Leah licked her lips. "It sure beats my catfish stew and cornbread."

He grinned. "Nothing beats your catfish stew and cornbread."

Her eyes met his warmly. "This is the happiest day of my life!"

His pulse quickened. "You take my breath away."

She blushed. "You take my breath away, too, especially when you make love to me over and over."

"*Shhh*!" He nodded at the couple beside them, stifling his laughter as they masked their own restrained mirth behind their napkins.

"What a charming couple," the woman commented to her companion.

"Yes, they seem to be," the man replied. "I feel as though I know him, but can't quite place it."

After finishing their meal, Clint ordered a doggy bag for the remainder and settled their bill.

The man leaned their way. "Excuse me, I'm John Roberts, and this is my wife, Mary. You look familiar. What business are you in?"

Clint shook his hand. "I'm Clint Long, and this beautiful lady is Leah. I drive in the American Racing Association Series."

Mr. Roberts snapped his fingers. "That's it! I must have seen you at the races. Would you and your lovely lady care to join us for an after dinner drink?"

Clint lifted his eyebrows to Leah, who nodded nervously. "I suppose we could finish our wine, Mr. Roberts." Clint pulled Leah's chair back for her and seated her at the couple's table before taking the chair across from her.

Mrs. Roberts turned to Leah. "That's such a lovely dress. And I love what you've done with your hair."

Leah looked lovingly at Clint. "Thank you, Ma'am. Clint bought it for me today. I've never had anything so pretty in my life. My hair was a tangled mess before he took me to one of those beauty parlors and got it all done up for me."

"You're a charming couple," Mrs. Roberts replied. "I wish John were as patient with me." She cast a glance at Mr. Roberts, who squirmed. "How long have you two been together?"

"Only three days, Ma'am," Leah answered. "Clint has taught me so much already my head is spinning."

Clint refilled his and Leah's wine glass with the last of their bottle. "Are you a race fan, Mr. Roberts?"

Mr. Roberts nodded. "Actually, we have a car in the ARA series of our own, the number twenty-six driven by Glen Johnson. I'm the president of the company that sponsors it."

Clint stiffened. "It's a small world, Mr. Roberts. I know your team and driver well. Glen hired my crew chief out from under me in the middle of the season and, as you may recall, he and I tangled in the last race. There's not a lot of love lost between us."

Mrs. Roberts turned to Leah with a smile to mask the sudden awkwardness that settled over the table. "Where are you from, child, and how did you two meet?"

Mr. Roberts stifled his discomfiture. "Yes, I recall now. You drive the thirteen car. I'm sure the last race was a most unfortunate incident and nothing personal."

Clint bristled. "Glen and I were racing each other hard. I suppose some could say I got the worst end of it. But my crew chief was all about money … *your* money, I presume?"

"I've lived in the bayou all my life," Leah replied to Mrs. Roberts nervously, distracted by the tension between Mr. Roberts and Clint. "Aunt Bessie sent Clint to me. My Momma passed on to the other side a week ago. I don't know what I would have done if he hadn't taken me with him this morning."

"We think a great deal of Glen and, err, your ex-crew chief," Mr. Roberts continued in the strained environment. "We're thinking of moving them up to the Cup Series if they continue with the success they've had thus far."

Clint masked his envy as he seethed. "I wish you all the luck." *Now just how in hell am I supposed to sit here and smile like a mule eating briars with one of the assholes that all but destroyed my career*!

"I'm sorry to hear about your mother, you poor child," Mrs. Roberts soothed. "So your Aunt Bessie introduced you to each other?"

"Oh, no, she didn't introduce us," Leah corrected. "She's my godmother in South Carolina that Clint stopped in to get a reading from as a lark, because he doesn't believe in fortune telling, and she sent him on along to me."

Mrs. Roberts frowned. "How … interesting. So your godmother is a fortune teller? And you two had never actually met before she decided he was right for you and sent him all the way to Louisiana to meet you?"

"Well, she didn't exactly decide he was right for me," Leah explained with a lisp from the wine. "You see, when I read his aura, there I was down on the floor with him, and me without a stitch of clothes on as naked as the day I was born. It liked to have embarrassed me to death. But I'd already taken his money, so I didn't have a choice but to tell him what I saw. And then he kissed me and I knew he was going to do it to me. I was so scared, because I'd never been with a man before and didn't know what I was supposed to do. But he didn't seem to mind too much and showed me how to do it. After that I couldn't bear to be without him and begged him to take me with him. He finally said we'd see how things go for a couple of weeks. I don't know what I'm going to do if it doesn't work out. I sure don't want to go back to that swamp for the rest of my life."

Mrs. Roberts cast a censorious glance at Clint, who smiled meekly and tried to catch Leah's eye. "How *intriguing* … and so you fell in love?"

"Well, I sure did," Leah admitted. "But it's just not the right time for him."

Mrs. Roberts glared at Clint as one might at a child molester as he tried to shrink himself into a tiny ball under her penetrating glare. "Well, I'm *certain* he'll come to his senses eventually," she replied dryly. "You said you tell fortunes, as well?"

"Well, it's not fortunes really," Leah advised. "I read people's auras."

"*Leah*?" Clint cautioned.

Leah placed her hand over her mouth. "Oops, I'm not supposed to tell people that because they'll think I'm crazy. You see, Clint's got his image to maintain."

Mrs. Roberts glowered at Clint. "Oh, I'm *sure* his *image* is very *dear* to him, child. Could you read my aura for me?"

Leah cast a cautious glance at Clint. "I wouldn't mind, Ma'am, but I don't want Clint to get mad at me. This has been the most wonderful day of my life and I don't want to ruin it."

Mrs. Roberts turned to Clint with a withering look, daring him to disapprove. "*Would* you mind?"

Clint swiped at the sweat beaded up on his forehead. "Mrs. Roberts, surely you don't believe in that sort of thing?"

"I think it would be entertaining," Mr. Roberts injected. "I've heard of people who are mystic, but I've never actually met one. Would it be an imposition?"

"I'm sorry, Clint," Leah whispered. "I promised I wouldn't do this, and here I've gone and done it. I think the wine made me forget. Would you be mad at me if I do it for her?"

Clint tried to dodge the darts emanating from Mrs. Roberts eyes and smiled sweetly. "No madder than I already am, I guess."

Mrs. Roberts patted Leah's hand as she shot Clint a sizzling look that promised bodily harm and major disfigurement if he dared mistreat the child any more than he already had. "You couldn't possibly be angry with her. She's so sweet and sincere."

"We didn't mean to create a problem," Mr. Roberts apologized. "I hope we haven't imposed ourselves on you in some disagreeable way?"

"Oh, no problem," Clint assured him as he worked up a mock smile. "When I get her home, I'll just strangle her and everything will be fine."

Mrs. Roberts turned to Leah. "There then, please read my aura for me, dear!"

Leah swallowed glumly. "Well, okay then, because I'm already in plenty of trouble anyway. Do you want to know anything specific?"

Mrs. Roberts frowned. "Well, let's see. John's been very evasive and mysterious all day. Can you do his aura instead and tell me what he's up to?"

"I can sure try." Leah took Mr. Roberts' hands in hers, rocked her head back, and closed her eyes. She sat for several minutes and then rocked forward beaming.

"Oh, you're going to be so surprised!" she gushed to Mrs. Roberts. "But I can't spoil it for you!"

Mrs. Roberts laughed. "That's not fair! You've simply got to tell me what you saw!"

"I just can't spoil his surprise," Leah insisted.

Mrs. Roberts turned to Mr. Roberts. "John? What have you done now? Can she tell me?"

Mr. Roberts shrugged. "Now *I'm* intrigued. By all means, tell her."

"Are you sure?" Leah asked.

"Please," he assured. "This is quite interesting."

"Ma'am, he's going to give you the most beautiful diamond necklace you've ever seen in your life," Leah gushed. "It's in his pocket right now!"

Clint hung his head in dismay in the total, stunned silence that followed.

Mrs. Roberts stared at Mr. Roberts. "John?"

Mr. Roberts turned his shocked expression from Leah to her, shifted, and dug into his pocket to produce a slim, leather-bound case. "I was going to give this to you on the Old River Bridge where I asked you to marry me twenty-five years ago tonight."

Mrs. Roberts opened the case and the necklace glittered as she swooned. "*Oh, John*!"

Mr. Roberts turned to Clint. "That's the most incredible thing I've ever witnessed. This is … quite a woman you have here …"

Clint, still staring at Leah in astonishment with his jaw unhinged, closed his mouth and tried to gather his wits. "Uh, yeah, she is … quite a woman … I guess. Well, it's been fun and all meeting you two, but we've got to go now!" He hurried around to pull Leah's chair back. "Good luck with your team and my crew chief."

Mr. Roberts stood. "Yes. Good luck to you too, Clint. It was … a pleasure …"

Leah tottered along supported by Clint's steadying hand on her elbow as he steered her to the door. "Are you really mad at me?" she whispered.

"Yes, *really-really* mad," he whispered back.

"Are you really going to strangle me when you get me home?"

"I'm leaning towards it! Will you turn me into a damned cat if I do?"

"I might."

"How *did* you do that anyway?"

"You were sitting right there … I read his aura."

"Okay … then maybe I won't strangle you when I get you home."

"Okay … then maybe I won't turn you into a cat."

She snuggled her arm through his and clung to him for support as she wobbled drunkenly along in her new high heels.

Chapter Twelve

The Council members settled into their chairs when the opening ceremony was completed and turned expectantly to Merle standing in the center of the circle as a hush fell over the assembled tribes outside the circle.

"I have called you to Circle because we have a problem," he advised. "Please address this issue directly with Council, Aunt Bessie."

Aunt Bessie shifted in her seat and clutched her Book of Shadows in her lap. "Things have taken an unexpected turn. Leah has left our world to join this one in his world." She waited for the murmurs to subside. "We have lost contact with them."

Drew stood. "Why wasn't this anticipated? We should never have trusted a Solitary. They are unpredictable. What were we thinking? Where could they have gone? Have you tried to communicate with Leah on this matter?"

Aunt Bessie turned to his voice. "Leah is true to our beliefs and shares her mother's same strong values. We need not find fault with her until we know more about her intentions. All I know is that she left with this one this morning. I have tried to communicate with her, to no avail. As I have said, she is very inexperienced in psychic communication."

Herschel stood. "This is due to the love spell you cast, Aunt Bessie. I'm certain of it! Bad karma is certain to follow. I think it imperative Council concede the spell was in no way authorized. In fact, it was expressly forbidden!"

Vaughn stood. "We need not place blame on an individual when all misjudged the situation. Obviously, in view of the fact a love spell was cast, with or without Council approval, we should have collectively foreseen that something like this might happen. The imperative thing now is to reestablish contact with Leah and bring the situation back under control, is it not?"

Shoshanna stood. "Does this one know he has passed his seed to Leah? Could she have possibly revealed that as an enticement to take her with him?"

"This is possible," Aunt Bessie replied. "I fear casting the love spell was indeed a serious mistake. I accept full responsibility for the act, and the reflected three-fold bad karma, as is my just due."

Hellene stood. "The question is unanswered as to why no one was watching over them? Why weren't *you* controlling the situation, Aunt Bessie, as Council charged you to do, through your familiar Jasmine?"

Jasmine hissed from her crouched position on the arm of the chair as Aunt Bessie sat immobile. "If fault is to be found, then the responsibility should rightfully rest with me. From what we knew of this one, I did not think he would be interested in a long-term liaison. Jasmine visited with them on the first day to cast the lust spell as directed by Council, and admittedly, I made a mistake in authorizing Jasmine to cast a love spell on Leah in my haste to help her. I am old and tend to think slowly now. Jasmine had to use all of her powers of suggestion to get this one to take the old road, and again to get him to take the lane to her house. Jasmine was tired and weak afterwards, for she is old as well. After they joined, I directed Jasmine to return here to rest. I did not anticipate this one would become smitten with Leah and take her to his world. I did not think she would leave her world behind."

Ginger stood. "I fear Jasmine may have cast the lust spell too strongly on this one in the first instance, as well. He remained for three days enjoying the delights of Leah's body. Under the circumstances, that would seem to be overly long for him to remain with her, and we should have anticipated that personal liaisons could develop between them."

Aunt Bessie nodded. "Perhaps this is so, but I remind Council that Jasmine was instructed specifically to cast a *strong* lust spell. But this is irrelevant. The issue is our loss of control of his seed based on Leah's action in joining him in his world, I believe."

Lola stood. "I disagree as to any reference of personal negligence on Aunt Bessie's part. I spent many nights with this one. I came to know him well in this period. I would not have thought he would be taken with one woman either. He gave no indication of having any interest in a lasting relationship with his focus on his racing career and preoccupation with finding a sponsor to support his team. Placing all the blame on Aunt Bessie for this unfortunate occurrence is unjust and serves no useful purpose. We need to quit pointing fingers and work on a proper solution to this issue."

Gretchen stood. "I agree with Lola. This one had no interest in women other than physical pleasure. I also came to know him well and would not have anticipated this happening, so to presume Aunt Bessie should have foreseen such an occurrence is unjust."

Adrian stood. "*Would of*, *could of*, *should of*, what does it *matter*? What we are going to *do* about it is the real question, is it not? This is what we should be focusing on now exclusively. That we have unwittingly managed to lose this one's seed is a serious malady for us, and the recovery and protection of it should be, and above all else, *must be*, our highest priority."

Vaughn stood. "I agree. When I met with this one as a potential sponsor, his only interest was in his race team and the upcoming season. There is no way any of us could have foreseen this unfortunate circumstance happening, but I caution you, we need to consider our actions carefully in correcting this distressing situation and avoid adversely imposing our will upon another. They are in fact together of their own choosing, even though an inappropriate casting of a love spell was involved, therefore, we cannot just assume we can persuade Leah to abandon this one she now loves and return to this world for our benefit."

The circle broke up into arguments, which Merle brought back to order by rapping his knuckles on his Book of Shadows. "*Here, here! We are not a rabble*! We are a *Council* guided by our collective wisdom. Each will have his say in an atmosphere of proper, moderate decorum!"

Lily stood. "Why do we feel as though we must do *anything* at this point? Is it so wrong for two young people to follow their hearts? The seed is not fundamentally endangered by this venture, because a warm and loving home would be a preferred and proper atmosphere to rear our future leader of Council."

Herschel stood. "But we have lost *control* of the lineage! We don't know *where* they are or *what* they intend to do. We must not lose contact with them. We have been five thousand years awaiting this event. We must consider this as we decide what course to take."

Ginger stood. "The only action we should take is to locate them. Then we should observe and determine what they plan to do with their future. As of now, they have done nothing to warrant our action or cause us to panic. If we do anything to adversely affect their relationship it would be an intrusion on their will and another serious violation of our Rede."

Merle stood in his stooped fashion. "I agree with Ginger. We need to find them and observe only. This could be a positive. If this one has indeed fallen in love with our Leah, she could be instrumental in guiding him to our Craft of her own accord. I find it hard to believe she would abandon our world so impulsively. This could be a good thing for us, not a bad thing."

Allay stood. "I agree no immediate harm has been done at this point. This could only be a fling on this one's part. He is young and leads a glamorous life. If Leah is as unworldly as Aunt Bessie claims, he will tire of her quickly in his world. Without him, she will be unable to cope there. We need to be ready to rescue her and the seed she carries when he abandons her. We must not overreact to this situation."

Gretchen stood. "Finding them will not be difficult. This one will return to his race shop in Charlotte. Racing is his passion and no woman will keep him from that for long."

Vaughn stood. "Should we send Lola and Gretchen back to watch for them and determine their intentions when they return?"

Lily stood. "This one would be very uneasy if either of them were around because he has mated with them both. If he has feelings for Leah now it would only complicate the issue. Why can we not send Allay for this purpose? She has offered her service to Council in the matter of this one on numerous occasions."

Allay stood. "I am ready to serve Council in this matter. I will journey to Charlotte to await his return, if Council so directs."

"Does Council object to Allay representing us in this matter?" Merle asked.

Shoshanna stood. "I think it imperative Allay be instructed to not interfere in any way without Council approval. She should locate and observe *only* until further directed by Council. We have had enough independent action concerning this one as it is."

Vaughn stood. "This is essential. We need have no further interference without Council approval."

Merle nodded. "It is then so directed. Is there any other business to address before the Circle is broken? Then let us enjoy our wine and cake. And if it harm none, do as ye will." He motioned for the maiden.

Chapter Thirteen

Clint lay in the tangled sheets with Leah snuggled under his arm and her head on his shoulder sleeping soundly. She insisted on putting her new nightgown back on after they made love, relishing the feel of the silky fabric on her body. That in itself was okay, but now one of her arms draped across his chest had a flimsy cuff that tickled his chin every time he breathed, which in turn was driving him insane with the desire to scratch where it fluttered. But he dared not move for fear she might wake up and want to do it again. Frankly, he was done out for the night. The girl was drunk and practically insatiable. *Just my luck that what appears to be every man's perfect dream woman turns out to be a witch who can't hold her liquor and a borderline nymphomaniac*!

He couldn't sleep, so he replayed scenes from the past three days around in his head searching for some logical explanation. To believe she was a witch was ludicrous. But she did seem to have some strange psychic power, or strong intuition, in any case. *You can bet the bank I'm going to keep my pendulant on from here on out. If she can really read minds, or auras, or whatever, I'll stay in trouble all the time.*

The scene with the Roberts was nothing short of amazing. Hell, it was unbelievable, but he had personally witnessed it. It would be asking too much of fate for the Roberts to keep the incident to themselves. They would probably tell everyone they knew and he would become the laughingstock of racers' row. *Damn, why did I have to order that wine? Why did the Roberts have to be sitting at the next table? Why did I feel the need to rescue a witch to begin with? Life just isn't fair!*

Could she really turn him into a cat? *Would* she? If so, what kind? Probably a damned alley cat if she was mad enough to do it in the first place. But then again, she probably wouldn't want an alley cat sleeping in bed with her, would she? That was some consolation—unless she intended for him to be a snack for Old Blue. It was probably best not to provoke her and find out.

But *if* she did, could she reverse the spell and change him back? If so, as a cat, how could he let her know when he had repented, just in case she was willing to reverse the spell? First thing in the morning he needed to buy a cat book and get to know something about felines.

Old Blue, as if sensing his troubling thoughts, came over to the bed and licked his hand. Had he really eaten her last cat? Would Old Blue be able to recognize him as a cat? Would he even care? He reached out and petted the mangy mutt's head. *Gooooood doggie!*

A lump of self-pity formed in his throat, making him idly wonder what a hairball felt like. *Damn*, was he losing his mind now? And double-damn that old Aunt Bessie hag for sending him there in the triple-damn first place. If only he had kept his pecker in his pants none of this would be happening!

Leah shifted and hugged him in her sleep, moving her hand away from his chin and down to his waist in the process. "*I love you, Clint*," she whispered in a sleep-laden voice.

Damn! Now where did *that* come from? He needed a shrink more than a cat book! He needed to get a grip on this situation, and fast.

He spent a restless night before slipping out of bed to shower and shave just before dawn. As he dressed, Leah stirred and moaned.

"*Ohhhh*, I feel *awful*," she whined. "My stomach is sour and my head is pounding."

"It's called a hangover, sweetie-pie," he replied smugly. *At least she wouldn't want to* do it *this morning*. "Hit the shower and get dressed. We've got places to go, people to see, and things to do! I'll take Old Blue for a walk and bring back some breakfast."

"I don't *want* any," she sulked as she stumbled to bathroom holding her head. "I'm going to be sick!"

"If you play you gotta pay, baby doll!" he sang out before slamming the door behind him and chuckling at the pitiful shriek from inside.

When he and Old Blue returned with coffee, aspirin, and Danish, Leah stood at the foot of the bed wrapped in a towel bawling pitifully.

He surveyed every piece of clothing he bought her the day before strung across the bed, set the tray down, and rushed to hug her. "What's wrong, Leah?"

She sobbed in slobbering quakes with liquid goop coming out of her nose as she clung to him. "I can't decide which outfit to wear! I've never had so many choices before! They're all so beautiful!"

"Here now, just calm down, I'll help you pick something out," he soothed, biting his lip as he quaked with suppressed mirth.

She jerked back and struck him in the chest with her fist. "*It ain't funny, Clint*!"

He pulled her back to his chest, shaking with laughter as she squirmed to pull free. "I'm sorry, Leah. I can't help myself. Come over here and sit down. Here's your coffee. Now take the aspirin for your headache and eat the Danish to help settle your stomach. Everything's going to be all right. I'm an expert at this." He seated her in the chair and handed her a Kleenex.

She gave a big honk into the tissue, wiped her nose, took a shuddering breath, gulped down the two aspirin, and sipped her coffee.

Satisfied she was regaining her composure, he turned to survey the clothes and rubbed his hands together expectantly. "Let's see, today is mostly a lot of travel and a quick meeting with my engine builder late this evening, so let's keep it simple—how about the blue jeans, this white blouse, and those tennis shoes?" He smiled at her, proud of his deductive reasoning in making the obvious perfect wardrobe selection for her.

She bit into her Danish. "No, I want to wear that gray pantsuit outfit."

He bobbled his head. "Sure, that'll work."

She took another bite of her Danish. "But I would really rather wear the brown one because I like the shoes better."

He nodded. "Brown it is—"

"No, I want the black skirt and the red blouse with the matching scarf for my hair."

"Red and black is definitely the better choice—"

"No, I—"

"*Leah*!"

She glowered. "Okay, then *you* decide!"

"*I just did*!"

"What are you so mad about then?" she shouted.

A loud knock occurred on the wall from the room next to them. "*Wear the god-damned blue jeans with the red blouse, matching scarf, and the brown shoes*! *I'm trying to sleep over here*!" a muffled male voice shouted.

"*Okay*," Leah called back happily. "*Thanks*!"

"*You're welcome*," the voice replied sweetly.

Clint stared beseechingly up at the ceiling. "Lord, this is Clint Long down here on earth. I hate to bother you this early in the morning and all, but I'd just like a minute of your time to point out that I've never done anything in my whole life to deserve this."

"*Amen, brother*," the voice behind the wall called out in a condescending tone.

The second crisis occurred when they were loading the suitcases in the car. As Clint stashed the last of them in the trunk, Leah came trotting out with her two paper sacks and thrust them at him.

"What's this?" he demanded.

"My old clothes," she replied.

"We don't need these anymore."

"They're mine."

"I know whose they are, but you don't need them."

"Yes I do."

"No you don't."

"*Yes I do, Clint*!"

"*No you don't, Leah*!"

"*I do*!"

"*You don't*!" He calmed himself. "Besides, we don't have enough trunk space."

He strolled over to the dumpster and tossed the bags in. When he turned back with a satisfied smile, Leah passed him lugging his own battered suitcase and swung it up over the top into the dumpster.

"That was my suitcase," he observed.

"I know whose it was," she replied pleasantly.

"Why did you do that?"

"To give us more trunk space."

"Leah, you're pissing me off!"

"Good, because you've *already* pissed me off!"

"So this is to be our first fight?"

"Second," she argued. "Remember last night?"

"Last night doesn't count."

"Does too—you were mad at me."

He smirked. "But *you* weren't mad at *me*. It takes *two* to fight."

"Says who?"

He sighed. "Leah, I'm going to crawl into that dumpster and get your bags and my suitcase. Then I'm going to load them into the trunk and we're going to go on about our business—*but I would greatly appreciate it if you didn't speak to me for awhile*!"

"Okay," she said.

"*Good*," he said.

"Good," she said.

"You've just *got* to have the last damn word, don't you?" he growled as he climbed up the side of the dumpster and dropped down into the interior.

"Yes," her muffled voice replied from outside the dumpster.

They drove for three straight hours in total silence until Old Blue finally whined from the back seat.

"Old Blue's gotta go potty," Clint advised as he slowed down at the next exit with a sign for a restaurant. "Are you hungry?"

She shrugged her shoulders.

He scowled. "Was that a yes or a no?"

"Am I allowed to talk to you now?"

"Yes, unless you intend to stay mad at me for the rest of your life."

"I'm hungry and I need to pee."

"How long are you going to stay mad?"

"Until you apologize."

"*Me*! How about *you*?"

"You started it."

"Okay, Leah, *I'm sorry*. Okay?"

She leaned across and kissed his cheek. "Okay."

Women are so damned complicated, and yet so darn simple, he concluded in bewilderment as he drifted onto the exit ramp.

Chapter Fourteen

At 10:30 p.m. that night, after fifteen and a half hard hours, two stops for gas, one for a quick lunch, and two more for Old Blue to do the doggie thing, Clint eased the car to a stop outside of Ronnie James's engine shop on the outskirts of Charlotte, North Carolina. He slipped out of the car and closed the door softly so as not to disturb Leah curled up against the door sleeping after spending the day staring out at the numerous states they were crossing and asking fifteen million questions once she had permission to talk to him again. Old Blue opened one eye and closed it in boredom from his position in the backseat.

Ronnie looked up from where he and three of his assistant engine builders were working on an engine hooked up to a Dyno. "Clint! How they hanging?"

"Low and left, Ronnie, how about you?"

"Can't complain, old buddy, can't complain."

"How're my engines looking?"

"On schedule. Three race, and two practice, right?"

"That'll get me started, but I'll need a couple more as soon as I get my sponsor signed."

"Getting real close to the start of the season, Clint, you don't want to get behind the old *power curve*, old buddy!" Ronnie cautioned as his henchmen chortled.

"That's a fact. When can I get these?"

"I'll send the practice engines over to your shop tomorrow. This is one of the race engines here." He patted the engine block. "She's a little balky at low RPM, but the bitch can churn out some bad-assed horsepower at max throttle. You'll be happy with it."

"You're the *man*, Ronnie!"

"I'll have another one by the end of the month, and the last the week before the season starts. *Good-god-almighty*! Just look at that *sweet thang* there!"

Everyone turned to the front of the shop where Leah was profiled beyond the picture window under the nightlight looking positively delectable as she leaned into a stretch with her taut breasts jutting out, the action emphasizing the pleasing curve of her derrière. Even at a distance, she was a conversation stopping, eye-popping beauty, with her tangled hair giving her a sultry come-hither centerfold look.

"*Grrruuu*!" Ronnie rasped as Old Blue sniffed at the base of a light pole and hiked his leg. "Is that little rosebud traveling with you, Clint?"

Clint scowled as the engine men leaned forward staring in a lecherous throng. "Yeah, that's Leah. I picked her up down in Louisiana a few days ago. She's a real beauty and as natural as spring water."

Ronnie winked at his helpers. "Well, knowing you, old buddy, you'll be tiring of her in about a week and looking to move on to greener pastures. You just remember old Ronnie and the gang when the time comes and drop that little Barbie Doll off here. Me and my grease monkeys will throw in a free rebuild for a night with that hot little honey-bunny, won't we, boys?"

One of Ronnie's goons snickered and rolled his chew of tobacco in his jaw. "Hell yeah, I'll even take sloppy seconds to ride that little filly! *Hee*! *Hee*! *Hee*!"

Clint clenched his jaw as he experienced the most astounding emotion of his life—damn all-mighty, he was *jealous*! His face flushed and his hands balled into knots as the group laughed. When another pursed his lips and kissed the air wickedly, Clint grappled with the urge to knock him on his ass. *It won't do for me to lose the best-damned engine builder in the whole damned world over one damned girl*! *But Leah isn't just one damned girl ... she's my damned girl*, *damn it*!

Ronnie tuned in to the fury in Clint's eyes. "Hey, old buddy, we didn't mean no offense. We're just cutting the fool. I've never known you to give a damn about anything but a racecar before, especially not a woman. No disrespect to you or the lady intended."

The smirks disappeared as the others hastily turned to tinker with the engine.

Clint spun on his heel. "None taken," he gritted as he stormed out. "See you at the end of the month."

"Hey, you take care now!" Ronnie called after him.

Clint lifted his hand in a wave without looking back and glared at Leah as he passed. "*Get in the car*!"

She hurriedly helped Old Blue into the backseat as he hit the starter, jacked the shift into reverse, and backed up with her still struggling to close her door as she stared at him wide-eyed.

"What's wrong?"

"*Nothing*!" he snapped as he shifted gears and spun the tires.

"Are you mad at me?"

"*No*!"

"You're acting like it."

He power shifted into second with another screech of rubber. "*Buckle up*!"

She clutched at the seatbelt as he hit third gear with another squeal of rubber. "Clint!"

"I ain't fighting with you again, Leah, so you can just cool it!"

"Did I do something wrong?"

"*No*, damn it!"

"I don't know unless you tell me," she insisted.

He downshifted, pulled into a gas station, stopped the car, stormed around to her side, jerked opened her door, reached in, pulled her out, and hugged her.

After the initial shock she lifted her arms to embrace him. "Are you okay, Clint?"

"Yes. Now get back in the car." He hurried back to his side, buckled up, and drove off at a reasonable rate.

"Are you hungry?" he asked.

"I … could eat something," she replied cautiously. "But mostly I'm just tired."

He hunched over the steering wheel. "I should have fed you and Old Blue earlier. Everything's probably closed by now. I don't know why I was in such a damned hurry to get here. I could have checked on my engines next week. They weren't going anywhere. You two haven't eaten since lunch. As usual, I ain't thinking about nobody but my own damn self."

She touched his arm. "That's okay. We can wait until morning. We don't want to be a bother."

He banged his fist on the steering wheel. "*No*, damn it! I've got to start taking better care of you and

Old Blue. I'm not used to having anyone to worry about but me. You've got to help me take better care of you two since I'm nothing but a self-centered jerk. You deserve better, Leah. You could have about any man in the whole damn world you wanted. Do you know that? Every damn man that looks at you wants you. Did you see how all those men looked at you in the restaurant last night, with their damn wives and girlfriends sitting right there in front of them? Do you think they gave a damn who saw them looking at you? Why, hell no! They were going to look and to hell with it if they got their face slapped in the process by their damned old wives and girlfriends. None of them broads could hold a candle to you anyway. Hell, I'd of been staring myself if you weren't with me. That's the damned truth, too."

"Clint, would you please pull over for me?"

"Sure." He pulled into a convenience store.

She got out, walked around to his side, opened his door, pulled him out, and hugged him. "Now I don't know what just happened back there, but I only care about how *you* look at me. You do take good care of Old Blue and me, and we both appreciate it. No one else matters to us. Now get back in the car." She walked back around to her side and slid in.

He glanced at her as he drove off. "You're one exceptional woman, Leah. Do you know that? A man like me is real lucky to have a girl like you."

"Just wait until I learn how your world works and I'll make you real proud of me. Wait and see."

"Hell, I'm already real proud of you. How about a Big Mac, some fries, and a shake?"

"I've never had that, but I'm willing to try it."

"You've never had a Big Mac and fries? You'll love it."

"I might like it, but I could only ever love you, Clint."

He slammed his palm on the steering wheel, causing her to jump. "Damn it, I could only ever love you too, Leah! *There*! I've *said* it!"

She smiled to choke back her tears. "Want to stop and get another one of them hugs?"

He swerved into the parking lot of another gas station "Hell yeah! But we ain't ever going to get anywhere at this rate."

She met him at the back of the car and embraced him. "Let's get that Big Mac thing and go make us some love."

He drew a deep breath. "Okay … and tomorrow we're going shopping for a ring."

"A ring?"

"I want all those jackasses out there to know you're *my girl*, damn it! Otherwise, they'll be sniffing around you all the time. You need a ring to protect you from all the creeps you're going to be meeting. My world is full of them hitting on every pretty girl they see. You just don't know how they are because you've never been around people like that. It would be in your best interest to have a ring so they'll know you're not on the open market. It's like having a gun in the house to protect you from burglars. Burglars won't fool with you if they know you've got a gun in the house. When those jackasses see that ring, they'll know you're mine and they won't fool with you then. It's for your own protection. Do you understand what I mean, Leah?"

She could no longer contain her tears. "I was afraid you would never want me, Clint. It just about kills me when I think of not having you in my life."

"If anyone had told me four days ago I would be getting engaged, I would have thought they had lost their damn mind." He tipped her chin up so he could look into her eyes and gently wiped away the streaks of mascara on her cheeks. "I know you'll think I'm crazy, but the first time I kissed you and scared you half to death, I felt something. It was the best feeling I've ever had, as if I was complete for the first time in my life. I probably ain't saying it right."

"You're saying it right," she whispered as she clung to him. "I felt the same way. That's why it scared me so bad. I knew you were the only one for me."

"Do we have to invite that old Aunt Bessie hag to our wedding someday?"

Leah laughed through her tears. "She'd put a hex on you if you didn't."

"I damn sure wouldn't want to end up as a cat on my wedding night."

"Toad," she corrected. "She'd be madder than that."

"Whatever. Uh, can witches reverse spells, Leah?"

She frowned. "What do you mean?"

"I mean if you ever got mad at me and turned me into a cat or something, can you reverse it? You know, if you wanted to, could you change me back to me?"

"It depends," she teased. "Some spells are stronger than others."

"Do witches have prenuptial agreements?"

"What's that?"

"It's sort of a contract before you get married where each party agrees to certain things."

"What kind of things?"

"Well, like if I wanted you to agree that you wouldn't get mad and turn me into a cat or something."

She giggled. "If I was mad enough to turn you into a cat, no stupid old contract would stop me from doing it, silly."

"I just thought it might be good insurance."

She hugged him as she laughed. "The best insurance is not to make me that mad in the first place."

"I'll keep that in mind, but sometimes women get mad and guys don't even know why."

"If I'm mad, you'll know why," she assured him.

"If I ever make you real mad, I want you to know right now that I'm sorry, and whatever I did, I won't ever do it again. Okay?"

"An apology only counts *after* you've made me mad," she argued.

"I'm just trying to stay ahead of things here."

"Okay, Clint. You're one apology ahead, depending on what you do to make me mad."

"What does it depend on?"

She glared at him. "Are you going to feed Old Blue and me, and then do the making love thing, or do you want to see me get mad right now?"

Clint drove to McDonald's, and then rushed to the nearest motel after stocking up on burgers, fries, shakes, and a dozen patties for Old Blue.

Chapter Fifteen

Clint drove Leah to his race shop, where she walked around his cars filled with curiosity. He showed her how to crawl through the driver's window feet first and wedge herself into the custom driver's seat, and then leaned in to fire up the engine with a throaty roar. She screamed and crawled back out of the window headfirst as he caught her, laughing at her panic. Afterwards she walked around the large open bay, impressed with how neat and clean the area was kept, with not a spot of dirt or grease, or even a trace of litter anywhere, and admired the shiny tools arranged in specific spots outlined by white paint.

He showed her his small office at the front of the shop and the cot where he slept. She became engrossed with the multiple pictures of him hanging on the walls depicting his previous cars of every color, pausing to study each of them in turn, and was equally taken with his many driving suits and racing helmets hanging on a rack against one wall, touching the heavy, fire-resistant fabric with her fingers. She then worked her way along the shelves holding his countless racing trophies, lingering over each in speculative appreciation.

Over her protests, he deemed the place unsuitable for her and Old Blue as a home and drove to an extended stay motel complex, where he rented a small suite, paying for two months in advance after putting down a hefty deposit for Old Blue. Leah wandered through it enthralled by the captivating luxury of the tiny kitchenette with electric stove and refrigerator, the large tiled bathroom, the king-sized bed, and stood spellbound as he showed her how to work the color TV and stereo in the living room, judging the remote controls pure magic.

Old Blue appeared nonplused by the setup until he discovered a cat lived in the unit next to them, and immediately set up a vigil by the door emitting low growls as the cat pretended to ignore him while parading back and forth on the porch in mocking scorn.

I'll bet that old dog really did eat her cat, Clint thought soberly as he watched Old Blue work himself into a lather over the cat.

He hauled their luggage in as Leah sorted it out, carefully placing her two brown paper bags in the corner of the closet and her cigar box on the top shelf.

"Let's go shopping to stock up on staples," he suggested when she finished.

When they entered the large grocery chain, she stood stunned at the multiple items lining the shelves on each side of the aisles.

"There's so much *stuff*," she gasped.

"You've never been to a grocery story before?" he asked.

"Only the general store near our house," she admitted apprehensively.

He grabbed a cart. "I'll show you the better brands and how to bargain shop by price and volume."

With the necessary chores finished and the groceries put away back at their suite, he loaded her in the car and searched out a jeweler. After selecting a sizeable one in a large shopping mall, he ushered her in under a large banner proclaiming:

Guaranteed highest quality and lowest prices!

50% OFF SELECT ITEMS

The diminutive man behind the counter rubbed his hands together and smiled. "May I help you, Sir?"

"I'd like to buy an engagement ring," Clint replied.

"What size?"

"I don't know. What size do you wear, Leah?"

The man smirked. "I meant in *carats*, Sir."

"I don't know," Clint replied. "Could we see some carats and decide then?"

"Of course, Sir. We have a rather large selection right this way." He led them to a counter near the back. "What sort of budget have you set?"

Clint shrugged. "I don't know. I've never done this before."

"I see, Sir. Depending on the quality of the stone and the cut, our diamonds generally run from three to five thousand dollars a carat. The setting is additional. The price varies with the quality and design, of course."

Butterflies danced in his stomach. *There goes another couple sets of racing tires*. "Okay. Can you show me a carat?"

"Certainly, Sir. This is a beautiful one carat stone here," he advised, extending a ring to Clint.

Clint frowned. "It's not very big."

"It's *beautiful*," Leah whispered in awe.

"I was expecting something bigger," Clint argued. *For that kind of money, the damned thing ought to be the size of a baseball.*

The attendant placed a large, glittering rock on a black velvet pad. "Here is a two and a half carat with a rather unique setting, Sir, and of the highest quality available anywhere."

"Oh, my goodness," Leah whispered, shrinking back as it shimmered like ice on fire.

When the jeweler picked the ring up and placed it on her finger, she held it up to the light as it sparkled in a glittering display, her cheeks flushing. "It's the most beautiful thing I've ever seen."

"We'll take it," Clint said. "How much?"

"That one will be eighteen thousand dollars, Sir."

"*Eighteen thousand*!" Clint shouted as his knees wobbled. He regained his composure and looked at the jeweler hopefully. "Is this on your select item list?"

The jeweler's eyes widened. "Oh, no Sir, *certainly not*! As I said, this is one of our *finest* stones with a *most unique* setting, definitely one of a kind. I have another couple coming in later this afternoon to see this one specifically. But we do have a large selection of lower quality, less expensive pieces, if you would care to see them?"

Clint gulped. "No, we'll take it." *A couple sets of tires hell, there goes two or three whole damned races*!

"No, Clint, it's too much!" Leah protested, slipping the ring off and placing it back on the velvet. "Could you please show us something less expensive?"

"No, that's the one I want," Clint insisted, swallowing with difficulty in an attempt to ingest the hairball lodged in his throat. "At least you can see it."

The jeweler smiled as he slipped the ring back on Leah's finger. "You certainly can, Sir. An excellent choice, I might add."

Leah swooned. "I think I'm going to ab-so-lute-ly *die*!"

Clint glumly whipped out his checkbook. *Me too*! *Damn that Ronnie James and his grease monkeys all to hell and back again*!

Chapter Sixteen

Leah fixed a simple dinner that night in her new kitchen. Afterwards Clint sat at the table with a small calculator and a pad figuring out his current economic status as she and Old Blue watched television.

Studying the few dollars he had left after buying Leah's clothes, engagement ring, and renting the extended stay suite, and then subtracting for food, gas, and a skimpy entertainment allowance needed over the next couple of months until the season began, he was practically broke. Nothing new there, he reasoned dolefully.

His racing budget was just as bleak, he assessed grimly. With the associate sponsorship he had in hand, he'd have to hire a part-time crew and a half-assed crew chief to even get through the first few races of the season. If he didn't land a primary sponsor by then, he would be forced to get a job during the week to support them and hang out at the tracks on the weekends praying for a ride.

He next made a list of potential sponsors he could approach in the next few weeks, knowing at this late date it would be virtually impossible because all the big money had been committed months ago. He would be forced to string together several small sponsors, if he could find them, and budget every dime if he was going to make it through the season. That meant this year would in effect be a write-off as far as being competitive and racing for the championship was concerned, or even for him to place in the top ten in points. He would have to use this year to build for the next one. There was no other choice open to him.

He sat back sick to his stomach with the repulsive image of crawling into a second-rate car and peddling around in the rear like he was driving Miss Daisy, just hanging on waiting for someone in front of him to wreck or suffer a mechanical malfunction so he could gain a position. He wanted to be a front-runner, and knew in his heart he had the talent if not the money. *And now I have a fiancée who is still trying to figure out how the real world works, and a big, hungry dog to feed and provide shelter for as well. What I really need the most is a swift kick in the ass for being dumb enough to get myself in this situation in the first place.*

Leah turned to him as he sighed. "Clint, can I help with your troubles?"

He swallowed the bile. "Sure, find me a million dollar sponsor. That would solve all my troubles."

She came over to the table and sat down across from him. "You look so worried. Tell me about this sponsor thing. Maybe I can help."

"It's complicated and there's really nothing you can do. It's all about positioning, and I don't have the money to get there without a sponsor."

"Well, let's go get us one of them sponsor people then."

"Oh, hell, I'm sort of bushed tonight—can we wait until morning?"

She glared. "Are you making fun of me?"

"I'm sorry for being a wise-ass, Leah, but I've been trying to get a sponsor for over a year now. They're damned hard to find."

"Mr. Roberts is a sponsor, isn't he? Let's talk to him."

"That's the one thing you *don't* do in this business," he snapped. "That would be the worst thing I could ever do."

"Why?"

He stood up and paced around the small room restlessly. "Trying to steal another team's sponsor is the kiss of death. You have to wait for them to approach you first. Otherwise you're an outcast forever. It's just not done."

"How do you get them to approach you?"

"By being a front runner."

She frowned. "How do you become a front runner?"

Clint slid back into his chair. "By having a sponsor that gives you the big bucks to hire the men and buy the equipment to put you up front. You see, Leah, it's all about winning. If you're a winner, everybody wants their name on your car and will pay big bucks to get it there."

She stared at him in bewilderment. "That sounds crazy. You said to get a sponsor you've got to have the right men and equipment, but to get the right men and equipment, you've got to have a sponsor. It sounds like you can't have the one without the other, and you can't get the other without the one."

"Of course it's crazy—otherwise everybody would want to be a racecar driver. It's the only way we can keep the competition down. Why don't you use some of that psychic stuff you used with the Roberts to tell me where I can find a sponsor?"

Her eyes narrowed. "Are you being a wise-ass again?"

"Yep."

"Okay, wise-ass." She hurried into the bedroom, returned with her cigar box, hesitated before selecting a red candle from the clutter inside, lit it, and then hurried around the room turning off lights before reseating herself and taking out the rose crystal heart. "Close your eyes and relax."

He sighed. "Leah, I was only kidding—"

"Hush and close your eyes," she scolded. "Just relax and let your mind drift," she soothed as she placed the cold crystal heart in his palm and cupped his hand in hers. "Oh, I forgot. You've got to remove that thing around your neck."

"Leah, please—"

"You ask me to do it, Clint. Are you scared?"

"This is silly," he grumbled as he used his free hand to pull the chain from his neck and place it on the table.

"Oh, that's so much better," she encouraged as he felt the heart growing warmer in his palm. "I see a picture of your racecar. It's brown and yellow—"

"That's the color of shit," he snapped, jerking his hand from hers and placing the heart on the table as his palm tingled. "Money is green and silver. Enough of this foolishness, let's go to bed. That'll help me relax plenty."

She smiled as she blew out the candle. "Can I turn on the light?"

"Nope," he replied, slipping his pendulant back around his neck.

"Why not?"

"Because I want your mind on me and not on that damned ring."

"That's selfish."

"Yep."

Chapter Seventeen

Leah had coffee, eggs, and bacon waiting when he awoke the next morning. He kissed her, slid into his chair with his appetite raging, ate quickly, and then showered.

"I've got to hit the road," he advised, emerging from the bedroom as he shrugged into his shirt.

"Where are you going?" she asked, the thought of being alone in a strange environment unsettling to her.

"To get that sponsor we talked about last night."

"Can I go with you?"

"You'd be bored."

"No I won't, I'll be learning your world."

"Okay, but keep in mind that one wrong word can send a prospective sponsor stampeding for the door."

"What do you mean?"

He hugged her to him. "I mean keep your big fat mouth shut and let me do all the talking. I'm the pro here and you're the rookie. And take your ring off—it won't look professional to have my girlfriend tagging along on a business meeting. I'll introduce you as my administrative assistant."

She laughed as she slipped her ring off. “Okay, Mr. Pro!”

He spent the morning with a national food distributor, presenting his bio and sales pitch as she watched. He got a commitment for $10,000 to sew their logo on his racing uniform.

After a quick lunch, they met with a regional Chevrolet dealer, where he got two diesel dually pickup trucks and a passenger van on loan until the end of the season for his crew and spare parts. His name, racecar number, and the dealership were to be placed on the sides of each, and he would be required to provide his own insurance.

They had an early dinner with a junior vice-president of sales and marketing for a regional sausage maker looking for national exposure, where Clint irritably regretted introducing Leah as an administrative assistant when the young vice-president spent the entire meal staring at her cleavage and ignoring his presentation. The best he got from the meeting was a commitment for the president of the company to come to his race shop in three days to talk further. On the drive home, Leah was thoughtfully silent.

“Pretty pitiful, wasn’t it?” he observed. “What’s on your mind?”

She scrunched up her face. “I’m just thinking about everything I saw today and trying to learn from it.”

“What did you learn?”

“The food guy’s budget had a surplus and he liked you. The Chevrolet dealer guy thought he got a bargain and would have given you more. The sausage guy could care less about you or racing. He was there because someone told him to meet with you and feel you out. He kept wondering how I looked without clothes on."

He grimaced. "Very perceptive."

"Did I do okay keeping my big fat mouth shut?"

"You did great. What else could I have gotten from the Chevy dealer?"

"I'm not sure. He was relieved you didn't ask for more. I don't know what else you might have wanted and neither did he, but he was happy with the deal you offered him. He also thought I was hot, but that was confusing since we were in his air conditioned office."

"By 'hot,' he meant you were pretty and sexy, but in a nicer sort of way than the sausage geek."

"It's hard to read people in your world without touching them."

"You just keep your cotton-picking hands to yourself, especially where that sausage nerd is concerned," he insisted. "And put your ring back on. That was a dumb mistake on my part. The whole purpose of buying it was to keep the jackasses at bay."

She smiled slyly as she slipped the diamond back on her finger. "You didn't think he was kind of cute?"

A flush flashed through him for the second time in his life. "How would you like a big bop in your little kisser?"

She laughed and kissed his cheek. "I'm just teasing, silly. He was a bore and gave me the creeps with his dirty thoughts about me."

"Oh really? I'm having dirty thoughts about you right now."

She giggled. "That gives me tingles and makes me think dirty thoughts myself. I didn't know what they were way back then, but did you have dirty thoughts when you first met me like that sausage guy did?"

"Way back then? That was only a week ago."

"Well, did you?"

"Absolutely. If you could have read me like you do others, I'm sure you'd have smacked me one."

She sighed. "I've learned so much since we met. Your world is very complicated."

He laughed. "All you've seen so far is the tip of the iceberg, but you're a quick study."

"I'm glad you think so. I feel so dumb sometimes."

Over the next two days, they met with five other potential small sponsors and garnered another paltry $30,000 in commitments. Clint figured that with the $100,000 he had from the associate sponsor, he was up to five, maybe six races now, provided he didn't screw anything up, and was beginning to feel panicky.

On the third day, he paced the floor of his race shop waiting for the president of the sausage company to arrive, acutely aware that this was his best, if not last, chance to land a primary sponsor that could carry him through the whole season. Leah had swept and mopped his former home the night before and straightened up and cleaned the small bathroom and shower at the rear of his office. She also dusted all of the pictures of him standing around his various racecars from past seasons. He had Skip, Ron, and Bobby pretending to work on two of his cars, one of which was a show car used at driver appearances and wasn't even capable of racing, but he wanted to give the impression of a dynamic race team preparing for the season.

When the Cadillac pulled up to his shop, he tried to squelch the nervous desperation as he walked out to greet them, while Leah seated herself behind the desk in his office pretending to handle administrative tasks as they had rehearsed.

"Mr. Long, this is Mr. Hutchinson, president and founder of Sunrise Sausage," the vice-president introduced.

Clint shook the president's hand. "Please, call me Clint."

The president clapped him on the shoulder as they turned to the shop. "Good to meet you, Clint. Call me Sam. What have you got scheduled for us?"

"If it suits you, I'd like to give you a tour of our facilities and then we'll talk business in my office over coffee."

Sam nodded. "Great! I've never seen a race shop. I didn't realize a driver had so many different cars."

"Each car and engine is designed for a different sized track. A short half mile track requires different handling characteristics and horsepower requirements than a larger track of a mile or better. It's very high tech today," Clint explained as he ushered Sam into the shop.

He spent an hour showing off his small, but well-equipped shop, as his make-believe team needlessly tightened bolts and managed to look professionally busy. The vice-president spent most of his time leering at Leah, who ignored him as she pretended to make calls and jot down messages. Sam was all business and very interested in everything Clint had to show him, asking well informed questions as the occasion called for or as his curiosity peaked on a particular topic. Skip made a point to interrupt politely with some vague situation he pretended to need advice on, nodding thoughtfully in concentration as Clint gave him the needed guidance. The whole production was well staged and impressive, Clint thought proudly.

When they moved to the office, Clint introduced Leah as his "fiancée and administrative assistant," enjoying the crushed look on the vice-president's face as Leah stood and extended her hand to Sam. "I'm glad to meet you, Mr. Hutchinson."

"Call me Sam, Leah. I'm delighted to meet you as well. Clint is a lucky to have both a lovely *and* talented fiancée."

She smiled. "That's very kind of you to think so, Sam."

Clint observed she held his hand for an extended time, somewhat relieved she didn't lean her head back and close her eyes as she normally did when she was doing her visionary thing. They seated themselves around the small table in his office and Leah poured coffee before seating herself back at her desk.

Clint curiously watched her light a green candle and a stick of incense in the background before he launched into an extended briefing on the demographics of race fans, the coverage ARA races received on television through the sport's fan base, and by the personal appearances of the cars and drivers. He pointed out that 51% of race fans were females, who controlled 76% of the purchasing power of the normal household, and ended with a strong pitch on the loyalty factor they displayed for the sponsors of the drivers.

He then produced a schematic showing the various sponsorship options, starting with the driver uniform and working his way through the various portions of the car, emphasizing that even the hauler itself was a rolling billboard when traveling to and from races, quoting prices for each position.

At the conclusion he sat back. “That about sums up the racing world, Sam. It boils down to more coverage for your advertising dollar than any other media outlet in the nation. On our side of the table, the symbol for speed is the all-mighty dollar sign. Motor-sports is the most competitive business in the world. To be a successful joint venture, a team requires the total focus of the driver on winning races, coupled with the best men and equipment money can buy to put him up front to win. What are your questions?”

“May I speak candidly?” Sam asked.

Clint nodded. “I would prefer you do.”

“Most of what you’ve told me has been confirmed by my marketing research team. Based on that, I’m sold on the concept. But to what extent, is the unfortunate question. Naturally, I would prefer a primary sponsorship, but my problem is the price. To back a top team requires a sizable investment. Sunrise Sausage is currently a regional commodity reaching out for a national market. That means that at this point in our growth pattern we don’t have a million dollars to spend promoting our product on a national level,” he explained as Clint’s heart sank.

“But let’s be honest here, Clint, your team is not a top caliber, proven winning team either, for that matter. That’s why I’m here. My research tells me you’re a better-than-fair driver who has a great deal of potential, but that you have very little sponsorship with which to run this season. Maybe we can find a way to help each other reach our goals.”

"I'm listening," Clint responded calmly, feeling anything but tranquil.

"I'm prepared to commit to a budget of three hundred thousand dollars for this season for the primary sponsorship of your team. If we deem our relationship a successful one at the end of the season, and if our product has found acceptance on the national level by that point, we can renegotiate to a higher level of commitment for next year. In other words, we can grow together if mutually successful."

Clint collected his thoughts, stifling his disappointment. *$300,000 beats the hell out of nothing, and will at least ensure I can run the whole season, albeit poorly. I really have no other choice at this late date but to accept, no matter how dismal the offer.*

In the ensuing pause, Leah refilled their coffee and slipped a note in his hand in the process, masking the transfer with her body as she poured. Clint glanced down and read: He'll go to 500.

He slipped the note into his shirt pocket as Leah sat back down and hunched forward, figuring he had little to lose by playing her hunch. "Sam, I appreciate your candor. I'd like to be as candid with you, if I may?"

"Please do."

"It takes a million dollar budget to be competitive in this sport at this level. Three hundred thousand dollars will allow us to race the whole season, but it won't really get either of us to our goals. Five hundred thousand may get us close. It won't put us in the championship hunt or anything, but with a little luck we might make the top ten in the points standing. I'd be willing to run Sunrise Sausage as my primary sponsor for that price for the first year. If we're both happy with our relationship, we'll renegotiate at the end of the season for next year. As you say, we'll grow together." He sat back hoping he hadn't overplayed his hand.

Sam sipped his coffee. "I'll go to four hundred thousand," he offered after a lengthy pause.

Clint did some quick math in his head. *That $400,000, coupled with the $150,000 I already have, will give me a sporting, but distant shot at the top ten. I can cut down on engine rebuilds, practice tires, and reduce my skimpy personnel roster even further. But at least I can race. I better not push it any further, or I might lose it all.*

"Mr. Hutchinson?" Leah interrupted as Clint opened his mouth to accept. Sam turned to her. "I know you're a good businessman and that you're used to getting your best deal. I respect that. Clint is an honest man, and I hope you respect that. The price he quoted gives him a fair chance to run good for both you and him, which you both need him to do for your own benefit. The price you quoted him does not give him a fair opportunity to do that for either of you. I read in a magazine somewhere that sometimes you can cut a deal so fine that both sides lose. I'm sorry for butting in with my opinion."

The silence that followed was heavy. Finally Sam stood and offered his hand. "Thank you for your time, Mr. Long. I'll have the contract prepared. Let's work hard to make this a successful year for us both."

Clint rose to take his hand. "Then you'll go to half a million?"

Sam nodded. "Yes, but I expect a million dollars of publicity for Sunrise Sausage."

"You'll damn well get it, Sam. Thanks! What are your racing colors?"

Sam hesitated. "Truthfully, I haven't given much thought to that. Our basic packaging is brown with a yellow rising sun. Do you think you can incorporate that into an attractive color scheme for the car?"

Clint looked beyond him to Leah in disbelief. "I'm sure we can find a way to make it work, Sam."

"Good. If you'll excuse me, I've got a meeting I've got to rush off to. Young lady," Sam added, turning to Leah. "If you decide to change career positions, come see me. I'm always on the lookout for good business people." He walked out as his vice-president hurried after him.

"What did I tell you about keeping your big fat mouth shut?" Clint demanded as he pulled Leah into his arms.

"Does that mean you're going to give me a big bop in my little kisser?"

"I'd sure hate to mess up something so tasty. How did you know he would go to a half million?"

"That number was in his mind when I shook his hand."

"And the brown and yellow car?"

"I saw it in your aura, but you wouldn't let me finish the reading."

"You're spooky. And what was the deal with the candle and incense?"

"Just a little extra enticement. The candle was to attract money and the incense to encourage friendship."

"Sometimes I think you really are a witch …"

Chapter Eighteen

After the opening ceremony, a hush descended around them as Merle turned to Allay. “Please render your report to Council.”

Allay stood. “Leah and this one returned to his race shop on the third day after they disappeared. They rented a suite at an extended stay facility. He bought an engagement ring for Leah, but they have not set a date for the wedding. He has found a sponsor to provide him with the funds he needs to prepare for his race season.”

Adrian stood. “This is excellent news! If the two of them marry, through Leah we can guide this one to our world and thus protect his seed. Casting the love spell could turn out to be fortuitous.”

Vaughn stood. “This one belongs in the world of his own *choosing*, Adrian. We must guide him nowhere. Why must this simple point be reinforced every time we discuss this one?”

Shoshanna stood. “I do not think it improper to give this one encouragement in the direction of our Craft in order to protect our future leader of Council.”

Hellene stood. “I agree. We have long awaited this event. It is for the good of all that this one turns to us. I feel we are justified in using whatever measures necessary to achieve this goal. Leah is in the perfect position to help us attain this objective."

Merle stood. "I agree we should find some means of introducing this one to our Craft in hopes he will choose of his own free will to join us, but how best to approach him in this quest?"

Hellene stood. "This one should be summoned to Council and made aware of his seed's heritage. He should be trained in our Craft at an accelerated pace in order to enter our world as quickly as possible."

Vaughn stood. "Hellene, we cannot *summon* this one to do *anything*, nor can we *require* him to accept training unless he *requests* this of us. What I am hearing here goes against our most basic beliefs. It *cannot* be *done* in this manner. Surely I am not the *only* voice of reason here?"

Hellene stood. "Under normal circumstances, I would be inclined to agree with you, Vaughn, but this one is *not* normal. This situation warrants unorthodox methods if necessary."

Lily stood. "I do not agree. What you are implying is that the end justifies the means. We are a society of *choice* and sworn never to impose our will over another. This one must come to us by his own path. We can only provide direction if he solicits our help. Anything else will do an injustice to him."

Ginger stood. "But how can this one make this choice without our help? He is a nonbeliever in our Craft. Without proper knowledge, how could he possibly make an informed decision to join us?"

Gretchen stood. "Leah is the key. She can provide the initial tutoring to this one to see our Craft in a more reasonable light. Our approach to him should be through her at first, and after he acquires adequate insight, only then introduced to Council. At that time he would logically choose to join our Craft as an informed and accepting participant."

Lola stood. "I agree with Gretchen. We must bring this one along gradually or he may be lost to us forever. Leah is the one to do this."

Adrian stood. "But Leah is a *Solitary*! How can we trust her to teach this one the necessary nuances of our Craft? She is young with much to learn herself, and the mere fact that she rejects the companionship of her tribe is cause for concern, is it not?"

Aunt Bessie spoke. "A Solitary does not necessarily mean she has less conviction, Adrian. It simply means she elects to practice alone. She is still devout in her faith."

Allay stood. "I propose Council direct me to return to Charlotte to speak to Leah openly. Perhaps we can invite her to appear before Council and give us advice on how best to approach this one on the subject of joining our world."

Herschel stood. "I agree. The key is Leah. She best knows this one and is in the most advantageous position to help us in turning him to our world."

Merle stood. "Does any member of Council object to Allay speaking with Leah and inviting her to appear before Council in order to seek her advice on this issue?"

Drew stood. "I agree this is a proper course of action. Invite Leah to Council and let us hear her views."

Merle stood. “Allay, approach Leah on Council’s behalf and invite her to appear. Is there any other business for Council before we adjourn? Then let us enjoy our cake and wine. And if it harm none, do as ye will.”

The strong maiden moved to serve refreshments.

Chapter Nineteen

Clint met with his chassis builder to order four new racing frames, his engine builder to order six new race engines, and five additional potential sponsors, where he managed to dredge up an additional $50,000, which left him $300,000 short of his full budget.

Leah helped around the shop as needed and sat silently by as he interviewed personnel and took care of business that should have been handled months beforehand. He added four new men to his staff in addition to the three he already had, and hired four part-timers to supplement his pit crew on race day. As he sat brooding over his only two candidates for the crew chief position, she sat down across from him.

"Walt Henning puts out strong vibes," she advised.

"He's an alcoholic," Clint replied.

"He's undergone a rehabilitation program in hopes of getting a fresh start and has experience on the Cup circuit," she countered.

"He was only moderately successful there before disappearing from the racing scene for several years while pursuing his new vocation of drinking himself to death. Now no one at the Cup level will take a chance on him, so he's slipped back to the ARA ranks looking for an opportunity to prove he still has the right stuff."

"What's wrong with wanting to prove yourself? That's what you're trying to do, isn't it?"

"He's in his mid-fifties and doesn't seem to have the proper respect for me," he argued. "Cal Roth seems the better choice, even though he doesn't have much experience."

"He puts out bad vibes," she advised.

He shrugged. "It's six of one and a half dozen of the other, I guess, since I don't think much of either of them. I guess I need to pick one and be done with it."

"Mr. Henning puts out strong vibes."

He shrugged. "Okay, the reformed drunk it is."

When he made the offer later that afternoon, Walt reluctantly accepted, clearly signifying he had hit bottom with this little rag-tag outfit and their skimpy racing budget. When Walt didn't even haggle over the salary offered, Clint knew he was just another stepping stone as Chuck had used him for the previous year. Shortly afterwards, Leah ushered a reserved young man into his office.

"Mr. Long, I'm Jeff Edwards. I understand you're looking for a crew chief. I'd like to be considered for the position."

"I just hired a crew chief."

"I'd settle for the assistant crew chief position," he offered quietly.

"Sorry, but I don't have the budget for an assistant crew chief."

"I'd be willing to work for a share of the purse," Jeff offered evenly.

Clint studied him doubtfully, as Leah, in the background, nodded vigorously for him to accept. "Dropping to assistant and working for a share of the purse is a big step down, Jeff. Why would you be willing to do that?"

"To gain national experience," Jeff replied. "If you'd like to check me out, you'll find I have a solid record at the regional level in Late Model Stocks."

Behind him, Leah balled up her fist and shook it at him threateningly.

Clint shrugged. "Okay, Jeff, come back in the morning and I'll introduce you to the rest of the crew."

With his team complete within his tight budget constraints, he took Leah out to dinner to celebrate at one of the more exclusive restaurants. After ordering, he sat back admiring her in her black strapless dress.

"Why are you looking at me like that?"

"Because I can't get enough of you."

She lowered her eyes. "Are you teasing me?"

He leered. "Not yet, but wait till I get you home."

She shivered. "Mmm, I like that!"

"Do you know you are one beautiful woman?"

"No, but I like for you to think it."

"By chance, are you wearing those black bikini panties with that dress?"

She blushed. "Yes. Why?"

He grinned. "I'm thinking of how much I'm going to enjoy peeling them off."

She rolled her eyes. "You're *embarrassing* me, Clint. What's gotten into you tonight?"

"You really don't have a clue how gorgeous and sexy you are. It turns me on."

"Either you stop talking like that, or you take me home right now," she complained. "I'm not going to be able to eat if you don't stop!"

He lifted his wine glass. "To you and everything you aspire to be."

She touched her glass to his. "Why are you being so romantic tonight?"

"Because I get so caught up in myself I forget how much you mean to me and have to play catch up."

"Are you really happy with me, Clint?"

"Yes. Are you happy with me?"

"I'm so happy it scares me. You've taught me so many things. I never knew a life like this existed."

They ate in silence in the intimate ambiance. When finished, the waiter pushed a cart laden with cakes and pies around to their table.

"Dessert?"

Leah flashed a flirtatious look. "The dessert I want is not anywhere on that tray."

Clint frowned as he surveyed the multiple wedges of enticement with exaggerated care. "I had something sweet in mind, but I don't see quite what I'm in the mood for here." He looked at Leah with arched eyebrows. "Do you have any suggestions?"

She smiled devilishly. "I've had the perfect dessert simmering for the last two hours."

He beamed. "Check, please!"

* * *

When Leah entered the laundry room at the motel complex to wash clothes, a woman in her early thirties with coal black hair followed her into the room.

Leah glanced at the pentacle around her neck and smiled. "Hi, I'm Leah."

"Yes, I know. I'm Allay, a member of Council. I've been sent to speak with you on their behalf. I've been waiting to catch you alone."

"Talk to me on behalf of Council?"

"Council would like to meet with you and get your advice concerning your fiancé."

"What advice does Council seek?"

"Council desires to consult with you about bringing this one into our Craft."

"Allay, Clint thinks our Craft is foolish and doesn't allow me to discuss our world with anyone because he's afraid they'll think I'm crazy. I can' help Council in this matter."

"Council feels it imperative this one be informed of his lineage and taught the basics of our Craft," Allay persisted as Leah placed her clothes in a washer and inserted coins. "They do not know how to approach him in this regard and need your guidance."

Leah turned to her. "But we are not allowed to persuade others to follow our Craft, Allay. We cannot go against our Rede."

"There are some among Council that feel this one is exceptional due to his lineage. They feel it is his duty to join our Craft so that his seed can be protected, and want to meet with him in that regard."

"Clint would never agree to meet with Council. He'd think they were crackpots."

"This is why we need your help on how to approach him so that he *does* take us seriously. Have you told him of the child you bear?"

Leah flushed. "He does not know of our child. I have not found the right time to inform him."

"If you won't appear before Council, will you consider meeting with your godmother on this matter?"

Leah lowered her eyes. "I left our world without Aunt Bessie's blessing."

"Are you happy in this one's world, Leah?"

"Oh, yes! But I do miss our Craft as well, and hope that in time Clint will become accepting of my beliefs and allow me to live in both worlds."

"You gave us cause for concern because we did not know your intentions. Our first thoughts were to protect the seed we entrusted to you. We did not anticipate you joining him in his world, but now that it has happened, many of Council feel this is a positive thing. You have our full support and need not fear reprimand."

Leah nodded cautiously. "Then I will try to meet with Aunt Bessie. This may take some time because we are so busy with the team. Please advise her of this."

Allay hugged her. "You are a faithful servant of our Craft, and one that we are all proud of. I will advise Aunt Bessie to expect your visit."

"Thank you, Allay. It is good to have spoken with you." Leah took her laundry basket and left, her spirits considerably lifted.

* * *

They pulled eighteen-hour shifts for the next three weeks, dressing out the new frames and installing the engines in a mad rush to get ready for the season. Leah was everywhere, providing coffee and sandwiches for the team members, putting decals on the cars, and even fetching tools when needed. On occasion Clint paused to watch in admiration as she took on any task assigned. With one week to go they completed the last car near midnight and sat back in exhaustion viewing the five gleaming machines before them painted a soft brown with the yellow rising sun of Sunrise Sausage on the hood. All of the league decals were on the front fenders, and the logo of their associate sponsor occupied the rear quarter panels, with the decals of their smaller sponsors occupying the bottom panels in prominent locations. A yellow, blazing thirteen decorated the doors and the top of the car, with “Clint Long” in yellow script above the driver’s door to match his new brown uniform with yellow trim.

Leah hugged him, her eyes shining. “I’m so proud, Clint. We did it. I knew we could!”

He turned to the tired men. “Guys, let’s take the weekend off and get some rest. Starting Monday, we hit the practice oval to shake out the bugs in these beauties as we start the quest for *victory lane*!”

Leah kissed him ecstatically and the crew cheered as Old Blue charged out in howling anticipation from his napping place on the rug behind the desk, all anxious for the hunt to begin.

Chapter Twenty

Clint awoke late the next morning and stretched lazily as he sniffed the tantalizing aromas of coffee perking and bacon frying from the kitchen, thinking that sleeping late was a luxury that he could seldom enjoy.

He lay in contentment counting his blessings. He had a beautiful, over-sexed woman who doted on him, an old hound dog that adored him, the makings of a decent, if Spartan, race team, five marvelous racecars that were as competitive as money could buy, and an adequate, though not luxurious, budget to run them the full season. If things got any better he wouldn't be able to stand it, he mused idly. Never had things come together so well for him after looking so bleak. And Leah is a large part of why things came together so well, he reminded himself soberly. *Maybe she really is a witch after all. If so, I'm not giving her back to her coven or whatever their social order is called. She's mine now and to hell with them.*

He eased out of bed, slipped on his pants, tiptoed to the bedroom door, and peeped playfully around the doorframe into the kitchen, where Leah was humming to herself with her back to him scrambling eggs at the small stove. The table was set, toast popped up in the toaster, orange juice poured, bacon draining on a folded napkin, and the coffee perking. He slipped into the small kitchenette and eased up behind her as she scooped eggs onto a plate.

"*Clint*! *Breakfast is ready, sleepyhead*!" she called without turning.

"How many times lately have I told you how much I appreciate you?" he asked.

She jumped in surprise. "You scared me, silly! What did you say?" She turned to set the plates on the table.

"How many times lately have I told you how much I appreciate you?"

She glanced at him. "Why are you asking me something like that?"

He slipped his arms around her waist and pulled her to him. "Because it's important to me."

She looked up at him uneasily. *He looks tired and drawn from his eighteen-hour days, and now he's talking nonsense.* "Is anything wrong, Clint?"

"Yes."

"What?"

"Me."

"What's wrong with you?"

"You."

A cold chill worked through her. *I've been so busy helping with his race team I haven't paid attention to him like I should. Lately I've been making sandwiches instead of hot meals and going to bed exhausted without even showering.* "What's wrong with me?"

"Me."

"You're scaring me, Clint. Are you unhappy about something?"

"I've never been happier in my life."

She frowned. "I don't understand what's wrong then?"

"I don't tell you often enough how much I appreciate you, Leah."

She relaxed. *He must be teasing me*. "I feel your appreciation all the time, silly."

"When was the last time I actually *told* you I appreciate you?" he demanded.

She extracted herself from his embrace to turn off the fire under the frying pan. "I can't think of a time right off, but I always know you do."

"See what I mean?" he argued. "Well, I *appreciate* you, Leah!"

"I appreciate you too, Clint. Don't you know that?"

"Yes, I do, but do you?"

He isn't making sense and this whole conversation is getting on my nerves. "Of course I do. Now sit down and eat your breakfast before it gets cold. Me and Old Blue are going to send you back to bed if you don't stop talking so crazy."

"Say you know I appreciate you first," he insisted.

"I know you appreciate me, Clint." She looked at him suspiciously as he pulled out her chair and waited to seat her. She sat, perplexed.

He kissed the back of her neck. "Good, now let's eat."

"Clint, you've been working awfully hard lately—"

He paused midway through forking eggs into his mouth. "Which means I've been neglecting you, right?"

"I didn't mean it that way," she argued.

"But it's true isn't it?" he insisted. "Go ahead and say it!"

She paused from buttering her toast. "Clint, are we fighting or something?"

"Today is your day, Leah."

"What does that mean?"

"You can do anything you want today. I'm at your disposal. You're the Queen and your wish is my command. Make a wish, Leah."

She took a bite of her toast and wiped her lips with a napkin. "I wish you'd quit talking crazy."

"I mean it. Anything you want is yours. The sky is the limit. For all of the sacrifices you've made for me, I give you this day. What do you want to do with it?"

"I want to spend it with you like I always do."

"Okay. Done. What else?"

"What else is there?"

"You name it, Leah."

She frowned. As long as he was in her sight, she was happy. Making *him* happy was her priority in life. The things that made her the happiest were a spontaneous smile or an unexpected warm look from across the room when he was busy. "I'm not good at making choices, Clint. You pick one for me."

"Hell no, it's not *my* day, Leah. It's *your* day. *You* pick one, damn it!"

She flinched. "Are we fighting now?"

"Getting close, Leah—getting pretty damned close," he threatened. *Why can't she let me do something just for her? She does so much for me. Today, I'm going to do something for her whether she likes it or not, damn it.*

"I don't want to fight, Clint."

"Okay, Leah," he encouraged. "You want to spend the day with me and you don't want to fight. It's your day, and if that's what you want, you've got it. That's two choices. Keep going, what else do you want?"

"How many more do I have to pick?"

"As many as you want, Leah."

Her eyes narrowed. "I've already picked two things. That's plenty enough."

"Pick one more thing that will make you happy today."

"I *was* happy before you started this nonsense."

"One more thing, Leah, just one more."

"Okay, one more, Clint, and then I don't want to hear any more of this foolishness. Promise?"

"Okay, I promise. One more. Whatever you want."

"Well, give me a minute to think … I know! I want you to make love to me. We haven't made love for three days because we've been so tired."

"That doesn't count, Leah. You've got to pick something else."

"Why doesn't it count?"

"Because I was going to do that anyway, so you can't pick that."

"Yes I can," she insisted. "You said anything I wanted. *That's what I want*!"

"Okay, we'll make love, Leah, but it *still doesn't count*! You've got to pick something else."

"*Yes it does count*!" she yelled as she jumped up, ran into the bedroom, and slammed the door.

Old Blue stared accusingly at Clint, lowered his tail to the floor, and laid his head on his paws.

"I didn't start it!" he argued.

Old Blue stood up, turned his back to him, and lay back down to stare out the door with a snort of disgust.

"Go ahead, turn your back on me, you little turncoat. But I'm telling you, we guys need to stick together on these things."

Old Blue lowered his ears, curled his tail around his legs, and sniffed in contempt.

"You just leave Old Blue out of this!" Leah yelled from the bedroom.

He eased over to the bedroom door and knocked.

"*What*!" Leah yelled.

He opened the door to find her curled up in the middle of the bed wrapped around a pillow, staring at the wall with her back to him. He sat on the edge of the bed and rubbed her back.

"That's not going to get you anywhere," she snapped.

"I'm sorry, Leah. I just want to make you happy."

"I *was* happy," she sulked, blinking back tears.

"I wanted to do something special for you today."

"You said I could have anything I wanted because I was the Queen and it was my day. I asked for three things."

"You can have those three things and anything else you want, baby doll, because you *are* a Queen."

"No I can't," she accused. "One of them was I didn't want to fight and we're already fighting."

"*I'm* not fighting."

"You *yelled* at me."

"It wasn't a mad yell. It was a frustrated yell."

"How am I supposed to know that?"

He felt the tension leaving her coiled body as he rubbed her back and shifted so he could use both hands as he worked around her neck and shoulders and down her back across her curvaceous posterior to her thighs, calves, ankles, and feet, and then slowly back up kneading and stretching. On the next trip down he slid her nightgown up to her waist as he worked his way back up. On the third trip she melted into a soft lump of putty in his hands, and on the fourth she was his. And she was magnificent.

Later they took Old Blue-The-Dirty-Rotten-Traitor for a long walk, and then drove leisurely through the countryside enjoying the tranquil harmony of Mother Nature's sprinkling of spring freshness. They ate a late lunch in a quaint country inn, took in an early matinee, and polished the evening off with dinner and a jug of red wine at a fine Italian restaurant.

Back home at last, he gave her another soothing massage, and she was even more magnificent than before.

Women are so simple if you don't go screwing around with them, he mused before drifting into a languorous slumber with Leah wrapped around him in sated bliss.

Chapter Twenty-One

Clint awoke early Sunday morning and stumbled out to the table as Leah prepared breakfast.

She placed a cup of coffee before him and sat down with her own cup as the bacon sizzled on the stove, fighting the butterflies in her stomach, having spent a lot of time the day before agonizing over broaching this subject with him.

"I know what I want now."

His radar went on full alert. "What do you want?"

"To go visit my Godmother."

Knots formed in his stomach. *The last thing I want is to see that old black woman again.* "Why do you want to go see that old hag?"

She glared at him. "Are we going to fight again?"

"*No*!" he assured her hastily, deciding they could make an outing of the trip and grab some good seafood along the way. *She rarely asks for anything, so this will be a small sacrifice.* "We can take Old Blue with us. He'll enjoy not being cooped up in the house all day. We can drop you off for a few hours and then come back and pick you up."

Her heart skipped a beat. She had expected him to vehemently refuse. “I’m so glad we don’t have to fight about it. I’ll go get ready.”

He drove the three hours to Charleston and pulled into the unpaved drive of the small, desolate clapboard house and sat idling. “Old Blue and I’ll be back for you in two hours and we’ll grab some lunch before heading back to Charlotte.”

He waited until she entered the decrepit old house before backing up and driving off hurriedly. He cruised aimlessly for a while before stopping near a bridge, where he and Old Blue walked along the banks watching fishermen drift by in small boats. When the time drew near, he drove back to Aunt Bessie’s and pulled into the dirt drive. Leah came out a few minutes later and he backed up and drove off, trying not to appear in too much of a hurry as she sat quietly.

“So, how was your visit?”

“My Godmother is getting old.”

“She’s already old. I bet she’s nearly a hundred if she’s a day. Are you hungry?”

“I could eat something. What did you and Old Blue do while I was visiting?”

“We watched some people fishing. There’s a great little seafood restaurant a few miles from here called Rebecca’s. Want to try that place for a late lunch?”

She shrugged. “Sure.”

He pulled over to the side of the road. “Okay, Leah, what’s wrong?”

She turned to him, dread rising in her. “I need to talk to you about something, and I don’t want you to get mad at me about it. I need you to hear me out. Will you do that for me?”

Goose bumps sprang out on his arms, a sure indication he was not going to enjoy this. “Okay, talk.”

She shifted around in her seat, unable to meet his eyes. “Drive while I talk.”

“Okay.” He shifted gears and drove off.

“I need to talk to you about our Craft.”

“*Witchcraft*! Leah, we’ve been through—”

“I thought you were going to hear me out!”

“Okay, I’m listening.”

“In my world we have a Council that governs our Craft. They want to meet with you.”

Icy chills ran down his spine. “*Forget that shit, Leah*! I ain’t meeting with a bunch of fruitcakes who think they’re witches. *No way, José*!”

She bit her lower lip. “It’s very important that you do. They have something important to tell you. They have asked me to bring you to them.”

He shook his head. “Nope! Forget it. If we need to fight about it, so be it. I flat out ain’t going to no damn witch meeting. Understand, Leah?”

She turned to him. “They have asked me to come if I can’t bring you before them. You once asked me to tell you what ‘being the one’ meant. I told you I was not qualified, but promised to help you find someone who could explain it to you. The members of Council can do that.”

“*No*! I mean it, Leah. When you came with me, you promised there was not going to be any more witchcraft stuff. Remember? You promised we were going to live in my world. Didn’t we agree to that?”

Waves of guilt washed through her. *I did promise him that*. “It’s not that easy, Clint. In spite of what you may think of us, we take our Craft very seriously, as seriously as others take their beliefs. If you would only open your mind to us—"

"Leah, I've *told* you, there is no such thing as real-life witches. It's all bullshit. People who run around naked in the moonlight are flakes, and maybe even dangerous. I don't want any part of their silly spells, or sick rituals, or animal sacrifices and such. They need to be in an asylum or something."

"We're not like that, Clint! We would never harm any living thing. You're talking about devil worshipers and Satanists, who we're as opposed to as you are. We're not witches like your world portrays us. Our Craft is about love of nature and our fellow man, and enjoying the peace and harmony of our universe."

"Yeah, and about casting spells, mixing potions, placing curses, and all that other phony baloney. I *knew* I shouldn't have brought you to see that old hag!" He pulled into the parking lot of the restaurant and killed the engine.

"Clint, please—"

"Leah, I *don't* want to talk about this anymore! Let's get something to eat. I'm hungry."

She sat in despair. "You go ahead. I'll wait here with Old Blue."

He cursed under his breath, re-fired the engine, and drove off at a fast pace. "Leah, I don't want to fight, but we had an agreement there wouldn't be any of that crazy crap. Remember? That was our deal. For you to ask something like that of me is not fair."

"I'm sorry, Clint. It's just that I'm in an awkward position. If you would do this, we could put it behind us and not have to worry with it again. All they ask is that you hear them out and the matter will be ended."

"No means *no*, Leah," he insisted.

Refusing her anything tore at him, but he drew the line when it came to lunacy and weirdo's. He gritted his teeth when he saw tears coursing down her cheeks and drove back to Charlotte in silence to retire early and sleep with space between them for the first time.

Chapter Twenty-Two

Over breakfast, both pretended all was normal, but each felt the lingering discord from their first fight.

When they pulled into the infield of the speedway later that morning, the first thing Clint saw was the big, fancy dual hauler of Glen Johnson's number twenty-six team, sponsored by the Roberts. His one-car rig squatted insignificantly on the other side, dwarfed by the huge double-decker and concealed in its shadow. Chuck, his former crew chief, had two cars at the rear of the hauler with his crew working efficiently under the raised hoods, with each team member outfitted in identical uniforms of Johnson's racing colors of red with white trim. Clint's team, dressed in blue jeans and assorted individual shirts because like everything else he was weeks behind in placing an order, sat around in bored disarray. He knew instinctively this was going to be another bad day as he made a beeline for Walt sitting in the cab of the dually with his feet propped up on the dash.

"What's the problem, Walt?" he demanded as he drew up at the open door of the truck.

Walt swallowed and sipped at his coffee. “No problem, Clint. Want a Bojangles steak biscuit and some coffee? We got extra.”

“No. I want my damned racecar out of the hauler and ready to go.”

“I’m not ready for it to come out of the hauler yet.” Walt took another bite of biscuit.

“Where is my second car?”

“Back at the shop.”

“Why?”

Walt wiped his lips with a napkin and dug into his sack for another biscuit. “I decided to concentrate on one car today.”

“I said I wanted to practice *two* cars today, Walt.”

“Let’s you and me take a little walk, Clint, and sort things out.” Walt slid his feet off the dash and walked off. Clint followed him out of range of the team.

“Now the way I see it, Clint, I’m the crew chief and these cars are my responsibility. I call the shots in the pits and you call them out on the track. I won’t tell you how to drive and you don’t tell me how to work on them. Do we have an understanding?”

“Walt, *I* own this damned team and all decisions are ultimately *mine*. *You* work for *me,* and you *will* consult me before you override my decisions. I’m more than just a dumb-assed driver, I’m the team *owner* as well, and as such, I *will* have input to all matters that affect this team. Do *you* understand?”

“What do you want to achieve here, Clint? Do you want to strut around like a rooster and pretend you know what the hell you’re doing, or do you want to win races? I can damned well put a car under you that will get to the winner’s circle if you’ve got the balls to drive it there. Now I'll tell you up front *I* can't drive, so what makes you think *you've* got the skills to do my job? I gotta trust you and you gotta trust me."

Clint calmed himself, aware that both his and Johnson's crew were watching. "Walt, things have changed a lot while you were away. I'd like for us to have a close working relationship built on mutual trust. That bond can't be forged with you ignoring my orders. If you disagree with me, pull me aside and we'll discuss it—but do *not* unilaterally *ignore* my instructions again. Is that clear?"

"Clint, your program, such as it is, is five months behind schedule. I've got five days to get our shit together. I've got a driver I've never seen drive, a team that don't know each other's names yet, and five cars that I'm not sure will even turn left. I recommend you concentrate solely on driving the beast I put under you, and let me prepare it for you to drive. You hired me to do that job, so let me do it."

"Those days are over, Walt. It doesn't work that way anymore. Racing is a team effort now. It requires that every man work in harmony with the rest of the team and for each member to provide input into the overall effort to be successful. Don't you realize that?"

"I realize there's got to be *one* boss, Clint, and that *I* can't have you second guessing every decision I make. That's a circus, not a team. Now, I've made a decision as to how I want to do things today—are you going to support me or not?"

"*I* don't have a choice, Walt, *you've* already made that decision for me. But if something like this ever happens again we're going to have a parting of the ways before our first race together." Clint turned on his heel and stomped back to the pits.

"If my way doesn't work, you won't have to fire me," Walt shouted after him. "I'll by-god quit!"

As Clint sat on the pit wall fuming, a banged-up, disheveled old truck pulled in next to his rig hauling an open trailer with a yellow, older model car on back without sponsor emblems. A scruffy crew piled out of the truck dressed in dirty jeans and grease stained T-shirts and began unloading the car. A tall, lanky, youth about nineteen years of age with blond hair and blue eyes waved at him and strolled over to extend his hand.

"Hi, you're Clint Long, Rookie of the Year last season, ain't you? I'm Bill Moyer, one of your fans. Folks call me *Wild Bill*. I'm new to the circuit."

Clint shook hands. "Glad to meet you, Wild Bill."

Wild Bill grinned. "I've been running Late Model Stock regionally. Did real good last year, so I'm looking to move on up now and decided to give it a try at the national level and see how you big boys do things. By the way, just call me *Bill*. The 'Wild' thing is for my fans."

Clint eyed his pitiful rig, old car, and ragged crew as they scurried around. "Do you have a sponsor?"

"Naw, not yet, but I'm looking to pick one up. Do you know anybody with a sack full of money looking for a hot driver on his way up?"

Clint shifted in annoyance. "Uh, the world's full of them, Bill. Just win a few races and they'll beat your door down."

"Thanks, Clint. I can call you Clint, can't I?"

"Sure thing, Bill."

Wild Bill hesitated. "Uh, Clint, I don't want to start off on the wrong foot or anything, but could I have your old tires when you get through practicing with them? My budget's kinda weak until I get me a sponsor signed. I guess I'll just have to make do until then."

Clint groaned to himself. "Sure thing, Bill. I'll have my tire man stack them to the side for you when he's finished with them, but they're pretty much used up by then."

"My motto is '*Give me the second best and I'll do the rest*'. Kinda catchy, ain't it? My Dad used to say that. It kinda stuck with me, you know?"

"Uh, right, Bill, well, good luck to you. I've got to get ready to practice now."

"Thanks, Clint. Anything I got you need in return, you just holler now, you hear? That's what friends are for, right?"

Clint suppressed a laugh. "I'll keep that in mind. Nice talking to you." He slid off the pit wall and hurried to his hauler to get away from the fool.

The twenty-six team fired up their first car with a throaty roar. A few minutes later Glen pulled out onto the track. Clint's crew finally began unloading his car from the hauler and preparing it as Glen cut a roaring swath around the track. Walt tracked him with his stopwatch as Clint sat on the wall fuming. Glen brought the car down pit road, parked it, and consulted with his crew chief on the various handling characteristics, with Clint enviously recalling how close he and Chuck had worked together the previous season, how they discussed every detail of the car's handling after each race and practice session.

Johnson climbed into his second car to repeat his practice secession. When he brought that car down pit road, Walt walked over to Clint.

"I'm gonna send you out in about ten minutes, but I don't want you running flat out until I say go. Get the feel of the car. Work your way up gradually to three-quarter speed and let's see what we've got."

Clint placed Leah on the observation platform on top of the hauler with a radio headset to monitor communications, gave her a clipboard, and taught her how to work a stopwatch to mark times on a lap sheet. He then changed into his driver's uniform, slid through the window of his car and buckled in, feeling a bit nervous because it had been months since he last drove.

He worked the car around the track a few times, checking his gauges and building heat in the tires, and then picked up the pace with each lap. The nose wanted to hunt the outside wall in turn three, but otherwise the car felt fine. Just as he was preparing to push it to its limits, Walt called him in. He drifted down pit road and parked as the crew swarmed around to make adjustments.

When Walt didn't come near him, Clint keyed his transmit button. "It's pushing a bit in turn three, Walt."

Walt keyed his mike. "I know that."

A few minutes later, Walt waved him back out on the track and keyed his transmit button. "Okay, Clint, same procedure. Pick up the pace each lap, but don't push it hard."

Clint gritted his teeth and did as instructed, building his speed with each lap in increments. Now the rear end was hunting the wall in the middle of turn one. When Walt called him back into the pits, Clint keyed his radio as he coasted to a stop and the crew again swarmed around him. "It's loose in turn one, Walt."

"I know that," Walt replied. A few minutes later, Walt waved him back out with the same instructions to pick up the pace slowly.

Clint sullenly ran three short practice sessions without saying a word about what the car was doing, nor did Walt ask. Finally, Walt instructed him to bring the car down pit road and shut it down. He slid out as Leah climbed down from the top of the hauler and hurried to him.

"Doesn't it scare you going that fast and coming out of the turns so close to the wall?" she asked breathlessly

"I never really got up to speed. What kind of times was I running?"

She consulted her chart. "You were running 23.40's and .45's."

"What was the twenty-six car running?"

She consulted her chart again. "19.10's and .15's."

"Damn, the track record here is 18.62!" He stalked over to Walt, who was checking the tires for wear patterns. "What's the deal, Walt?"

"Heavy inside wear on the right front. I've got Jeff changing the camber now. I'm gonna add a little more cross weight as well."

"Johnson's running in the low 19's."

"I know that," Walt replied.

He stood around for a few minutes with Walt ignoring him, and then went back over to Leah and sat on the pit wall as Wild Bill pulled onto the track and began building speed. Leah clocked him in the high 28's and he lost interest. Glen Johnson came out of his hauler, talked to Chuck for a few minutes, and then strolled over to him.

"Clint?"

"Glen. How's my crew chief working out for you?"

"Good to see you back," Glen replied, ignoring the trite remark.

"Did you expect I wouldn't be?"

"Hear you got a new sponsor at the last minute. Lucky break. Congratulations."

Clint shrugged. "That's what life's all about—lucky breaks."

Leah offered her hand. "I'm Leah, Clint's fiancée."

Glen took her hand. "Ma'am, Glen Johnson. Glad to meet you."

Leah held onto his hand as he attempted to withdraw it from her grasp. "We met Mr. and Mrs. Roberts at dinner in Shreveport."

Glen stiffened and looked at Clint. "Did you now?"

"They said a lot of good things about you."

Glen extracted his hand from Leah's with a determined tug. "That's good to hear. They're nice people to work with."

"I've got to check on my crew," Clint murmured as he stormed off.

When Glen hurried off to his fancy driver's lounge in the front of his elaborate hauler, Leah followed Clint into their hauler. "He's nice and puts out good vibes. You were rude to him, but he still respects you. He was really nervous about us talking to Mr. and Mrs. Roberts."

"I'd really prefer you didn't go around holding hands with every damned person you meet," he fumed.

"I saw you treat him badly and wanted to know what he thought of you. It had something to do with a race, but I couldn't figure out exactly what. Why don't you like him?"

"For starters, the jackass stole my crew chief in the middle of last season, and then stuffed me in the wall in Florida on the last lap. It destroyed my best car and banged me up pretty badly. What goes around comes around and he'll remember that when the time comes!"

"He intended to apologize, but you didn't give him a chance."

"An apology's a waste of time. He knows what to expect and that he has it coming."

Walt sent him back out and they spent the rest of the day trying different setups on the car. By mid-afternoon Clint was running flat out, but his best time was a 20.04, which was nowhere near good enough when compared to Glen Johnson's 18.82 on his last run of the day, a mere two-tenths off of the track record.

As Clint changed out of his driver's uniform, Walt strolled over for the first time. "Clint, I'm happy with today's practice, and even though you didn't show a lot of patience, it helped me and the crew a lot. We'll get better tomorrow. See you in the morning."

"The twenty-six car ran an 18.82 today, Walt."

"I know that," Walt replied as he walked off.

Clint instructed his tire man to give Wild Bill his used tires and drove off in a sulky mood.

"Why are you so quiet?" Leah finally asked.

"I didn't see anything about Walt today that impressed me as a crew chief who knew what he was doing," he replied grimly. "If today is any indication of things to come, we're in deep trouble. I probably ought to fire him right now and look for someone else."

"Maybe things will get better tomorrow," she soothed. "How many cars will you be running against?"

"They start forty-two in a field."

Her stomach convulsed. "My goodness! How do you keep from running over each other?"

He laughed. "We do a lot of running over each other out there, Leah. That's part of the show."

"I'm going to be watching you with my eyes closed then! I can't bear to think of you getting hurt."

"If we don't find some speed, you won't be watching period. I'm so slow right now I won't even make the field. I don't understand Walt's refusal to talk to me about what the car is doing."

"I think he wants to show you he knows his job."

"That's the way they did it in the old days, Leah. The crew chief prepared the car and the driver showed up on race day and drove the wheels off of it. But today everything is high-tech. It takes everybody pulling together as a team to find that razor edge. Things are so competitive now there's no room for error. One second can separate the first place car from the last place car in a lot of races. It's not a one man show anymore. And another thing, at the speeds we're running these days, the driver has to have the confidence the car will stick when he slams it into a turn at a hundred and fifty miles an hour. The price for a miscalculation on the race setup is a sudden stop against a cement wall, which hurts real bad and destroys a fifty thousand dollar car."

"It's really important to him that you do well."

"It's only important to him so he can move back up to Cup racing. I'm just a stepping stone for the man."

"Jeff doesn't agree with Walt on some of the things he was doing to the car today. He thinks you don't drive like other drivers and he's trying to figure out if that's good or bad."

He glanced at her. "How do you know all of these things everybody is supposedly thinking?"

"I read them, Clint. But it would be a lot more reliable if I could touch them. Sometimes their thoughts get mixed up with others around them and I get confused."

"No touching, Leah! They'd think you were coming on to them if you put your hands on them. You just don't realize the impact you have on men. In our society, touching is taboo."

She frowned. "I noticed Glen was uncomfortable shaking hands with me today. He was hoping you wouldn't punch him in the mouth. I don't understand why he would think something like that just because he was shaking my hand."

"If he held on to your hand like you did his today, I *would* punch him in the mouth."

"I don't understand this not touching thing in your world."

"Touching another person is limited to a quick handshake, and women don't even normally do that. It's just something that's considered bad manners."

"Why?"

"Hell, I don't know. I guess it evolved from the medieval times when the male warrior protected a woman's virtue or something like that. Or maybe it's a male jealousy thing, you know, where we men are so insecure about ourselves we're overly protective of our women. If the truth be known, I've never cared enough about a woman to give a damn if she touched someone else or not, but I'm damned conscious of who you touch. And I don't like it when another man touches you. It's just the way things are."

She laid her hand on his arm. "I like you being protective of me, even if you are being silly about it. I like knowing you care, and I don't ever want to do anything to make you insecure. There's no other man I could ever care about but you, don't you know that?"

He cleared his throat. "I care about you too, Leah."

She squeezed his arm. "Why does the 'L' word bother you so much?"

"Damn, women sure have a way of turning a conversation around! We were talking about Walt."

"I love you, Clint …"

"Damn it, Leah, that's not talking about Walt! All this girly gibberish is annoying. Can we just drop the subject for now?"

She flashed a wicked smile. "If I don't, what are you going to do about it—take me home and make love to me until I pass out so you can shut me up for awhile?"

"That's a thought," he threatened darkly.

"Ohoooo, I *love* to think about you doing something like that, and I *love, love* it when you're actually doing it, and I *love*, *love, love* the thought of us doing it as soon as we get home!"

He scowled and sank lower in his seat. "I'd *love* for you to just drop this whole damn subject, Leah!"

Chapter Twenty-Three

On Tuesday Walt brought cars two and three to the practice oval, where they spent a long, fruitless day chasing a race setup, ending with a best lap time of 19.34 on car number three and car number two not even breaking into the teens. Wild Bill Moyer, practicing on Clint's used tires, improved to the 24's, and seemed pleased with his progress as he again gathered up Clint's old tires. Johnson and his crew were nowhere in sight, signifying they were race-ready.

On Wednesday they ran cars four and five, with car five getting to a 19.84, and car four wobbling around in the low 20's at its best. Wild Bill Moyer ran a few laps in the low 22's before filching every tire he could get his hands on from Clint's team and any other team who happened to be practicing that day who would give them to him. Clint joined his dispirited team at the race shop to review their progress.

Walt studied the race setups, shocks, springs, and tire pressures in seclusion, looking for the right combinations to find the additional speed they needed. He selected car number three as their primary car for

Saturday's race, number five as the backup, and what he considered to be the best mechanical settings.

On Thursday they ran both cars in their last session with this new setup, marginally improving on each of them. In Clint's opinion, they were still somewhere out in left field as serious contenders. Wild Bill ran in the low 21's before ecstatically grabbing Clint's used tires and departing. Walt loaded their heavy-hearted team up to return to the shop, out of time and ideas as to where to find the needed additional speed.

Jeff was thoughtfully mute at that evening's pre-race meeting as Walt dictated his final selection of settings to be used. The crew went to work on the changes, working through the evening going over every part, nut and bolt, checking and rechecking each component for signs of wear or potential malfunction. They spent the remainder of the evening loading the primary and backup cars into the two haulers, and inventorying and storing the necessary mix of spare parts and other accessories needed for the race. At midnight the two rigs pulled out for the track, and the remainder of the exhausted team headed home to grab a few hours rest before the big day facing them in a matter of hours.

Clint spent a restless night as Leah attempted to soothe his frayed nerves and gloomy attitude. They departed at 6 a.m. for the track, arriving in the pits at 9:15 for a practice session that started at noon. Clint attended the driver's meeting as the crew unloaded the primary car and made last minute adjustments to the chassis.

A few minutes before noon they pushed Clint's car to the practice grid and he fired up the engine to warm to the proper operating temperatures. Minutes later they were waved onto the track for the official start of the four allowed practice sessions before the qualifying runs scheduled at 5 p.m. that evening.

Clint was all over the track as he fought the wheel, one of the slowest in the field of fifty-three teams searching for thirty-seven official qualifying positions, with the remaining five positions awarded based on driver points from the previous year. Being near the bottom of the list, he would have to qualify or pack up and go home as one of the eleven drivers who would not make the race, a humiliating prospect.

Walt made a series of changes for the second practice session and the car was worse, with Clint ultimately spinning in turn three trying to force more out of it than it was capable of giving, narrowly missing the wall as he looped in a swirling cloud of tire smoke and frustration. He was forced to use a second set of tires for the third practice because he had flat-spotted the first set in the spin, an expense he could ill afford with his limited budget. Walt made another series of adjustments, and Clint drifted around in the back of the pack in the third practice session unable to maintain a modicum of respectable speed.

"This is the next to last practice—you've got to quit pussy-footing around out there and push it harder," Walt counseled over the radio.

"I can't push it any harder!" Clint radioed back angrily. "It's loose as a goose in turns one and two and pushing like a freight train in three and four!"

"You need to drive it like you've got a set of balls," Walt replied.

Clint pulled into the pits, jerked his helmet off, crawled out, and shoved Leah aside to confront Walt as his crew looked on in mortification. "This is the worst piece of shit I've ever sat in!"

"You're running the wrong line!" Walt shouted back as the teams around them watched in wary amusement. "You've got to drive it to the bottom of the track, not float around at the top like a jaybird! You gotta get focused out there."

"The son of a bitch won't go to the bottom!" Clint yelled, throwing his helmet into the driver's compartment in disgust. "It's tight in one end and loose in the other. When I go into a goddamn turn I've got no idea where I'm coming out at!"

"You're driving it too hard into the turns—you've got to set up for them!"

"I'm driving it hard because I'm a goddamn brick in the turns!" Clint yelled. "I can't get out of my own goddamned way out there!"

"I can't set the car up properly unless you drive a consistent line!"

"I can't drive a goddamn consistent line because the goddamn car won't run in the same goddamn groove for two goddamn consecutive laps!"

"Do you want to crew the goddamn thing?"

"I want to *drive* the goddamn thing if you can get your *head* out of your *ass* long enough to make it turn left!"

"I need a *real* driver to show you how it's done!"

"I need a *real* crew chief who knows the front end of a car from the ass end!"

"*I need you both to quit making fools of us*," a quiet voice grated as Clint and Walt glared at each other with their noses inches apart. They turned their heads in unison to stare at Jeff in surprise.

"I've had about all of this I can take," Jeff admonished in a level voice. "Right now we're set to go home after qualifying with our heads up our butts. Mr. Long, you go on in the trailer there and calm down. Mr. Henning, you give me a hand with the car. I've been watching the way Mr. Long drives a high line much like Richard Petty ran in his day. I'm going to set the car up to suit his driving style for the last practice instead of trying to change his groove, and we don't have time to argue about it."

Walt glowered. "Fine by me! You can't *fix* it if it ain't *broke*!"

Clint glowered back. "Fine by me! You can't make it any *worse* than it already is, and right now it's one sorry-assed piece of *shit*!"

Jeff issued orders and the team rushed off to get the shocks and springs he wanted as others jacked the car up and began making changes to the chassis.

Leah rushed in after Clint stormed into the hauler and kicked a container which sent Old Blue scampering as it ricocheted off the wall.

"Are you okay?" she asked apprehensively.

"Hell no, I ain't okay!"

She hugged him. "It's just one race, Clint. There'll be others."

"*Every* damned race is important in the points' series, Leah!" he shouted. "I look like a monkey out there! At this rate, I won't make a race all year! This is goddamn humiliating! I *knew* I should have gone with Cal Roth, strong vibes on your part be damned!"

She clung to him as he trembled in rage. "I'm sorry it's not working out between you and Walt, Clint. Jeff says for you to calm down now and he's right. You need your wits about you when you go back out there."

He took a deep breath. "I'm sorry about the smart-assed vibes quip, Leah, and I didn't mean to yell at you like that. This is all my fault and no one else's."

"You're just frustrated." She kissed him and sensed him calming as Jeff appeared at the end of the hauler.

"Mr. Long?"

"What's the deal, Jeff? Is it going to turn left?"

"This is just a SWAG on my part, so take it easy the first few laps to get the feel of the car. We don't need to tear anything up at this stage. It's either going to be fast or we're going home."

"Don't worry, Jeff, a *scientific-wild-assed-guess* is better than what we had before, and at this stage, I'd rather carry the car home in one piece than wreck it trying to force something that ain't there anyway."

Jeff nodded. "Yes, Sir, that's good to know. Better get strapped in. We go out in about two minutes."

Clint climbed into the car, which was still up on jack stands with crewmembers under it bolting on parts at a furious rate. They dropped the jacks as the last practice session began and he roared down pit road and fell in on the end of the line. He made two cautious laps and then pushed it harder on each successive lap as the car responded with a stable feel. He pushed it nearly to its limits on the last three laps, finding it had a slight push going into turn one, but otherwise held the line like it was on a rail, shocked to find himself passing cars inside and out on the last two laps. He pulled down pit road at the end of the practice session knowing they had a chance of making the field as the crew swarmed around him.

"Tell me exactly what the car was doing," Jeff requested as he climbed out.

"It was damned near perfect!" he praised. "The nose wanted to chase the wall just the tiniest bit going in turn one, but otherwise it stuck like glue. What kind of times did I run?"

"Your last lap was one-tenth off the fastest time run today," Jeff replied.

"Hot damn! I left a little bit out there on the track because I didn't have my full confidence yet. By golly, I think we're going to make this damn race now!" he proclaimed as his crew cheered.

"Congratulations, Clint." Walt hung his head. "I guess I'll pack my bags. Looks like you've found yourself a new crew chief."

"Mr. Henning, I believe you have a contract with this team," Jeff said evenly. "I know chassis and I can make a car turn left as good as most, but we as a team still need your experience to guide us during the race. Do you agree with that, Mr. Long?"

Clint hesitated. "Jeff, from now on call me Clint. Walt, I'll let you out of your contract if you want out, but in spite of our differences, you know race strategy better than any of us. I'm willing to give you another shot if you're willing to give me one."

"Under what title?" Walt asked.

"Crew chief … but I make the calls on the track and Jeff makes the calls on the chassis setup. You have control over the pits, the shop, and race strategy."

Walt clapped Jeff on the back. "I can live with that. Let's get this bugger set up to qualify. Oh, and Clint, I want you to cut my pay in half and give it to this young man. He's working for peanuts right now and he just saved our ass!"

"Done! Now let's go get it done!" Clint shouted as everyone rushed about with a new attitude and hope gleaming in their eyes.

On his qualifying run an hour later, he ran the fourteenth fastest lap in the fifty-three car field and pulled into the pits with his crew dancing merrily around like kids, knowing he could have run even faster if not for fighting the confidence factor. He couldn't get the grin off of his face as Leah hugging him and the crew pounded his back whooping in joy.

From the back of the group Walt winked at him over his own grin, and Jeff nodded his head in quiet satisfaction. He was even more elated when Glen Johnson qualified fifteenth, one position behind him. To his utter surprise, Wild Bill Moyer qualified in the last position at the thirty-seventh starting spot … on Clint's old tires.

He strolled over with growing respect for the feisty little guy and his scrappy team. "Congratulations, Bill. Not many rookies qualify for their first race the first time out of the chute. I'm impressed. I was worried I wasn't going to make it there myself."

"Thanks, Clint," Wild Bill replied. "I knew you'd get it figured out eventually. You know, I couldn't find it myself, so I started watching you run that confounded high line you were running in the last practice session there, and I said, heck, nothing else I'm doing is working, I think I'll try it myself. Worked like a charm. Took some nerve to let it drift up that high in the turns at first, but once I got used to it, I just ignored that old wall and let her rip. Uh, would it be okay if I got your used tires during the race tomorrow?"

"You don't have new tires to race on?"

Wild Bill shook his head. "Naw, them things cost over a grand a set. I figure I can afford some eventually if I get in a few good finishes."

Clint shook his head in wonder. "I'll ensure my tire man sets them aside for you."

"Thanks, Clint, I won't forget how you've helped me. I never forget my friends."

"Uh, Bill … you *do* know that when the green flag drops tomorrow, you don't *have* any friends out there, don't you?"

Wild Bill shrugged. "I know how the game is played, but a man always has his friends."

Clint nodded. "Good luck tomorrow."

"You too, Clint."

Clint hesitated. "Look, I'm heading for the motel. We could grab a bite to eat together if you'd like?"

Wild Bill ducked his head. "Aw, we'll probably just sleep in the truck tonight and eat some sandwiches we got in the cooler. Ain't no use in wasting good money on a room when we'll only be there for a few hours anyway. See you tomorrow, Clint."

Walt and Jeff insisted Leah take him to the motel, feed him, and put him to bed early, explaining to her that preparing the driver for a grueling race was every bit as important as preparing the car.

Leah took her assigned duties seriously and soon had him fed, bathed, and tucked into bed, where he was asleep almost as soon as his head hit the pillow.

Chapter Twenty-Four

Aunt Bessie sat as erect as her diminutive body would allow. “I have met with Leah. This one brought her to my home and dropped her off. She has reluctantly agreed to approach this one about meeting with Council, but does not believe he will agree to do so, and fears he will only become upset with her for even broaching the subject.”

Drew stood. “When will we know if this one will agree to meet with us?”

Aunt Bessie’s unseeing eyes turned in his direction. “She could not say for certain. She thinks it will take some time to convince him, if she can do so at all. I urge Council to be patient with her, and to be tolerant of him as well. I fear if we push too hard we will cause unnecessary conflict between them and only harden his opposition to our Craft.”

Lola stood. “Has she told this one she is carrying his seed yet?”

“I discussed the seed with her, and encouraged her to tell this one as soon as possible. She promised to do so this weekend after the race. I also gave her some pointers to discuss with him to encourage him to meet with Council."

Hellene stood. "Perhaps Leah is not the one to approach this one on Council's behalf after all. She seems unsure of herself. Perhaps we need someone of stronger faith to meet with him instead of relying upon a young lady of somewhat questionable convictions."

Aunt Bessie turned in her direction. "Leah's convictions are not called into question here, Hellene, unless you are in fact doing so now. I feel the issue is a matter of this one's lack of belief in our Craft."

Adrian stood. "What guidance did you give Leah?"

"I encouraged her to discuss the merits of our Craft and attempt to dispel some of the repugnant myths and falsehoods that others have attached to us over the ages, and to give him as much insight as possible as to what we actually represent."

Vaughn stood. "Again I take the floor to protest what I hear today. We are getting dangerously close to recruiting here. We must not cross the line with this one any more than we would with another who does not have the good fortune to possess his noble lineage. We must not lead him to us, nor should we inflict our will upon him in any manner. What we sow, we shall reap three-fold! I urge patience and caution in our approach to him and feel strongly Leah is our best chance of reducing his opposition to our Craft because she has his love and trust. I am convinced a member of Council, a mere stranger to this one, would not be well received."

Hellene stood. "It is not simply *another* we are talking about here. Our normal practices do not necessarily hold true in this instance. We would be negligent in our duties if we did not properly inform this one of his seed's birthright. We have harmed none by such disclosure. I do not disparage Leah in this matter, only point out that others may be better suited for the task."

Merle stood, using the back of his chair to steady himself. "Perhaps we do not harm, but we do run the risk of further alienating him. I think it better we move at a slower pace and allow Leah time to lessen his opposition to our Craft. We have waited five thousand years—a few more weeks will be of no significance."

Shoshanna stood. "I agree. We cannot risk alienating this one when we are so close to gaining our full Council. Leah is the key. Let her educate this one as Aunt Bessie suggests. Give the knowledge she imparts time to take hold and break down his barriers to our society. Caution and patience is the mode we should select in our approach in this matter."

Aunt Bessie nodded. "I propose that if we do not see a softening in this one's opposition to our Craft in a few months, we can then consider a more direct approach."

Merle stood. "Does any member of Council object to this course?" After a silence, he nodded in satisfaction. "Then let us enjoy our fellowship over wine and cake. And if it harm none, do as ye will."

He motioned for the strong maiden to serve the council members.

Chapter Twenty-Five

Clint drove Leah to the track the next morning four hours before the start of the race and was a bundle of nervous energy as he darted around his crew making their pre-race checks. Walt eventually begged Leah to drag him off to the hauler and settle him down so they could get their job done.

As he paced impatiently mentally running every lap of the upcoming race in his mind, Mrs. Roberts appeared at the ramp of the hauler.

"Hi, Leah, I wanted to stop by and say hello before the race begins."

"Mrs. Roberts!" Leah hurried to meet her. "It's so nice to see you again. How is Mr. Roberts?"

"He's fine, child. I'd like to invite you over to watch the race in the comfort of our lounge which has air-conditioning and closed circuit TV."

"I sure appreciate it, Ma'am, but I've got to stay here with our crew since I'm the official lap time keeper for the team," Leah said proudly.

"How thrilling! I wish Glen's crew would let me do something. John says they get nervous when I'm around, but I'd love to be a part of the action instead of just sitting around being bored. Child, what *is* this on your hand?" Mrs. Roberts grabbed Leah's left hand to admire the diamond sparkling there.

"Isn't it beautiful?" Leah gushed.

"I'm so pleased for you!" Mrs. Roberts hugged her. "Have you set a date yet?"

"No, Ma'am, we're waiting to see how the season goes."

"I want you to promise John and me an invitation."

"I promise, Mrs. Roberts. You're the only real friends I've got outside of our race crew."

"You can count on us being there, child. I better get back. Please stop by our place if you get the chance. Good luck out there today, Clint, and please be careful," Mrs. Roberts called to him in the back of the hauler.

"Thank you, Ma'am, and good luck to your team as well," he called back, meaning it on a basic level, but mindful that he still had a score to settle with their driver, where a transgression on the racing circuit carried the weight of a Mafia edict to be assuaged only by sweet revenge.

Leah came back to him with eyes shining. "That was so nice of her to come by and visit, Clint."

He grinned. "At least I seem to be off her shit list."

"It's almost noon. Would you like a sandwich?"

"No," he replied and resumed his nervous pacing.

At 12:30, he joined the other drivers on the starting grid beside his car with his crew decked out in their full race attire for the first time, admiring their new yellow shirts and brown pants received just the day before by special delivery. When the announcer called his name, he waved to a scattering of applause from the crowd and slid into his car. Leah leaned through the window to give him a good luck kiss as he tightened the straps. The crowd grew silent as a local pastor recited a prayer for their safety and encouraged them to exercise good sportsmanship before some celebrity sang the national anthem.

"GENTLEMEN! *START YOUR ENGINES*!"

Clint took a deep breath as the command blared over the speaker system, sending a thrill through him as he hit the ignition switch on the panel. His engine roared to life, sending gauges leaping to their marked dial positions, the thundering din of forty-two cars engulfing the infield and reverberating over the fans as they surged up into a cheering mass. The pace car led them out onto the track, where he swerved back and forth building heat in his tires and clearing off any accumulated rubber. On the third lap around the pace car turned off its flashing yellow lights, signaling one lap to go, and he moved up onto the bumper of the car in front of him as the field tightened up.

"Focus. Wait for my signal." Jeff, his designated spotter, called over the radio.

"Roger," Clint acknowledged as the pace car pulled off the track in turn four. A second later, his earphones crackled to life.

"*Green flag*! *Go*! *Go*! *Go*!"

He jammed the throttle to the firewall and felt an exhilarating surge of power as the air erupted into ear-splitting thunder. He held his line as the pack screamed down the front stretch and poured into turn one in a flashing, colorful mass of chaos as the war began.

"Settle in now," Jeff encouraged calmly. "Clear left. Outside. Outside."

He pulled down into the inside groove and tore out of turn two down the backstretch on the bumper of the car inches in front of his hood. Going into turn three, the car to his front pushed up the track a few feet and he stuck his nose under him to force him higher. They came out of turn four door to door and roared down the front stretch. He again forced the car beside him high in turn one and took the position coming out of turn two as he set his sights on the next car in front of him.

"Good move," Jeff called. "Clear around."

Fifteen laps into the race a spin in turn two brought out the first caution flag, and he eased back on the throttle to fall into line behind the pace car gathering up the field in front of him as he drew a deep breath to relieve the tension.

"You're looking good. Any problems?" Jeff called.

"All instruments are green. No vibrations. She's on a rail. Where am I running?"

"You're ninth. Maintain that position. Save your tires."

"Roger."

"One to go. Wait for my signal."

For the next hour and hundred laps, Clint raced the car hard, but was careful not to abuse the tires or put himself in a position to get caught up in a wreck or to cause one, taking what the track gave him without forcing the issue with cars around him. He was running sixth and feeling good when two cars crashed on the front straightaway. As the pace car gathered them up, he held his hand out the window to curl air into the 150-degree interior as sweat trickled down his face saturating his uniform and flexed his legs to relieve the strain on his back from the constant G forces through the turns.

"Bring her to the crib, Clint. Let's feed the baby and put some new booties on her," Jeff called, indicating Walt wanted a full pit stop.

Most of the cars peeled out of line in turn four with him to growl down pit row with the crews leaping the walls and charging around them as they came to a stop. Twenty seconds later, after fifteen gallons of gas, four new tires, and a drink of water, he pulled back onto the track in a disappointing eleventh position after losing five track positions.

"Sorry about that, Clint," Jeff called. "We need some work on our weekend pit crews. Be patient and work back to the front. Tighten up, one to go."

Another hour and another hundred laps found him running fourth, but unable to do anything with the third place car because of a push going into turn one, which was costing him momentum coming out of turn two. He drove grimly, catching the car in front of him in turn three, falling back again in turn one, catching him again in three, and falling back in turn one in a see-saw battle of wills waiting for the opposing driver to make a mistake so he could gain the advantage.

Forced to make a green flag pit stop with fifty laps to go, Walt elected to change only right side tires and give the car a splash of fuel. Clint came out in third place ahead of the car he had been battling with, who took on four tires. In spite of an air pressure change to his right front, the car still wanted to push in turn one and he again played the tag game of catching the second place car in turn three and then falling back in turn one. Through two more cautions in the last fifty laps, he couldn't improve his position, and in fact was now fighting a hard charging Glen Johnson off, who was all over his rear bumper trying to find an opening.

With three laps to go, Glen got under him when he drifted high in turn one from the push, and they rubbed fenders down the backstretch with sparks flying between them. He beat Glen into turn three and regained the position, but Glen again dove under him going into turn one. They swapped paint down the backstretch as the crowd rose to their feet screaming for the one to pass and the other to hold him off, but Glen couldn't pull the pass off going down into three. On the last lap Glen again dove under him in turn one and they battled down the backstretch elbowing each other aside and slamming back together in a determined duel as they entered turn three door to door with the crowd going wild. He pulled Glen coming out of turn four and took the checkered flag in third place, half a car length ahead of the twenty-six car's hood planted firmly at his door. He throttled down, realizing he could not have held Glen off another lap with him on the inside and the push working against his car in turn one.

He eased around and coasted down pit road feeling like spaghetti, with a pounding headache and arms of molten lead, but supremely happy. As his delirious crew pulled him from the car, Leah jumped up and down behind them with her fists in the air and streaks of mascara staining her cheeks as Old Blue howled in excitement from his chained position at the hauler. The crew carried his exhausted body to the pit wall and sat him down, where he nearly collapsed from fatigue. One of them thrust a bottle of water at him, which he drank deeply from before pouring the rest over his head as they pounded his back in jubilation. Leah fought her way through the crew and planted a kiss on him amid the bedlam.

"Hell, I'd kiss you too, if you weren't so ugly," Walt allowed, shaking his hand as Leah settled in his lap with her arms clasped around his neck.

His crew parted for a camera crew, and with Leah still perched on his lap, he plugged his sponsors and praised Glen Johnson for running him hard but clean in the last few laps. Someone unchained the howling Old Blue, who loped over to rear up and lick his face as his tail cut a furious swath amongst the packed bodies around him. Jeff set the crew to loading the equipment back into the haulers as Walt accompanied the car to the TEC station for the post race inspection.

Wild Bill grasp his hand. "Heck of a job, Clint. You passed me on the outside in turn one like I was standing still."

He laughed. "I was pushing so bad I couldn't get below you. How'd you finish?"

"In twenty-second place, two laps down. You boys play rough out there. I see what you mean by not having any friends when the green flag drops. This is a different ballgame altogether than the regional level."

"In this league it's all about intimidation. Hold your ground and they'll learn to respect you. Give way and they'll eat you alive. Twenty-second in your first race is damned respectable, especially on used tires."

"At least the boys can eat at Hardees tonight. Those baloney sandwiches are getting old." Wild Bill turned to the crowd pouring through the gates into the infield. "Well, let me get on out of your way now as I expect a lot of them folks want to get next to you."

Clint laughed. “See you next week, Bill.”

“Count on it, Clint. Thanks again for the tires.”

Wild Bill stepped back as the fans mobbed Clint wanting autographs and pictures taken with him, the crush elbowing Leah to the back of the pack, where she tried to control Old Blue, who was distraught with all the strangers clustering around them.

* * *

“I can’t believe they gave you so much money,” Leah said later as they departed the track, staring at the twenty-two thousand dollar third place check.

“First place pays twice as much,” he advised.

“Is it all yours?”

“Sixty percent is. The rest is divided among the crew as an incentive bonus,” he replied, relieved that he could now afford to pay the rent on their extended stay motel due on Monday since he had less than two hundred dollars remaining in his personal bank account. “This little payday will give us some breathing room. How do you feel about a furnished apartment? It’ll help cut our overhead and give us more room as well.”

“We can live in the back of your race shop for all I care,” she replied. “I’m so proud of you. I never knew anything could be so thrilling. It gave me as many goose bumps as the first time you made love to me.”

He laughed. “I plan to work up a bunch of those bumps for you tonight.”

“I’ve never seen so many people in my life. There were thousands of them standing and screaming when you and Glen were beating on each other at the end. I couldn’t even watch because I was so afraid you were going to wreck, but I kept peeping through my hands because I couldn’t stop watching either.”

"I'm glad Glen and I could give them a good show for their money."

"I don't like all those girls hugging on you and taking their picture with you though. I was just about to bop that one girl who kept hanging on your arm."

"She's just a fan. She didn't mean anything by it."

"I saw the way she was looking at you. She'd eat you up like a candy bar if she got the chance."

"Leah, it's all harmless," he protested. "Are you really jealous?"

"Yes I am!"

"You're all the woman I could ever want."

"I sure hope so, otherwise one of them gals might end up holding you in her lap and petting you while you purr," she snipped.

"*Leah*!"

"Either that or the first time they pucker up to kiss you, they'll find themselves kissing some old toad with warts!"

"Okay, okay, I get the picture," he said, laughing.

"I was so proud of you today I could just die."

"It was a good race, but I was still the second loser. Just wait until I win one. There's no feeling like it."

"Jeff thinks you have the most natural moves in a racecar he's ever seen. He thinks you not driving like other drivers is a good thing and that you can even be great. He's excited to be a part of your team."

"Jeff's a good man. He sure pulled our butt out of the fire yesterday in qualifying."

"Walt thinks you've got good instincts, but that you're too stubborn and it will keep you from making the big time if you don't control it, but he was really proud of you for hanging in there against Glen."

"They *think* those things, Leah?"

"I was so excited I grabbed their arms when I was jumping up and down and trying not to watch, and there it was in their minds thinking you could be great."

He shrugged. "Time will tell, I guess."

After a short silence, she drew a deep breath, her heart pounding, knowing the time had come. "Clint, how do you feel about us having a baby? Would that be okay with you?"

He lurched and almost ran off the road. "Where in hell did that come from? A baby is the *last* thing I need right now. *Definitely, absolutely not*!"

She stared straight ahead. "Why not?"

"I've got to get my career on track and have some financial security before I bring a baby into this world. Something like that is way-way off in the future."

"What if it's too late?"

"What do you mean? Too late for what?"

"To think about having a baby."

"Why would it be too late? You're on the pill aren't you?"

"I don't know anything about any pill."

"*What*! Are you kidding me? *Everybody* uses birth control these days. I'll get you an appointment with a doctor first thing next week to get you on the pill. It'd be a disaster if you got pregnant right now."

"What if I'm already pregnant?"

He clenched his jaw. "Then you would have to get an abortion, Leah."

She recoiled. "You'd want me to *kill* our *baby*?"

"Abortions are legal now."

"I'm not talking *legal*, Clint! I would *never* kill our baby!"

"Okay, okay, let's just drop it," he soothed. "Just don't get pregnant in the first place and we won't have to worry about it."

Tears streaked down her cheeks. "I got pregnant the first time you done it to me, Clint."

He hit his brakes and lurched into a supermarket parking lot before turning to her. "Leah, don't kid around about something like this!"

"I haven't got my period in two months, and I can feel the baby inside me. It's the greatest feeling I've ever known. I was hoping you'd be as happy as I am."

"Leah, please don't say that," he pleaded. "We've only been together a little over two and a half months. It takes three months to know if you're pregnant. Even I know that much. We'll see a doctor Monday to get you on the pill."

"I'm pregnant, Clint, and I won't have an abortion," she whispered. "This is our baby and I won't give it up. This is why you came to Louisiana. I was supposed to receive your seed to protect your lineage. If you'll agree to meet with Council they'll explain everything to you."

He studied her intently. "Leah, you're not making sense. Let's don't fight about this until we see a doctor and confirm it one way or another, and then we'll decide what we need to do."

He put the car in gear, his mind in complete turmoil. *How could I have been so stupid to assume she was on the pill? A baby just is not an option. If she is pregnant, I need to find a way to get her to agree to an abortion. I'm the potential father, and by god I have some say in this matter as well! And what the hell is this Council crap? What did she mean by she was supposed to get pregnant to protect my lineage? I should never have carried her to see that nutty old hag. All of this foolishness seems to revolve around that crazy old black woman in some way or another.* He drove in the heavy silence, his emotions scattered.

Leah slumped against the passenger door, her heart frozen, her stomach as if it held rocks. The mere suggestion of killing her baby was the single most repulsive thing she had ever heard in her life. Though she loved this man with every fiber of her being, she would never allow that to happen. The mere fact that he had even suggested such a horrible thing hurt to the core of her soul and filled her with anguish. Somehow, she had to get him to agree to meet with Council so he could understand what was at stake and be as happy about the baby as she was. She had to teach this man about the wonder of life and the compassion of humanity, because if he could do something like that he was truly lost. She silently grieved for him deep inside where the ache of his words still stung, as tears coursed down her cheeks and she mindlessly, mutely hummed a chant of forgiveness for him.

Chapter Twenty-Six

Sunday continued to be stressful as the strain between them lingered through the day, which Clint spent on the sofa watching a Cup race on TV while Leah busied herself elsewhere in the small apartment.

Monday morning he accompanied her to see a doctor, who ran preliminary tests to confirm she was pregnant and in excellent health. He prescribed vitamins and made an appointment for her to see a gynecologist after offering his heartfelt congratulations.

Clint drove them to the race shop in stunned silence. Leah appeared near tears throughout the day as they went about their tasks with hardly a word exchanged between them. The crew, sensing the tension, busied themselves with the number five car they intended to run the coming weekend. Clint received a call from Sam Hutchinson at Sunrise Sausage congratulating him on the race and expressing his satisfaction with the TV interview.

They left the crew working that evening and drove home in heavy silence. She prepared dinner as he sat at the table watching her quietly while Old Blue lay on the floor, his eyes doleful. She sat two plates of stew on the table, poured them a glass of tea, and seated herself.

When they finished, she began clearing the table. "We can't go on like this, Clint."

"You know how I feel about having a child right now."

Tears slid down her cheeks as she turned to the sink to wash the dishes. "I don't understand how I can be so happy about something that makes you so upset."

"This just can't be happening!" he swore. "What in *hell* did I ever do to deserve this?"

She turned to him. "I'm sorry this has brought you so much sorrow. I never wanted to do that."

"Can we at least *discuss* an abortion?" he pleaded.

She shuddered and turned away. "That's something I can never do. I care more for you than anything I have ever cared about in my whole life, but I can't kill our baby for you, so please don't ask me to. It hurts me so bad to say no to you, but it hurts me even more when I think about doing something as awful as that."

"Leah, it's *not* killing! It's been proven that—"

She raised her palms to her ears. "No, Clint! I don't want to hear anymore!"

"I should have a say in this too!" he shouted. "I'm not ready to be a father yet! Don't you understand that? This ruins everything I've worked for my whole life. I'm on the verge of making it to the big time. To the *Cup*, Leah! Saturday's race proved I can drive with anybody if I have a car under me. People will be watching me now and evaluating me, looking to sponsor me, maybe even move me up. We can have a kid anytime, Leah, but you're lucky if you get *one* shot at the big-time in this business."

"Clint, please don't yell at me," she pleaded. "I'm not deaf. I don't see how me having our baby is going to keep you from doing the things you need to do in your racing career. I can take care of it all by myself. It's not going to interfere with your racing. If you would agree to meet with Council you would understand why this baby is so important beyond you and me."

"Oh, *I* understand, Leah! *It's you* who doesn't understand!" he shouted. "That's the whole damn problem here—you're so *dumb* about things. And *hell no*, I won't meet with a bunch of damned *weirdo's* to enlighten me on a bunch of *bullshit*! I wish I had *never* stopped to see that old Bessie hag! My life has gone to hell ever since!"

"Are you saying I'm bad for you, Clint?" she sobbed. "Have I made things so wrong in your life?"

He stood, glaring at her. "I've got to get away for awhile and think things out! I'm going to stay at the race shop tonight." He turned to the door.

She hurried after him. "Please don't leave me like this—I'm so confused!"

"I need some space, Leah," he threw over his shoulder. "I can't think right now!"

She watched him storm off in near panic. *How can he be so upset about me giving him something so marvelous*? His world was so confusing, so filled with wonders on the one hand, and with such cold harshness on the other. To suggest that she take a life he had helped her create was so repulsive she became physically ill and rushed to the bathroom to lose her dinner in gasping heaves. She lay slumped against the cold ceramic bowl shaking uncontrollably as tears spilled down her face, having never known such pain deep in the pit of her stomach, where even now one of the wonders of the universe was incubating. She shuddered, realizing she had no one outside of him to turn to, and that she had driven him away.

He drove off with his tires spinning. *This can't be happening*! *Not now. What am I going to do with a kid? I can't even take care of Leah and Old Blue properly! She isn't being fair about this. I've got to make her see what she is doing to our life. Abortion isn't like murder. It's done every day. It's simply preventing a child from being born that can't be taken care of properly—like this child. I'm just not ready for that. Maybe someday, but not now—Leah will just have to understand that!*

He slept on his cot at the shop, tossing and turning as he wallowed in self-pity. The next day he worked feverishly to keep his mind off Leah and the baby as his crew went about their business in a subdued manner, avoiding him and his bad temper as best they could. He worked until midnight, long after the rest of the crew had gone home, and then took a shower in his small stall at the back of the office before falling into his bunk in exhaustion. He was already working the next morning when the crew arrived and set a torrid pace for them. At noon, one of his crew came to where he was working under the car to inform him that Leah was on the phone.

"Tell her I'll call her back later!" he snapped.

Later another crewmember informed him a Mr. Sellers was on the phone for him.

"I don't know a Mr. Sellers. What does he want?"

"He said it was personal, Clint."

"Have him leave a number."

Later another crewmember approached. "Leah is on the phone again, Clint. She says she it's urgent."

"Tell her I'm in the middle of something and don't answer the phone anymore. Let them leave a damn message."

That evening when the crew departed, Walt lingered behind. "We need to talk."

"About what, Walt?"

"What's going on with you and Leah? She called here twice today with some sort of an emergency and you wouldn't even talk to her."

"She and I are having a little disagreement. It doesn't concern you or the crew."

"It's very difficult for us to work in this environment and keep our focus on the race this weekend. Ignoring a problem doesn't make it go away. Why don't you go home tonight instead of staying here and try to talk things out? That girl loves you to death, Clint, and we all think highly of her ourselves. This is not the right way to handle things."

He hung his head. "Walt … she's pregnant …"

"Congratulations," Walt said sincerely.

"You don't understand. I'm not ready for this. I've got too many things going on in my life right now to raise a kid. I want her to get an abortion. She refuses to talk about it. I should have a say in this matter too."

"Well now, I guess you should and you shouldn't, Clint. It's her child too, and her body completely. Ultimately, she has the final say, just as you do out there on that track in the heat of battle. No one can second-guess you in that situation or her in this one. I know a child is a big responsibility and can scare the hell out of you initially. I know that because I've got two daughters of my own out there somewhere."

"Walt, I'm not financially secure enough to raise a child. Hell, I live in a motel. I don't own a damn thing outside of these damned old racecars here and the clothes on my back. Do you know what I mean?"

"That's only a part of it, Clint. When my girls were growing up, I was in the big time in Cup racing bringing down the dough with both hands. They always had a good home, and clothes, and all of the other material things in life. I took pride in that and thought it was enough. I've since discovered all of that don't matter much if they don't have love, and that's the one thing I never provided for them. I never gave them any of my time when they were growing up, and now they won't give me any of their time now that they're grown. They're ashamed of me for being an alcoholic, actually. But even though I all but ignored them when they were young because I was so busy with my career, and later because I was drunk night and day, I can honestly say there's never been a day when I didn't love them. Children don't care about anything but love. If they have a parent's love, they're happy. You and Leah have more than enough of that to provide to a child. The material things will come in time."

"But what about my career, Walt? I've worked my whole life for this moment. I'm on the verge of making it, I can just feel it."

"Clint, you're a talented driver, one of the best at your young age I've ever seen. I predict you'll make it in this profession if you get your head out of your ass long enough to listen to other people. This child won't change that. This child is as important to Leah as your career, so embrace it with all of your heart and just do the best you can for the both of them. You'll find in the long run that will be more than enough. Now get on home and work things out with that little gal. Don't add to your worries, or hers either, by acting like this. This thing is disrupting our whole team."

He hung his head. "I guess you're right, Walt. I am acting like a stubborn jackass, and I've got to get this thing resolved one way or another. Lock up for me, will you?"

"Thanks for hearing me out," Walt called. "And good luck!"

Clint drove to the extended stay suite, where there were no lights on inside, he noted as he inserted his key. When it wouldn't unlock the door, he knocked, waited, and knocked again.

"Leah? Open the door, please."

The lady living next to them opened her door. "She and her dog left today."

"Left?"

She glared at him. "She got evicted. She used my phone twice to call you."

"Evicted!" He suddenly recalled the rent was due on Monday. In all the confusion with the pregnancy, he had forgotten to pay it. *That's why Leah was trying to call me today!*

He whirled and ran to the motel office. After some persuasion, the night manager called the day manager at home. When he hung up, he turned back to Clint.

"It seems your lady friend was informed the rent was three days in arrears and that the past due balance and the following weeks' rent would need to be paid by 5 p.m. today or she would be required to move out. The personal belongings left in the suite have been boxed up and stored in the back of the office here."

"That's crazy! Why didn't somebody call me? I want to speak to the day manager! I want to know where Leah is, goddamn it!"

The night manager edged away from him cautiously. "Sir, it would do no good to talk to Mr. Sellers. He assured me he called your place of business today and was informed you were unavailable. He assured me he also left two urgent messages on your recorder as well after that. He done everything he could do. He explained that to the lady when she left. He doesn't know where the lady has gone. She and her dog sat out on the curb for an hour after she moved out, until the police came by and explained to her that she could not stay on the premises any longer. That was the last he saw of her. I'm sorry, Sir, but there's nothing else I can tell you."

Clint raced out to the curb and looked up and down the busy boulevard as his heart pounded. He looked at his watch and calculated they had been gone some two and a half hours. He ran back to his car and drove up and down the boulevard for two miles in each direction looking for some sign of them as the guilt ate at him, and then drove the boulevard again in both directions for four miles, becoming frantic. *How could I have allowed this to happen*?

He drove back to the motel and stood on the curb again, trying to think of which way she would have gone. He chose south and drove in that direction, stopping at every gas station and convenience store, but no one had seen a woman accompanied by a large dog. He drove north and at the second service station an attendant remembered such a woman walking with a big dog and crying.

He drove up and down the northern portion, and then branched out through the side streets, tears stinging his eyes as the enormity of what he had done sank in. *She's helpless, broke, and alone in a big city, in a world she's ill-equipped to deal with. She has nowhere to go and nobody to turn to but me, and I rejected her pleas for help. Think, damn it! What would I do if I were her?*

He flagged down a police cruiser and explained what had happened to the officers. They called dispatch and asked every cruiser in the area to be on the lookout for Leah and her dog, and requested that other cruisers check the bus stop and train station, but he knew she didn't have the money for a ticket to go anywhere and wouldn't leave Old Blue behind even if she did.

He drove until daylight in circles around the boulevard and all of the side streets, both north and south, and even swung by his race shop twice on the off chance she had gone there, but found no trace of her or Old Blue. He checked in with the police again and got a negative report. She and Old Blue had simply disappeared into the night.

The next morning he called Walt at the shop from a phone booth. "I won't be in today. Can you and Jeff handle things?"

"Sure, Clint. What's the problem?"

"It's Leah, Walt. She's gone."

"Gone? Gone where?"

"Walt … I forgot to pay the rent on Monday. I was so upset I didn't even think about it. That was why

Leah was calling yesterday. They were evicting her. I'm so ashamed."

"Take it easy, Clint," Walt soothed. "We'll all pitch in and help you look for her. I'm sure she's checked into a local motel or something."

"She doesn't have any money, and I've already got the police looking with me. Just get us ready for this weekend. I've got to find her, Walt."

"You do what you need to do, Clint. Jeff and I've got things under control here. You go find that little girl. She couldn't have gone far if she's broke."

He drove randomly around Charlotte, looking along the Interstates and in any conceivable place he could think of that she might have gone. He went back to the motel in hopes she had returned there. The day manager was of no help to him, and insisted he get all of his personal gear out of the storeroom. He loaded it into his car and deposited the boxes back at his race shop, where Walt was distraught to learn of his fruitless search for her.

"What are you going to do next, Clint?"

"Keep looking. That's all I can do. Get the cars to the track tomorrow. I'll meet you there."

He drove all over Charlotte looking for them until midnight. Exhausted, and with no hope left of finding her and Old Blue, he drove the three hours to the track and slept in the back of his car until morning.

Chapter Twenty-Seven

Clint qualified sixth in his depressed state after four decent practice rounds, and afterwards, collapsed in a rented motel room consumed with guilt because Leah had no bed.

The next day he drove like a madman, wanting to get the race over with, paying scant attention to anything other than staying out of the multiple wrecks occurring around him and passing the next car in front of him. After a green flag pit stop where he lost considerable track position due to a jammed lug nut, he found himself passing Wild Bill Moyer's yellow sixteen car for tenth place, briefly wondering how the determined little rookie could get that high up in the rankings while running on used tires in an outdated car with a makeshift pit crew.

Thereafter he pitted when Walt told him to, took on whatever Walt called for without question, and drove mindlessly when the green flag waved, his only desire to get to the finish line so he could resume his search for Leah. Paying scant attention to the race itself, he was shocked when he slipped under the car in front of him in turn three and came down the front stretch with the white flag waving indicating he was leading on the last lap. He took the checkered flag and coasted around the backstretch indifferent to having won, as Wild Bill and a host of other drivers drew up beside him to salute his victory. He pulled into victory lane feeling empty inside, and went through the motions of the interview in the winner's circle as his crew riotously splashed each other with Gatorade, performing like an animated robot for the TV crews before withstanding the crush of fans seeking autographs. When the crowd finally thinned, he turned to Walt.

"I'm not in the mood to celebrate. I need to get back to Charlotte so I can continue searching for Leah. Take the crew out for a victory dinner and I'll see you back at the shop."

Walt nodded. "You go find that little gal, Clint. I'll see to the crew and get us ready for next week."

Back in Charlotte, the police reported no sign of Leah or Old Blue, and the extended stay manager assured him she had not returned. He drove to his race shop, showered, and opened some of the boxes searching for clean clothes. On top of the second box, he found a letter addressed to him with her engagement ring inside and the rose quartz heart she had kept in her cigar box. He sat at his desk and unfolded the page.

My Dearest Clint,

I don't know how to say this right and hope you will understand if I say it all wrong. I love you. I have always loved you even if I couldn't say it out-right very often because it annoyed you. I have left you my sacred heart as a pledge of my devotion to you, for there will never be another for me. My only regret is that the time was not right for you to love me. I am so grateful to you for making me the happiest girl in the world and teaching me so much by sharing a part of your life and world with me. For a while, I could pretend I was just like those beautiful women in the magazines and live a regular life like them. I realize now I should never have made you take Old Blue and me with you. That was wrong of me and changed the order of things, but if I had it to do over, I would still trade the few months I had with you for all the rest of the years of my life with no regrets.

I am so sorry for the anxiety and grief I brought you in our time together. I never meant to hurt you in any way. I just loved you so much I thought I could make it right for us.

Please forgive me.

Leah

He sat with tears streaming down his face staring at the letter, and then searched the boxes for anything else from her, but found only the clothes he bought her with the exception of one set of blue jeans, one blouse, and a pair of tennis shoes. He sank to his knees sobbing as the life drained out of him and a great cavity expanded within him. He grasped the crystal heart and lay back on his cot in exhaustion, his mind filled with troubling images of Leah and Old Blue. A tingling in his palm drew his attention to the crystal and he was startled to see the rose color fading to a frosty white as it grew warmer in his palm. He turned the point of the heart away from him towards his fingers as the frost melted to a surreal clear depicting Leah sitting on a patch of green grass, her eyes filled with enduring joy as she watched a female child with ringlets of golden hair at play before her, whom he instantly recognized as his own. The image was so startling he collapsed back on his bunk shaking and felt himself sinking into oblivion. He awoke at dawn filled with tender remorse and a deep longing for his daughter that Leah carried, and an even stronger sense of desperation to find them.

He scribbled a note to Walt informing him he would be gone for a few days and that he had full confidence in the team to prepare for the next race. He quickly packed, shoved Leah's engagement ring and rose quartz heart into his pocket, climbed in his car, and drove to the small sign advertising *Readings by Miss Bessie* attached to a fence post. He pulled into the drive of the weathered little clapboard house and anxiously knocked on the door.

"Come in, youngster," the frail voice cracked with age invited.

Filled with trepidation, he entered and paused to allow his eyes to adjust to the gloom, finding Aunt Bessie at her table wearing her old black smock, her eyes staring straight ahead without focus, her weathered face mired in wrinkles below her sparse white hair, her wrinkled hands resting on the table. "Why do you fear me, youngster?" she challenged. "Sit down and tell me why you have come back to me."

He eased into the chair across from her. "It's Leah, Ma'am … I need to find her."

"And why do you need to find her, youngster?" she asked curtly.

He cleared his constricted throat. "I made a mistake with her, Aunt Bessie … she's gone and I'm so worried about her."

"It's *Aunt* Bessie now, is it, and not the *old hag*?" she cackled. "Why the sudden respect, youngster?"

"I'm sorry for disrespecting you … please help me find her … she's going to have my child."

"Yes she is, youngster. I sent you to plant your seed in her womb, but I didn't expect you to take her out of our world. You changed the natural order of events and altered her future."

"I … don't really understand all that, but I never meant to harm her. Will you help me?"

"Why do you want her back, youngster?" she demanded. "You have proven yourself unworthy of such a one as my Leah."

"I was upset and made a stupid mistake, but I swear it wasn't intentional. I'll take care of her and make her happy for the rest of my life if she'll still have me. I admit I'm not worthy of her, but I promise I'll try to be in the future if she'll give me another chance."

Her unseeing eyes searched his face. "Did you appreciate her when she gave you her virginity, or her heart and soul afterwards, youngster? Did you appreciate her when you paid so much money for that fancy stone in your pocket? Did you appreciate her when you discovered she was carrying your child in her womb?"

He wiped at the tears as guilt stabbed at him. "Aunt Bessie, I might be lacking in many ways, but I swear to you, I *love* Leah. I didn't know how much until I lost her. I'll do anything you ask if you'll help me find her."

"And what of the child you want her to give up?"

"I was foolish to ask that of her. I know you're sworn to protect her. I promise I'll take care of her and our child for the rest of my life. Please help me." He removed the rose heart from his pocket and held it out to her. "She called this her sacred heart and left it for me. When I held it in my palm, I saw an image of Leah and my daughter. They were so happy together. I want to be in that picture too, Aunt Bessie. I swear to you on this heart I will never do her wrong again."

"Take off your talisman, youngster, so I may read you to ensure I make no mistake in assisting you."

He removed the gold chain with the Tiger's Eye stone and laid it on the table as his heart pounded. Her gnarled hand grasped his and held it tightly as a tingling warmth grew in his palm from the crystal heart.

"Yes, I see you more clearly now," she rasped after a time. "You are worthy, for your heart is pure, even though you have proven to be foolish in many ways."

"Can you tell me what all this means?"

"You were invited to Council to learn of these things, youngster."

"Please, Aunt Bessie, tell me what I need to know so I can try to understand all this."

"Very well, youngster, listen closely, for I haven't much strength. You and Leah are destined to bring the great one to our world who will enlighten all mankind."

"I-I'm sorry … but that sounds crazy to me …"

"The ancient ones were from a dying galaxy now extinct, and were unable to adapt to this planet in their physical embodiment. They therefore infused their genetic makeup into the early human species to breed modern man, which harbors their soulful essence. The ancient ones deliberately engineered a specific genetic order for each of our twelve tribes to spawn the diverse ethnic and cultural genres of our world.

"During the last visit by the ancient ones some five thousand years ago, the purest member of each of the tribes was chosen to serve on Council and sanctified to preserve their twelve direct bloodlines throughout the generations by passing their seed to their firstborn, who in turn passed their seed to their firstborn. The twelve members of Council today descended through this secular process. The ancient ones ordained each member of Council to collectively govern our Craft, and decreed that it be one of choice thrust upon no other, whilst allowing us diversity in our individual rituals and freedom to pursue our convictions as we please, if it harms no other.

"The ancient ones also gifted us twelve sacred crystal skulls which collectively contain all the wisdom and knowledge they possessed. They further decreed the key to this vast knowledge would lie in a thirteenth crystal skull, which will come through a new soul who carries the genetic code of each of the original tribes. As such, this new soul will take the revered place as head of Council and unlock the knowledge awaiting us. We have continuously tried to complete this linkage over these thousands of years, but due to war, disease, and naturally occurring disasters, we have never reached the twelfth linkage.

"Your mother unknowingly possessed ten of the genetic seeds of our twelve tribes, when by chance she married a member of the eleventh tribe to birth you, who now magically holds eleven of the twelve linkages. Leah is a member of the twelfth remaining tribe, and thus chosen by Council to bear your firstborn child to complete the preordained genetic linkage. Bearing your firstborn is a great honor for her, for that seed will grow into a High Priestess and take her rightful place on Council to usher in the golden age of enlightenment.

Unfortunately, we did not anticipate Leah becoming your life mate."

"I'm having trouble understanding all of this, Aunt Bessie. You say my daughter will become a High Priestess in your world and serve as head of your Council?"

"That is correct, youngster. Through these thousands of years, we have tried to engineer the genetic feat you currently possess. When I discovered that you by a freak of nature held eleven of the necessary twelve links, our first priority was to complete the lineage through Leah. Our second priority was to inform you of your daughter's heritage in hopes you would join our world where she will assume her rightful place as head of Council and release all the collective insight of our ancient ones to usher in a new age of enlightenment."

"I-I don't know if I can … give you my daughter, Aunt Bessie …"

"She is not ours to take, nor yours to give, youngster. She is by birth of our world."

"I … have rights as her father … there are laws and—"

"This is not a matter of law, youngster, it is a matter of destiny."

"But … if I don't want her to be part of your world and …"

"… take her away from us, youngster? Then she would eventually find her way back to us on her own accord. It is preordained."

"Please, I-I don't understand any of this …"

"Our religion is one of choice. As such, you may choose to serve our Craft, or you may choose not to, but we must protect your lineage in any case, as is our scared duty. Regardless of your choice in assuming a place in our world, or to remain forever in your current world, you are rearing a beacon of light in the darkness which we revere."

He hesitated, fighting disbelief. "Aunt Bessie, I mean no disrespect, but I don't believe in witchcraft or whatever. All I care about is Leah. Will you help me find her?" He waited through a long silence. "Aunt Bessie—"

"Quiet, youngster," she commanded. "I am trying to locate her." She sat for an intolerable time before cocking her head. "She is on a highway in a large vehicle, she and her canine mastiff," she stated in a trance-like voice. "The road is rushing by under her and the tires are making a steady humming sound, which is lulling her to sleep. She is tired and scared due to the swiftness of her journey to a destination she does not desire to arrive at. There is a man with her wearing a hat, but I cannot make out his features. A sign ahead says Montgomery, 65 miles." She snapped out of her semi-conscious state. "Leah has gone to sleep. I have lost her."

He stood with pounding heart. "It sounds like she's in an eighteen-wheeler 65 miles this side of Montgomery, Alabama, heading back to her old home in Louisiana. Is she in any danger from the man with her?"

"Her mind was only on you and the ache in her heart."

"Aunt Bessie, can you use your powers to let her know I'm coming for her?"

"She is not strong in this method of contact. I can only see and feel what she sees and feels when I dispose myself to her, but this is very tiresome for someone as ancient as I."

"Do you have a telephone? I'll call you in case you are able to communicate with her and let her know I'm coming for her."

"Leave your talisman off and concentrate on me when you want to converse. Believe what images you see and what thoughts you receive in your mind."

"I … don't believe that will work with me."

"You believe or you wouldn't be here, youngster," she scolded. "But you don't trust your beliefs. Keep your mind clear and concentrate on me. You have strong psychic powers that you do not even know you possess. Believe what thoughts I place there for you to read."

He hesitated, and then leaned over to kiss the top of her head. "Thank you, Aunt Bessie. I'll try to repay you someday for your kindness."

"You have been a long time coming," she said softly. "Go now, youngster, find our Leah and prove worthy of her!"

He turned and ran for his car.

Chapter Twenty-Eight

Clint stopped to gas up and guzzle down a coke and pack of cheese crackers before setting sail in earnest, cruising at over 100 miles an hour on the Interstate, slowing only for traffic, or when his fuzz-buster alerted him of radar signals. Four hours and forty minutes of hard driving brought him to the sign announcing Montgomery, 65 miles. Pangs of anxiety flashed through him, as it was now 3 p.m. After driving cross-country like a demon and traveling a distance that should have taken over seven hours under normal conditions, he was still four and a half hours behind the eighteen-wheeler. He pulled off the Interstate into a gas station, anxious to refuel and be back on his way, hoping they had stopped for lunch or made a cargo pickup or delivery, or encountered some other delay, and that he had gained even more time on them. He had been so intent on his driving he had not attempted to communicate with Aunt Bessie. He eased back onto the Interstate at a leisurely 70 miles an hour and forced himself to relax and imagine her in her chair at her table, focusing on her diminutive figure sitting in the gloom, feeling a little foolish, but desperate enough to try anything.

"Aunt Bessie, can you hear me?" he thought.

"*Hello, youngster,*" flashed into his brain with startling clarity. "*I have been waiting for you.*"

No, that was too easy—my imagination is working overtime. This mind thing has to be harder than that.

"*Trust in your beliefs,*" flashed into his mind.

"Aunt Bessie?" he thought tenuously.

"*I am here, youngster,*" flashed back, leaving his heart pounding.

No way, his logic reasoned, *you're getting as nutty as a fruitcake and beginning to hallucinate.*

"*Don't fight me, youngster,*" filled his mind. "*What took you so long to contact me*?"

"Aunt Bessie, if I'm not going crazy, I hear you," he thought. "Is this for real or am I losing my mind?"

"*Where are you, youngster?*"

"Near Montgomery," he thought. "Have you communicated with Leah?"

"*They are still moving. She is not open to my telepathy. Her thoughts are on you only.*"

"Do you know where they are now?"

"*A sign said Interstate 10 some time ago. The farther away Leah gets from you, the more intense her pain.*"

"I'm so sorry," he thought. "I'll make it up to her, I promise."

"*What are your intentions now*?"

"I'm going to Interstate 10," he thought. "Please keep trying to reach her."

"*I am growing weary. I will need to rest soon.*"

"Please hang in just a little longer," he thought.

"*I will do my best, youngster.*"

He hit the throttle and pulled his mind back to the task of driving at over 100 miles an hour, part of him arguing this was a foolish waste of valuable time, but another part urging him to believe, as improbable as it seemed. *What other alternative do I have*? One hour and ten minutes later, he slowed after pulling onto Interstate 10 and imagined Aunt Bessie back in her home.

"Aunt Bessie, are you still there?" he thought.

"*I'm very tired, what took you so long, youngster*?"

"Traffic is heavy. Have you reached Leah?"

"*She is in a restaurant eating now.*"

"Do you know where the restaurant is?" he thought, checking his watch, calculating it was an hour earlier in this time zone.

"*A sign said Mobile some time ago. Another said Pascagoula just before they stopped.*"

"I'll check in later," he thought.

"*Be safe, youngster.*"

"I'm not losing my mind or anything, am I?" he wondered.

"*No, youngster, your mind is sound—it's your judgment that is suspect.*"

He grinned and picked up the pace, fighting his logic, but willing to believe anything if it could possibly lead him to Leah.

Damn! I guess my luck can't hold forever, he groused as a flashing blue light fell in behind him on the outskirts of Pascagoula some time later while hitting better than 110 on this stretch, realizing that kind of speed meant jail, not a fine, if the state troopers caught him. He pushed it up to 150, knowing he could outrun the trooper behind him, but not his radio, and that his Smokey-bear buddies would be waiting up ahead with a roadblock and be in a sour mood when he got there.

He down shifted and took the next exit at better than 80 miles an hour, ran the stop sign at the bottom, and power shifted back up to high gear as he flashed down a narrow ribbon of blacktop away from the Interstate. He switched off his headlights and slowed, took a side road, and coasted to a stop. He got out and listened intently to sirens blaring from both directions trying to catch him in a vise between them, knowing he had done well to choose this exit.

He drove back onto the Interstate at a sedate 65 miles an hour after the police car flashed past the exit. Ahead he saw four sets of blue lights flashing as the two groups met and pulled over to confer. He drove by them with baited breath and then eased back up to 70 as their lights faded in his rearview mirror, grateful luck was still with him.

"*Are you there, youngster?*"

"Yes, Aunt Bessie. I'm at Pascagoula now. Have you seen any more signs that will help me?"

"*A sign said Gulfport-Biloxi some time ago, but I could not read the miles. I need to rest, I am an old woman.*"

"Please hang with me, Aunt Bessie! I'm close now, less than an hour behind them."

"*Try to contact Leah yourself, youngster. You are all that is on her mind. Maybe you can break through to her where I cannot. You are closer to her and your thoughts will be much stronger. My mind is growing weary from the effort.*"

"How do I do that, Aunt Bessie? I'm new at this mind stuff, if I'm not crazy and just imagining all this."

"*Send your thoughts out to her and see if she receives them ... I must go now ... I am very tired.*"

"Leah? Can you hear me? I'm somewhere on Interstate 10 trying to find you. Can you hear me, Leah?" he thought as hard as he could as he eased the speedometer back up to 100.

He repeated the message in his mind, waiting after each thought transmission, praying for a reply. After an hour his head throbbed and he gave up and eased his speed back down as he approached a sign reading Slidell. He pulled into a truck stop to fill his tank, go to the bathroom, and purchase some aspirin for his headache. When he exited the restaurant, he drew up in surprise when he saw Glen Johnson's show rig parked at the diesel pumps, apparently on its way to a sponsor event somewhere in Louisiana. He vaguely recognized the driver, who was preoccupied with filling his tank, and hurried past with his head averted, in no mood to offer himself up to ridicule on the racing circuit if his personal situation became public knowledge. He reentered the Interstate with fatigue tugging at him and shook his head to relieve the tension.

"*Youngster?*" the thought popped into his mind.

"Yes, I'm here," he shouted, and then remembered to think.

"*Where are you?*"

"Have you heard from Leah?" he thought.

"*She is at a truck stop in a place called Slidell. They have stopped for fuel.*"

"Slidell! I just left there! I'm going back."

"*I must leave you now.*"

He found a reasonable spot, cut across the median of Interstate 10, and headed back to Slidell, where he cruised through the first truck stop he came to and made inquiries to ensure Leah and Old Blue were not in the two rigs parked there or the restaurant. He hurried back to the Interstate and the next stop, where he spent a half hour talking to several of the drivers in the ten rigs there without receiving any useful information concerning a beautiful lady and her dog riding in a truck. He rushed to a third truck stop and found five rigs there, but none of the drivers could help him. He then went back to the first two stops to recheck them, without luck. He took Interstate 10 West and raced along, checking all stops and rest areas that had eighteen-wheelers parked in them, without results. Even worse, he could not communicate with Aunt Bessie at all now to get additional leads and assumed she was resting since it was well past midnight. He was beyond mere fatigue himself and reluctantly pulled into a rest area, crawled into the backseat, and slept until 5 a.m. When he awoke, he drove to a truck stop, shaved, showered, changed clothes, and had a large breakfast, the first food he had eaten in nearly forty-eight hours. He drove back to Slidell focusing on Aunt Bessie, frantic to have a direction.

He stopped at the larger truck stop in Slidell, bought a map, drank a cup of coffee as he studied it, and realized Slidell was the logical place for her to turn north to get back to her old shack in the swamp. He arrived there a little before noon and knew as soon as he saw the place Leah was not there. He noticed someone, most likely kids, had vandalized the wood headstone on Hazel's grave with spray paint. He sat in the old rocker on the front porch to wait, and tried to communicate with Aunt Bessie, but received no return thoughts. As darkness settled around him chilling his soul, he went back to his car, crawled into the backseat, and slept fitfully, dreaming of Leah.

At dawn, he again searched around the old shack before giving up hope and backing down the narrow lane to the asphalt. On his way back to the Interstate, he tried to imagine where Leah and Old Blue could have gone, but could think of no place other than here or Aunt Bessie's. Despondent, he attempted to contact Aunt Bessie, to no avail.

Chapter Twenty-Nine

With no other known direction to search, Clint headed back to Charlotte to help his crew prepare for Friday's qualifying trials, driving at a more reasonable pace while trying throughout the fifteen-hour trip to contact Aunt Bessie. At Columbia, South Carolina, on an impulse, he turned to Charleston and pulled into Aunt Bessie's driveway just after sundown, where he found a multitude of people gathered. He paused before a group of black men sitting on the porch steps.

"I'm here to see Aunt Bessie."

"Aunt Bessie done passed on to the other side, Mister," the man replied. "They found her early Monday morning."

"What happen?" he asked with a sinking sensation. *Am I responsible for this? Did I push her too hard?*

The man shrugged. "Her poor ol' heart just give out. She be mighty old. Nobody knows for sure how long she be here on this earth. She be around as long as folks can remember."

That explains why I couldn't contact her. I'm the root cause of her death by keeping her up so late and working her so hard in my search for Leah. She repeatedly told me she was weak and tired, but I selfishly begged her to stay with me. "May I pay my respects to the family?"

The man shrugged. "Ain't but one great grandchild left that I knows of."

"She was very special to me … and the godmother to my fiancée," Clint said.

The man looked at him with new interest. "You that racing man that took up with her little god-daughter down there in Ne' O'rlan's, is you? Go on in tha' house there then, and ask for Dorothy. She got somethin' fer you."

Clint stepped up onto the porch and entered through the screen door to pause before a chalk Pentagram drawn on the rough wood floor encircling a simple pine box with a dozen women chanting in soft, hushed tones as they stared in reverence at the casket in the candlelight.

"Excuse me, I'm looking for Dorothy."

A woman with a black lace shawl over her head turned. "That'd be me. What you want?"

"I'm Clint Long, Leah's fiancé."

"You that racing man?" she demanded. "My great grandma Bessie left a message with me just before she passed on to the other side. She say to tell you she can't help you no more. She say you too far away, it take too much energy for her. She say give you this." She handed him his gold chain with the Tiger's Eye he had left on Aunt Bessie's table when he ran out to find Leah. "She say she think Leah is safe and she hope she try to contact you. Say for you not to block her with your talisman if she do. She say for you to keep trying to reach Leah on your own. Say to not give up. Say to believe in yourself."

"Thank you, Ma'am." He bent over Aunt Bessie's body and kissed her forehead. *I'm so sorry …*

"You best go now, racing man," Dorothy advised. "We got to put her down soon. You ain't no part of that."

"She was very special to me," he replied bitterly. "Did she say why she thought Leah was safe, or why she thought she might try to contact me?"

"She say what I done told you she say," Dorothy replied. "No more. Goodbye, racing man."

"Thank you, Ma'am."

After a respectful distance, he picked up speed filled with elation, hope, sorrow, guilt, and fear in a kaleidoscope of jumbled emotions. He reviewed Dorothy's message from Aunt Bessie in his tortured mind, sent as she lay dying. She had seemed timeless, and he deeply regretted hastening her departure by placing such a heavy burden on her. She had contacted Dorothy and directed her to return his mother's pendulant to him. Why? And she alerted him that Leah might attempt to contact him. How? She also thought Leah was safe. Where? What did it all mean? He drove mindlessly working her messages around in his head, and then focused on Leah in her shack by the swamp.

"Leah, can you hear me? I love you so much," he thought in desperation, willing the message back to Louisiana.

"*I love you too, Clint. I miss you so much I think I'm going to die*," flashed into his mind.

"Leah! Is that you?" he shouted in excitement, forgetting himself. "Leah, talk to me!"

No answering thought returned. He tried again, and then again, and again. Nothing came back to him. He was convinced it had not been his imagination, that he had been close, that she had heard him. If so, why didn't she answer him now? Did she not want to? He couldn't blame her if she didn't. Was he blocking her? He quickly dug the pendulant out of his pocket and tossed it in the glove compartment before valiantly trying to reach her all the way to Charlotte, to no avail.

He pulled into his shop at three in the morning and fell into his cot in utter exhaustion. As he drifted into sleep, a distant message played through his mind: "*I love you so, Clint.*"

"I love you too, Leah," he thought as he slipped into a deep, troubled sleep.

He awoke at noon with Walt prodding his shoulder.

"Sorry, Clint, I let you sleep as long as possible. We're loaded and we've got to roll within the hour. Grab a quick shower. I've got you some Bojangles chicken and biscuits you can eat on the way."

He stumbled into the shower, shaved, and dressed in a mindless haze, realizing the last twelve days had taken a heavy toll on him as he studied his haggard face in the mirror. He crawled into the back of the dually, ate in ravenous gulps as they pulled out of the shop for the fourteen-hour drive to Florida, and then dozed during the long journey, his mind filled with worry for Leah.

Chapter Thirty

Clint awoke when they pulled into the track the next morning and struggled through the four practice sessions trying to keep his thoughts on the car, but the two weeks of searching for Leah had taken its toll on him and he couldn't seem to maintain his focus.

After the last practice he pulled into the pits and his disgruntled crew stumbled out to put the qualifying setup on the car, none speaking to him as all knew he had not given his best effort. Mrs. Roberts glared at him as she walked past on her way to another location. He dipped his head in humiliation, realizing there were few secrets on racer's row and certain everyone on the circuit knew what had happened by now.

"Oh, Leah, where the hell are you?" he pleaded despondently. "I'm so worried. Please forgive me for being so stupid."

"*I need you so, Clint*," entered his mind, causing his heart to jump before he realized he was only imagining it, leaving him aching with longing and shocked by the sudden realization that even his racing career was secondary to finding her. *Why didn't I see that before I drove her away*?

"Leah, I beg your forgiveness," he thought as he watched the crew work feverishly on his car. "I am no good without you, to myself or anyone else. Please come home. I'm so very sorry for what I did to you."

"*You are so close I can't stand it,*" entered his mind. *"I can almost reach out and touch you, but I dare not. I would give anything to be in your arms right now, my love. I'm so sorry for making you unhappy.*"

"Oh, Leah, how can I make it right between us again?" he answered to the imagined thoughts rambling around in his head.

"Clint? Got a minute?"

He looked up sourly at Glen Johnson standing in front of him. "What's on your mind, Glen?"

Glen shifted cautiously. "I try not to get involved in anybody else's business, and I appreciate them staying out of mine. You and I've had our differences in the past, but I hope we've got them behind us now."

"Have you got a point, Glen?"

"My point is that I had nothing to do with this thing between you and your girl. I just wanted you to know that so it doesn't cause us any problems on the track. I didn't even know about it until today. That's all I wanted to say."

Now what the hell was that about? Clint wondered as Glen turned back to his rig several rows down.

When his team pushed his car out onto the qualifying grid and he strapped in, Jeff leaned down to peer at him through the window.

"I think we're close. It might want to drift a little going into three, but it'll stick everywhere else as far as I can tell."

"You and the crew have done your job, Jeff," Clint replied miserably. "I know I've let you down today because I can't seem to get it together. I take full responsibility for that."

"Well, you've had a hard couple of weeks and all," Jeff encouraged. "For now, just focus for two laps when you get out there. We don't need to bend this baby up or get you hurt in the process. We've got a long season in front of us."

"Thanks, Jeff. I'll give it my best shot."

Halfway through the qualifying, he snapped out of his mechanical state of mind and tuned in to boiling smoke and a resounding crash out of his vision in turn two. He keyed his mike. "Who bought the farm, Jeff?"

"The yellow sixteen. Wild Bill is alright though, he's climbing out."

"Damn. What happened?"

"He blew a right front going into one and looped it before slamming the wall backwards. The rear deck is all the way up to the back windshield."

"Some people never get a break," he replied, his sympathy going out to Wild Bill and his rag-tag team.

"He'll spring back," Jeff replied. "That boy don't have quit in his vocabulary."

Stabs of guilt flashed through him. Was Jeff implying *he* had quit? He gritted his teeth in shame and tried to erase Leah from his mind, steeling himself for his qualifying run.

Glen, in second place in the point's series three points behind Clint, was the next to last car out and set a new track qualifying record, sending his crew into wild jubilation when the time was posted on the board in flashing numbers. Clint watched with envy as they swarmed around him when he pulled down pit road, their previous conversation nagging at him as the official waved him onto the track for his qualifying run. He shook all thoughts out of his mind, fighting to focus, reminding himself he was leading the point's series and needed to run a good lap. His attention was shattered as he swooped into turn one when '*Good luck, my love*,' seeped into his consciousness. He was so startled he wobbled around the track like a lame duck and posted an embarrassing qualifying lap that put him in the thirty-second starting spot, good enough to make the field, but a long way from being a legitimate contender for a win.

He pulled down pit road in mortification as the crew hung their heads and avoided his eyes. When he climbed out they stoically set about preparing the car for tomorrow's race, trying to mask their bitter disappointment. Humiliated by his weak effort, he walked to Glen's pit to offer his hand in humble congratulations for posting a new track qualifying speed record.

"Hell of a run, Glen."

Glen shook his hand with a cautious grin. "Thanks, Clint. Sorry about your run. I know you'll make it up tomorrow."

"Yeah," he mumbled before turning back to his pit.

Wild Bill approached him. "Clint, I don't guess you have room for me on your crew, do you? I'm a good hand and I'll work for an occasional sandwich just to keep my finger in the pie and learn what I can while I'm getting myself put back together."

"You don't have a backup car, Bill?"

"Naw, I didn't even have this one paid for yet. I guess I'll be a pit rat until I can get back on my feet. Maybe somebody will offer me a ride here and there so I can keep the rust knocked off these old bones."

"Come on, let's go see Walt and find a place for you. Where are you currently living?"

"Awe, I been sleeping in my truck. But don't worry about me, I'll be fine."

"I'll fix you up a cot back at my shop with me. It's not the Hilton, but it's got a shower and a hot plate."

"I sure appreciate it, Clint. You're a good friend."

"We've all been through bad times. You'll be back in the seat before you know it."

"Much obliged, Clint. I'll earn my keep."

Clint motioned to Walt. "Bill here will be staying at our shop and working for us until he can find himself another ride."

Walt nodded. "We're shorthanded and can use you. Do you have any particular specialty?"

Wild Bill shrugged. "I can do about anything on a racecar you need done, but I can get more out of a tire than any man alive."

"I can believe that," Walt replied. "You've run on nothing but used tires since you got here. Welcome aboard."

Wild Bill shook hands with Walt. "Thanks, Mr. Jennings, I sure appreciate it."

Walt turned to Clint. "You need to get on out of here and get some rest. We've got a lot of ground to make up tomorrow and we need you at your best."

Clint hung his head. "Sorry, Walt, I feel pretty rotten about letting the crew down today."

Walt nodded. "We can overcome it. We'll be counting on you to be right in your head for us tomorrow. Get some rest and bring our real driver back here for the race."

"I'll do my best, Walt."

"If I was still a drinking man, I'd get you drunk tonight. I've learned there are no answers in the bottom of a bottle, but sometimes it can help you face your true feelings and get them out so you can deal with them. You're no good to yourself or us like this, and you've got a lot of people counting on you. You've got to find some way to get her out of your system."

"That's the biggest problem I have, Walt," he replied as he turned away. "I don't *want* to get her out of my system—and I know *exactly* what my true feelings are for the first time in my whole sorry-assed life!"

Chapter Thirty-One

Clint's stomach clutched as he lay back on his bed in the motel after trying to eat a meal that was unpalatable and shoving the plate away in disgust. He loathed the self-pity within him, but nothing seemed to matter anymore. He needed Leah to fill the void within him. *Somehow I've got to find her and make things right between us.*

He abruptly decided to put Wild Bill in as his substitute driver and take time off to search for her. Even as a rookie, Wild Bill had more talent than most of the hopefuls hanging around the pits, and Wild Bill could certainly concentrate more than he could at the moment. *I'll fall out of the point's series and right now I'm leading,* but *I don't care, Leah is more important than a championship will ever be.*

He resolved to announce to Walt and the crew first thing in the morning that Bill Moyer would be his alternate driver while he was away. With the decision made, he relaxed, freeing his mind to drift to Leah. *What if I never find her? I will find her!*

"Leah, I'm coming for you," he vowed, willing her to hear him.

"*Oh, Clint, I'm driving myself crazy thinking about you. Now I even think you're talking to me in my mind. I can't take this much longer*," came softly to his mind.

"I *am* talking to you, damn it!" he thought cautiously. "Can you hear me?"

"*I've got to stop this. I'm losing my mind*," drifted into his thoughts.

"Leah, are you really hearing me?" he thought intensely.

"*Oh, Clint., if only this was really happening!*"

He sat up slowly, his heart pounding, afraid to hope, afraid to even breathe. "Leah?"

"*Clint*?" came into his mind.

He fought to maintain his poise. "Leah, either I'm going mad or I can hear you."

"*Clint, I hear you too. But it can't be you. I'm longing for you so much I can't think straight anymore and now I'm pretending you're here in my mind*," he read in his thoughts.

His heart beat wildly as hope replaced disbelief. "This is real, Leah! Trust it," he insisted.

"*I couldn't read you before, so how could this be real?*" the thought drifted back to him.

Butterflies fluttered in his stomach. "My mother's lucky charm blocked you out before, remember? I took it off so I could communicate with you."

"*Oh, Clint, this can't be so*," drifted through his mind. "*I've got to stop torturing myself like this. It hurts so bad I can't stand it anymore*."

"Leah, don't go! Please! Give me a test. I'll prove it's really me," he thought in near panic, terrified she was tuning him out.

"*A test*?"

"I'm afraid to believe it myself, but I want it to be true so badly, I'm willing to make a fool of myself. Tell me where you are and I'll come to you right now," he pleaded in his mind.

"*Come to me*? *Where are you*?"

"In a Holiday Inn near the race track in Florida."

"*Look out your window and tell me what you see*," came back to him.

He hurried to the window. "A red truck, a white car, and a brown dumpster at the end of the parking lot. Why?"

"*I'm in the same motel as you. I'm looking out my window. I see the same car and truck and even the brown dumpster*," he read in his thoughts.

"Leah, I'm going outside. If you really are here, come out to me. That way we'll both know we're not going nuts." He hurried out to the middle of the parking lot on quaking legs and turned to face the motel.

"*Oh my goodness*! *It really is you*!" seared through his mind.

He started shaking all over. "Leah! Come to me!"

A door opened on the second floor near the end and Leah stepped out to look down at him as Old Blue barked in delight and brushed past her bounding for the stairs.

"Leah!" he shouted as Old Blue hit him on a dead run nearly knocking him over as he reared up and licked his face in delight, his tail wagging in delirious fury. Clint hugged the dog as he watched Leah edge down the stairs in disbelief staring at the two of them as if traumatized. He took a hesitant step towards her. "Leah? Am I just imagining it's you?"

"Clint, what's happening here?"

"I don't know." He hugged her to him, desperate to know she was not an illusion, and felt the empty cavity inside of him filling, confirming she was real.

She clung to him, burying her face in his chest, sobbing. "This can't be, can it?"

He blinked through his own tears. "Where did you come from? How did you get here?"

"I flew down with the Roberts this morning in their private plane."

"The Roberts?"

"One of their truck drivers drove me to their home in Shreveport."

His mind flashed back to the truck stop in Slidell when he had walked right by Glen's hauler. That was obviously what Glen was talking about at the track today—he had found out one of his men drove Leah to the Roberts' in Louisiana and wanted to assure him he had nothing to do with it.

From the room next to Leah's, Mrs. Roberts walked out to the railing to stare down at them, her composure benign. "I hope she has the courage to forgive you since she's nearly grieved herself to death. Frankly, I'm not sure you're worth it." She turned, reentered her room, and closed the door.

Tears trailed down Leah's cheeks as she stared up at him. "Mrs. Roberts made me come back, Clint. She said I had to get you out of my system or the stress would harm the baby."

He could barely answer around the constriction in his throat as he saw the vein pulsing at the base of her throat. "I'm so grateful—I've been so worried!"

"I saw Glen's trailer at a gas station after they made me leave our motel. I didn't know what else to do, so I asked the driver if he could help me contact Mrs. Roberts. I was hoping she could tell me what to do."

"I'm so glad you're safe," he gasped.

"I was so scared. Mrs. Roberts wanted to fly me to Shreveport, but I told her I just couldn't leave Old Blue. She had the driver put me up in a motel room and give me some food money. He was carrying a new show car up to them on Sunday for a company promotion they were doing, so he picked me up at the motel and took me to Shreveport." She hung her head in misery. "Clint, she said … the baby and I can live with them if you haven't come to your senses yet and … still don't want us …"

"I *do* want you! *And* the baby. I *love* you! Don't you understand that?"

"Aren't you mad at me for getting pregnant and ruining your life?"

"Leah, you didn't get yourself pregnant! *I* got you pregnant."

"That's not true, Clint. I meant to take your seed. But Mrs. Roberts said that wasn't the right thing to do because you hadn't agreed to it. She said a woman should never trap a man like that, and that it was wrong of me to do so. But I never intended to do you wrong. I never meant to trap you. Honest I didn't. I was just doing what Council asked of me. Do you believe me?"

"I don't know much about this Council thing, Leah, but I believe you. In any case, you didn't ruin my life—you're giving me a new life and a daughter! That's all that matters to me now. You've always given me more than any man could ever hope for. I've been so selfish and dumb I couldn't see it. Losing you made me understand that nothing is as important to me as you are, and nothing will *ever* be more important to me than you are."

"When I told Mrs. Roberts what had happened, she made me come back to talk to you. I was supposed to wait until after the race tomorrow so I didn't disrupt your concentration because you're the national point's leader now. I was so excited when she told me that. I was in her hauler watching you practice the whole day and could hardly stand not coming out to you."

"I don't care about being the point's leader." He squeezed her to his chest. "I wasn't even going to race tomorrow. If you had waited until after the race, I would have missed you."

"Not going to race? What do you mean?"

"I was putting Wild Bill in as my substitute so I could go back to Louisiana and look for you."

"Clint, that's crazy. You're the point's leader! Every race counts."

"Without you, I didn't have the heart to race. I don't have the heart to do anything. I didn't know they evicted you until later that night, but that's no excuse for what occurred. I'm so ashamed of myself for allowing that to happen to you."

"I thought you didn't want me and our baby."

"My mind was so screwed up I forgot to pay the rent. I wouldn't take your calls because I was being so pig headed about everything. Walt pulled me aside and made me see what a damned fool I was for leaving you in the first place."

"Oh, Clint, I thought I was going to die I was hurting so bad." She clung to him. "I couldn't bear the pain of being without you."

He dug in his pocket for her ring. “Leah, I want us to get married as soon as possible. Will you still have me after what I did to you?”

She searched his eyes, her own filling with hope as he took her hand and slipped the ring back on her finger. “I must be dreaming all of this, Clint. That’s all I’ve ever wanted. When I imagined I heard you in my head telling me you loved me and wanted me, I wanted it to be true more than anything else in the world.”

“I gave myself headaches trying to reach you. Aunt Bessie taught me how to do it.”

“Aunt Bessie?” she asked, her eyes widening.

“I searched everywhere for you. When I couldn’t find you, I went to her. She tried to help me. She kept seeing places you were passing and sending messages to me. I missed you at a truck stop in Louisiana, when I walked right by Glen’s hauler. But then Aunt Bessie died when I was so close to you and couldn’t help me anymore. I even went back to your old home in the swamp.”

Leah pulled back in shock. “Aunt Bessie has passed on to the other side? I’ve been trying to reach her too, ever since Mrs. Roberts insisted I come back to see you. I needed for her to tell me what to do for having unknowingly wronged you.”

“She died Sunday night after guiding me all the way to Louisiana. I pushed her too hard trying to find you, Leah. I’m responsible for her death.”

She hugged him. “Hush thinking like that, Clint. If she passed on to the other side trying to help you, it was because she wanted to do it for you.”

“She was trying to communicate with you … to tell you I was coming for you.”

"I got a strange message in my mind that night when I was asleep that said to open my mind to you, but I didn't trust it because my own mind was so messed up. I thought it was just what I wanted to believe. I didn't want to talk to her because I was so ashamed of how things turned out, so I went to Mrs. Roberts instead."

He pulled the rose heart from his pocket and handed it to her. "Thank you for leaving this with me. I saw you and our daughter in it. It was the most beautiful sight in the world."

She folded his fingers over the heart. "It's no longer mine. Once passed, it is bad karma to return it. It must remain yours until you pass it to another."

"Then it will remain mine forever, for I will never pass it to another," he vowed.

Old Blue stopped his impatient circling and reared up on them, his tail thrashing like a windmill as Leah laughed and hugged him to them. "He got sick on the plane coming back. He's missed you something awful and has been sulking the whole time we've been gone."

Clint slid the heart in his pocket and laughed as Old Blue licked his face in a frenzy of delight. "I never want either of you out of my sight again."

She hesitated. "Clint, there is one other thing that would make me happy. When I first met you, I thought if I acted normal I could live in your world and be with you for the rest of my life. But I found out I can never be normal. I can only pretend to be around others. If you could learn to accept me for who I am, maybe I wouldn't have to pretend with you anymore."

He hesitated. "What do you mean, Leah? What do you want me to do?"

"Just let me be myself around you. Let me practice my Craft, what we call the old religion. It's truly a wondrous thing. I miss my rituals so much."

"What is the old religion all about? I mean, what exactly do witches do?"

"We don't think of ourselves as witches, or Wiccans, as they're called today. We don't call ourselves by any name, really. We use the term Craft for our religion, and we use the natural flowing forces of nature coupled with the vast powers of the universe to help all living things."

"Then why does the whole world think you're something evil?"

"There is both good and bad in your world, Clint. As the once largest and most revered belief in the world, other religions denounced us because they were jealous and feared our power. They persecuted us in horrible ways to diminish our influence during the Burning Times. But we are still tolerant and accepting of all other religions, even though most abhor our own way of life. Our Rede does not allow us to harm anyone or anything, nor impose our influence over another. We are dedicated to the good of all mankind."

"That's a far cry from cutting up animals and blinding people when you look them in the eye. Okay, I promise to be tolerant of your beliefs in the future. Maybe someday I'll understand it all, but right now all I want is you."

She clung to him. "I'm afraid I'm going to wake up and none of this is going to be true."

"In time I'll prove it true, Leah—if Mrs. Roberts doesn't kill me first."

She laughed. “I don’t think she’ll kill you just yet. She said she thought you would come around with a little coaching, and that a woman always has to show a man what he really wants, and then give him a little time to figure it out on his own.”

“She’s a wise and true friend. And Leah, thanks for not turning me into a cat when I did you wrong.”

She smiled slyly. “You had your one pre-apology coming, remember? So be extra careful from now on because you won’t have that protection anymore.”

He pulled her to him. “Heck, I’ll be a cat if it means being with you. I’m nothing without you.”

Her eyes danced. “Do you want to take me to your room and do that making love thing to me now?”

“*With* you, Leah, not *to* you,” he corrected. “Yes, I’d like that very much.”

“Well, come on then …”

She grabbed his hand and led him to his room with Old Blue in eager tow.

Chapter Thirty-Two

Merle stood in his half stoop as the chants died out.

"As elder member of Council, I have called us to Circle to honor Aunt Bessie, who has passed on to the other side as we all eventually must, and to greet our new member of Council, her great grand daughter, Dorothy, who takes her chair. We honor Bessie's spirit and devoted service to Council and our Craft. May her life-force be enriched through her reunion with her loved ones on the other side, and may she enjoy a swift rebirth and timely return to our world."

They chanted in unison, lifting their voices in harmony in praise and well wishes for her long journey. A hush fell over the assembly when Merle lowered his arms.

"In view of our loss of Aunt Bessie, we have severed a vital link with Leah. I solicit your recommendations to this end."

Hellene stood. "I feel we must approach this one directly. To do otherwise would be a travesty."

Vaughn stood. "I advise caution on how we approach this one. I recommend we seek Leah's counsel on how best to approach this one in a manner that does not further dissociate him from our Craft."

Lily stood. "I agree we should approach Leah on this matter, and propose we dispatch Allay to her as our emissary."

Gretchen stood. "The most urgent matter before Council is bringing the just heir to the sacred chair. I agree that Allay should be sent to Leah to facilitate a meeting as soon as possible with Council."

Lola stood. "I feel to approach this one prematurely will be a mistake and alienate him further. Leah has advised us of this one's strong aversion to our Craft. We must patiently bide our time until he is ready to embrace us of his own free will. After waiting over five thousand years, another few months will not be of any significance, and would be preferable to losing him entirely if we force his decision prematurely."

Drew stood. "I agree with Gretchen. Council must make this one aware of his seed's inheritance whatever the consequences."

Shoshanna stood. "I too feel we should approach this one directly, but I think we should first approach Leah so that the presentation is made in the most favorable manner possible. As Lola points out, we already know he is vehemently opposed to our Craft, therefore I see a risk of pushing him further away if not presented in the most favorable manner possible."

Herschel stood. "I favor soliciting Leah's advice before we approach this one directly."

Allay stood. "I favor seeking guidance from Leah on how best to approach this one."

Ginger stood. "I feel that dispatching Allay to consult with Leah in the matter is essential."

Adrian stood. "I urge Allay be dispatched to consult with Leah beforehand."

Merle stood. "Council has spoken. Allay will be dispatched to consult with Leah. Let us give our thanks and good wishes to our Deity and each other in the name of our avowed unswerving love for all of nature and humankind. Let us enjoy our cakes and wine. And if it harm none, do as ye will."

Chapter Thirty-Three

Clint awoke with Leah snuggled next to him and pulled her closer, enjoying her warm softness.

His thoughts wandered to the last two weeks and the confusing revelations concerning his bewildering lineage, finding it all almost unbelievable—but the extrasensory communication with Aunt Bessie and Leah was definitely real. What did Aunt Bessie mean by him being genetically linked to their Council and Leah groomed to bear his child? What were the mysterious powers his daughter was supposed to possess?

Leah stirred and frowned with her eyes still closed. “I can’t sleep with all your thoughts whirling around in your head like a washing machine. What time is it?”

He kissed the top of her head as she snuggled into his chest. “It’s late. We need to get going or we’ll miss the race. Can you really read what I’m thinking?”

“Yes, but it’s all confusing. Your mind is going about a thousand miles an hour, and it’s all jumbled up. I’m going to make you sleep with that dumb old talisman on from now on.” She kissed him, slid out of bed, and headed for the shower.

He dressed, took Old Blue out for his morning walk, and picked up coffee and ham biscuits on the way back. While he showered and shaved, Leah rushed up to her room to dress and pack her clothes to relocate to his room.

They drove to the track, where his crew greeted Leah and Old Blue with relieved enthusiasm. Walt gave him a knowing wink, Jeff a nod of quiet satisfaction.

Wild Bill and two of his former crew members approached. "Clint, I don't want to impose on you, but I want you to meet Mike and Jessie. They're homeboys who have been with me since I started racing."

"Mike, Jessie, good to meet you."

"They've asked me to approach you on their behalf," Wild Bill continued. "If you will have them, they'll crew for you until we get our act back together. They know they won't get paid, but if they could sleep in our truck at your shop and you could throw a sandwich their way now and then, they'd be satisfied. You'd need to foot their pit passes and such, of course, but they'll sleep in the hauler at the races and you won't even have to spring for a room for them. It would mean an awful lot to me."

"Your guys are more than welcome to stay at my shop, if you'd like," he replied. "I'll get a couple more cots so you don't have to sleep in the truck, you can share in the purse with the rest of the crew, and I'll ensure you don't go hungry."

"We're mighty grateful, Mr. Long," Mike said, shaking hands. "You'll find us hard workers. We just want to hang on until Billy gets himself sorted out."

"Thank you, Mr. Long," Jessie said, shaking hands. "We just need a place to lay our head until we can get our team back on its feet. We'll earn our food and shelter, and you'll have no cause to find fault with us."

"I'm grateful to have you guys. Bill, take them to Walt and get them assigned a place on the team."

He attended the drivers' meeting and afterwards slipped over to Glen Johnson's hauler and knocked at the crew quarters. Mrs. Roberts opened the door and looked down at him.

"May I come in for a minute, Ma'am?"

She stood back as he stepped up inside the crew compartment, trying to hide his envy for the large, air-conditioned room occupying the front part of the hauler equipped with leather sofas built into three sides of the forward half forming a horseshoe with a small kitchenette and bathroom located at the rear. Three televisions built into the wall over the rich carpeting played as Mrs. Roberts crossed her arms and waited.

"I wanted to thank you for taking care of Leah for me, Ma'am. I was sick with worry. If you'll tell me how much I owe you for her new clothes and food and lodging, I'll repay you."

She sat down on one of the sofas and indicated for him to sit across from her. "That is of no consequence. We were glad to be of assistance to her. Our concern is her and the child."

"I plan to marry Leah at the earliest opportunity, and to provide for her and our baby as best I can. I'm not in the best of financial positions to be starting a family right now, but if I have to give up racing to provide a home for them, then that's what I'll do."

She visibly relaxed. "That's admirable. In spite of your … rough ways … I've always thought you a decent man. John and I have grown very fond of Leah in the short time we've known her. We've never had children of our own, which was always our greatest wish. We've come to think of Leah as we would a daughter. We talked last night after you two got back together. We would like to be godparents to your child. How do you feel about that?"

"I'm honored."

"We'll go to dinner tonight after the race and talk further. Now clear your mind and go out there and win today. And for goodness sakes, be careful."

He frowned. "To win, I've got to beat your team."

"Leah can pull for you. John can pull for Glen. I'll pray for both of you to have a safe race. Get going."

"Yes, Ma'am, and thank you again."

As he exited the hauler, Glen walked over to him warily. "Visiting, Clint?"

"Glen, I don't want you to feel uncomfortable about things with me and your sponsor. They think a lot of my fiancée. It ends there."

"I guess I don't have a lot of say in the matter …"

"Nor do I, Glen."

"Okay, then."

"Okay, then." He turned back to his pit.

The race evolved into a grueling event. Starting thirty-second in the field was bad enough, but his car was poorly prepared due to the bad practice sessions of the day before. From the first lap he struggled with the ill-handling machine and the poor track position, deftly avoiding the multiple wrecks occurring around him, taking what the track gave him, slowly working his way through the field.

At the halfway point he was running seventeenth and grateful for a pit stop to correct some of the handling problems. Wild Bill worked magic on the tire change, giving him a combination through air pressure adjustments and stagger that softened many of the rough handling short-comings of the ill prepared car. With fifteen laps to go, he was running tenth and ready for the race to end, having used up his tires getting there, and no longer a threat to win, barely hanging on to what he had with the eleventh place car worrying his rear bumper. Glen Johnson led most of the race and was in position for an easy win that would give him the point's lead in the series when lap traffic held him up and the second place car caught him. The two got into a bruising duel for the lead and tangled coming out of turn four with ten laps to go, resulting in both wrecking on the front straightaway and collecting the third, fourth and fifth place cars in the carnage, moving Clint into fifth position on the restart. He limped to the checkered flag in fourth place after a cut tire forced the third place car to pit with three laps remaining.

"Well done, Clint!" Jeff radioed as he drifted down the backstretch.

"We got lucky and backed into this one, Jeff," he radioed back, unwilling to celebrate the top five finish.

"Luck or not, we'll retain the point's lead, and even pick up some additional points over the twenty-six team. I calculate he's dropped back from his second place position to seventh place, which gives us a nice cushion."

When he pulled into the pits, his crew bounded around him filled with pride and relief.

"Wild Bill, that was a critical tire setup you gave me on the last pit stop," he praised as Wild Bill hung his head in embarrassment. "It enabled me to hang on at the end. Much appreciated."

"I'm just thankful we dodged a potential crippling race," Walt said.

Clint hung around for the obligatory interviews, praised his sponsors and crew, and gave credit for the luck he had encountered during the race to put him in the top five and then withstood the crush of fans and autograph seekers. Exhausted, he drove Leah back to the motel to shower and change in preparation for their dinner engagement with the Roberts.

"Why are we having dinner with them?" she asked as she dressed.

"They want to be godparents to our child."

She paused. "How do you feel about that?"

"I owe them for taking care of you for me. I'm fortunate they care so much about you."

She slid into his arms. "They've been very kind."

Chapter Thirty-Four

They were ushered to the Roberts' table, where Mrs. Roberts hugged Leah as Mr. Roberts shook Clint's hand.

"Great race today," he greeted warmly. "You hung in there and fought your way back. I admire your skill and patience."

Clint seated Leah and sat down across from him. "Thank you, Sir. There was a lot of luck involved. I put myself in a bad position to begin with on the qualifying run. Sorry about your team. I thought they had it won after setting a new track record and leading practically the whole race."

Mr. Roberts nodded. "I'm learning nothing is a given in this sport. Glen was especially disappointed."

"I can imagine. He's an excellent driver. He'll put you back up front."

Mr. Roberts grew solemn. "So you plan to marry Leah?"

"As soon as possible, Sir, if she doesn't come to her senses first. I'm powerfully embarrassed by what happened, but it made me realize just how much she and our baby mean to me."

Leah squeezed his hand. “I’m part of the blame as well. I should have been more honest with Clint in the matter of our child. He had a right to be upset with me.”

Mr. Roberts nodded in satisfaction. “Sometimes bad experiences have a way of making you aware of the blessings in life. Mary and I want to give you two a first-class wedding. If it’s agreeable to you, we’ll have it in Charlotte so your family and friends can attend.”

Clint frowned. “I don’t have any family, Mr. Roberts, and very few friends outside of my race team. Whatever Leah wants is fine with me.”

“I don’t want you to go to a lot of trouble,” Leah replied. “I don’t have any family either, and the only friends I have are our team and you and Mrs. Roberts. If you’re there it would be special enough for me.”

Mrs. Roberts placed her hand over Leah’s. “Surely your godmother will want to attend, won’t she, dear?”

Leah lowered her eyes. “I just found out she passed on to the other side a week ago, Ma’am.”

Mrs. Roberts patted her hand. “I’m so sorry to hear that, dear.”

Mr. Roberts looked thoughtful. “If I can’t give you a big wedding, I’ll give you a first class honeymoon. Where would you like to go, all expenses paid?”

Leah looked uncertain. “I don’t think we can go anywhere right now, can we, Clint? There’s so much for us to do.”

“It would be tough getting away right now,” he acknowledged. “I’ve neglected my responsibilities with my team for the last two weeks and it’s beginning to show up on the track. That’s not fair to them or my sponsors. I’ve got some serious catching up to do.”

Mrs. Roberts laughed. "You're making this difficult for us."

"I'm sorry, Ma'am," Leah apologized. "I'm so grateful for your kindness, but all I really want is a simple ceremony and to get our life back together. Clint's career is very important to our future and I don't want to do anything to distract him from that. If you come to our wedding that will be enough."

"I agree," Clint offered. "A simple ceremony and getting our life put back together is the most important thing right now. The first thing we've got to do is find a furnished apartment with room for a nursery."

Mr. Roberts pursed his lips. "Mary and I have discussed that and have a proposition to make. We purchased a three bedroom, two and a half bath condominium last year in Charlotte. We planned to spend time there when we visited our race team, but as things have worked out, we spend no time there and fly directly to the races from Shreveport. I'd like you to consider living there."

"That's very generous of you, but we probably couldn't afford the rent," Clint replied.

"Mary and I will fly you to Charlotte tomorrow to look at the place. If you like it, I'll cut you a deal and it'll be yours outright."

Leah's eyes lit up. "I've never had a real home of my own before."

Clint shook his head. "Sir, my income is so sporadic I probably couldn't qualify for a loan even if I could make the mortgage payments. But I appreciate the offer."

"Let's order dinner and I'll give you the details of my proposal," Mr. Roberts suggested. "I think you'll find it's something you can live with."

After placing their orders, Mrs. Roberts turned to Leah. "Child, as my wedding present, I want you to have all of the furnishings in the condo. I hand selected and decorated the place myself. I'm so excited about it becoming your new home!"

Clint shifted. "Mrs. Roberts, please understand, this is not something we can financially do at the moment."

Mr. Roberts leaned forward. "Clint, you are a rare and honest man. I greatly admire that about you. What I have in mind is for my firm to be a co-sponsor on your car. The condo would be part of the package."

"Co-sponsor?" he asked. "I don't understand. How would the condo be part of the package?"

"My advertising budget is shot this year. However, the condominium is appraised at $350,000. Mary has spent another $150,000 decorating and furnishing it. I will deed it over to you and Leah for a partial sponsorship on your car for the remainder of the year."

"Sir, that's … too generous. I couldn't possibly accept …"

Mr. Roberts waved his objections aside. "Nonsense, Clint, you're the point's leader. That pays big money and you know it. If you don't accept my deal, someone else will snap you up. I know I could probably get you for three or four hundred thousand, but I don't have that in my budget. It's a good deal for you and for me because it gives you and Leah a beautiful home and my company double exposure with two chances at winning the championship."

Clint sat for a minute, composing his answer. “Sir, my team is already seriously under-funded for the year and I don’t have a lot of room for error. I’m skimping on engines and tires, and have got a partial crew with part-timers and outright volunteers keeping me afloat. A couple of bad races would drop me from the top back into the middle of the pack, and I don’t have the resources to pull myself back up. What you’re proposing would benefit Leah and me personally, but would be of no help to you or me in winning the championship, and as such, would not be fair to you if bad luck comes my way.”

Mr. Roberts nodded. “Let’s keep this strictly on a business level and let the chips fall where they may in the future. The fact is, we need to sell the place, and you and Leah need a home. I need additional national exposure and don’t have the ready cash to purchase it. Two cars would give me that, especially with two quality drivers like you and Glen on the same team.”

“It still wouldn’t work, Sir,” Clint argued. “Keep in mind Glen and I are competitors and could be throwing punches at each other in the next race. I’m surprised we haven’t done so already. I’m sure Glen would never be agreeable to such an arrangement because it would be of no benefit to him.”

“Glen speaks highly of you and seems to genuinely respect you,” Mrs. Roberts argued.

“I agree, and you’ve indicated you respect him,” Mr. Roberts added. “Why wouldn’t it benefit both of you to be teammates?”

“Sir, I do respect Glen. But in our arena, friends can become enemies and enemies can become friends in the next race. Glen is one of the best there is and you've got an excellent team behind him, to include my old crew chief, which is still a sore point between us. My team is struggling along and has had a few lucky breaks to put us at the top of the series. Glen is going to have to knock me out of that position to do right by you and his team, as well as to ensure his own racing future. I'm not about to let him do that for the very same reasons. It's inevitable that one of us is going to lose that battle. By the nature of our sport, we're natural enemies. Even Leah being friends with you and us having dinner together makes him nervous because he's concerned I might be trying to undermine him and steal his sponsor. It's an unnecessary distraction to him that hurts your team."

Mr. Roberts sighed. "I understand what you're saying. I have a great appreciation for you drivers and the level of competitiveness you live under. But couldn't you and Glen become quasi-teammates? Couldn't there be some common ground between the two of you that would benefit the both of you? There are several two car teams out there, and more than a few who share sponsors."

"I couldn't honestly do that, Mr. Roberts," Clint replied. "I plan to win the championship, and to do that I've got to beat your team, which is my strongest challenge in reaching that goal. It wouldn't be fair to you or Glen if I ultimately did that with your help."

"I'll talk to Glen and reassure him there is no conflict between him and our friendship with you and Leah, or with my company's co-sponsorship of your team. The fact is, with you leading the series, it's a good investment for me. You two gladiators can do what you need to do out on the track to ensure your own success and I won't interfere. If you or Glen gets the short end, you can deal with it in your own way. I want the national exposure for my company and to double my chances of winning the championship. It's strictly a business decision on my part."

Mrs. Roberts looked at him sternly. "Clint, it's not business on my part, it's personal. You need to think about Leah and your child. If you won't do this for John, you need to do it for them. They need a home. I implore you to give this serious consideration."

Clint reached for Leah's hand. "How do you feel about this?"

"I would love for our baby to have a permanent home. You told me that you never approach another team's sponsor—that you had to wait for them to approach you. You said they only do that if you're a front runner." She squeezed his hand. "You're now a front runner and another team's sponsor is approaching you. This is what you've worked for and earned. I think you should accept their offer if it helps them get the national exposure they need for their business. They've been so good to me I'd do anything to help them. But I'll support whatever decision you make."

Mrs. Roberts smiled triumphantly. "She makes sense. We really need this for our company, and your wife and child need a home. Quit being such a stubborn jackass about it. We all benefit, just like John said."

Clint sighed. "You need to understand that I'm going to do what I have to do to win, and so will Glen. If we get crossways with each other, we'll handle it between ourselves. I hope if that happens you'll still be godparents to our daughter in spite of what you think of me afterwards."

Mrs. Roberts laughed. “Or your *son*?”

He squeezed Leah’s hand. “It’s our daughter, I’m certain of it.”

Mr. Roberts held out his hand. “Then we have a deal?”

“Yes, Sir … we have a deal …”

Chapter Thirty-Five

Clint and Leah flew to Charlotte with the Roberts in their private jet after dropping Old Blue off to travel back with the race team. A driver in a limo whisked them from the airport to the condominium complex, an exclusive gated community with sweeping green space around a large swimming pool, a grand clubhouse with fully equipped exercise room, tennis courts, and an adjoining golf course.

They entered into a small, arched enclave with a crystal chandelier, which opened into the main room with an even higher arched ceiling and thick gold carpeting. A big screen TV, dual VCRs and a stereo with surround sound built into an expensive wood cabinet occupied one wall, and a large marble fireplace adorned the other. Two brown leather sofas with matching easy chairs bordered by expensive end tables and a huge coffee table stood in the center with soft, indirect mood lighting along the walls. A tiled patio overlooking the golf course opened out on the far end with a built-in gas grill and plush patio furnishings.

The all-white kitchen contained built-in refrigerator and freezer, a walk-in pantry, and every conceivable modern appliance. A matching white dining table, chairs, and buffet festooned the adjoining dining room. A large laundry room off the kitchen contained a washer, a dryer, a folding table, and storage cabinets. A marbled half bath was situated at the bottom of the stairs leading to the second floor.

Upstairs, a large balcony with sturdy cast-iron patio furniture overlooked the swimming pool. The huge master bedroom had a large bath with gold fixtures, big mirrors over his and hers counters, an oversized bathtub with water jets, a large shower, and two walk-in closets. A luxurious comforter covered the king-size bed surrounded by matching wallpaper, plush carpet, and a love seat.

The other two bedrooms were tastefully decorated and shared a second big bathroom. Expensive paintings and appealing fixtures adorned the walls throughout, with beautiful figurines and vases holding flower arrangements spaced strategically about, giving a warm, natural freshness to the home.

Leah turned to Clint, struggling to speak as she hugged him. “It’s so beautiful!”

Mrs. Roberts beamed. “I took great pride in putting it together. It was a labor of love.”

Leah hugged Mrs. Roberts. “I’ve never seen anything so beautiful. How could you give it up?”

Mrs. Roberts patted her back soothingly. “It makes me so happy knowing you appreciate it. You and I’ll build a nursery in the bedroom next door. It’ll be so much fun to do together!”

Leah turned back to Clint, sobbing. “I just know I’m dreaming all this.”

"Let's let the girls get themselves together," Mr. Roberts suggested, leading Clint downstairs. "There's beer in the refrigerator."

"Mr. Roberts, I don't know how to express the gratitude I'm feeling right now. This is far beyond anything we ever dreamed of."

"It's a good business deal for us both, Clint. I've wanted to sell this place for over a year now, but Mary put so much of herself into it she couldn't bear to part with it. When I mentioned that I wished I had the funding to put a partial sponsorship on your car, she immediately suggested we do a trade."

"Leah and I will be forever grateful to the both of you. This is not something we could have afforded for years. I don't know how I can properly thank you."

"Win us a championship. Here's to a successful run this season." He clanked his bottle to Clint's.

"I'll do my best, Sir," Clint promised.

"Here are the keys. I'll have the deed and a contract drawn up and get my decals over to your shop in the next couple of days. Mary and I have to rush back to Shreveport, but we'll fly back on Wednesday to complete all the legal work. Thanks for allowing me to be a sponsor for your team, Clint."

"Thank *you*, Sir, and I especially appreciate you looking after Leah while I was being stupid."

Mr. Roberts laughed. "We guys are a little slow on the uptake sometimes, but I have no doubt you were meant for each other." He finished his beer and walked to the bottom of the stairs. "Mary, we need to be on our way now."

"Coming, John," Mrs. Roberts called down to him.

She and Leah came down together and Mrs. Roberts paused to hug Clint. “You take good care of this girl for me, or you’ll have me to answer to.”

“Yes, Ma’am. Thank you for all you’ve done.”

“Leah and I have decided you will be married on Wednesday when we return. Does that suit you?”

“Yes, Ma’am, the sooner the better.”

“I’ll make the arrangements. John and I will arrive around noon.” She turned to hug Leah, who was crying again, as Mr. Roberts shook hands with him.

Leah turned to him after waving the Roberts off in their limo. “I hope you’re not too disappointed in not getting money for the sponsorship. I know you need it real bad.”

“Taking care of you and our baby is the most important thing to me right now. Having a home for the two of you takes a big load off me. We’ll do the best we can on the budget we’ve got. If it wasn’t for you, none of this would be happening.”

“It’s just like you said, when you’re winning, everyone wants to have their name on your car. I love all of this, Clint, but I would give it back today and go live in my shack on the bayou if that’s what you wanted us to do. You’re all I really care about.”

“Having you for the rest of my life is enough for me. When the team gets back, we'll get my car, Old Blue, and get moved in properly.”

“While we’re waiting, let’s go get in that big tub and work our way slowly out to the bedroom ...”

* * *

The Roberts flew in Wednesday with their lawyer to complete the legal requirements. Later that evening,

Clint and Leah exchanged vows before a local priest on the deck near the pool. Both race teams attended in their race uniforms, with Leah attired in a stunning white lace wedding dress provided by Mrs. Roberts, and Clint in a rented tuxedo, forming a colorful group.

Clint dourly watched Glen's twenty-man team and his own ten-man team gleefully kiss Leah when the vows were completed. Afterwards they attended a catered reception in the clubhouse, where Mr. Roberts danced with Leah and Clint danced with Mrs. Roberts in front of a live band. He and Leah danced together next, and then Walt and Jeff led Leah out and the trio danced together as the rest of the crews and their wives and girlfriends joined them on the dance floor. Mr. Roberts beamed like a proud father throughout. Mrs. Roberts cried over Leah and fussed over the arrangements for the reception. As the evening wore on they worked their way through the tubs of beer, bottles of champagne, and tables of bountiful food with the crews in a full swinging celebration together. Standing off to the side, Clint watched Glen Johnson approach with his wife on his arm.

"Congratulations, you're a lucky man."

"That I am, Glen," he agreed.

"This is my wife, Sheila. Shelia, Clint Long."

Clint nodded. "Ma'am, glad to meet you."

"Glen speaks highly of you."

Glen looked him in the eye. "This has all happened so fast we haven't had a chance to lay out the ground rules. Let's plan on dinner Friday night after qualifying. The girls can get to know each other and you and I can try to iron out our differences."

"That's fine by me, Glen."

"In the interim, do I need to be looking for a new sponsor for next year?"

Clint held his stare. "I don't know what arrangements exist between you and Mr. Roberts, Glen, or what this season will bring. I do know that Mr. Roberts seems to think a lot of you, and as far as I know, he intends to stay with you. I have never tried to undermine you or steal his sponsorship from you. We met by accident and they took a fancy to Leah."

"Which one of us is to be the favored team now?"

"My deal was specifically that you and I are free to do our own thing. We can work together or not, and what we do on the race track is between us."

"Mr. Roberts pretty much said that to me, but he did indicate he would prefer we work together."

"My budget is not as strong as yours, and I would probably get more benefit out of it than you would, but I'm willing to try if you are."

"The way things are shaping up, Clint, it could very well come down to you and me fighting for the championship this year."

"It's still early in the season, and a lot of racing is left before we get there, but if it comes down to that, I'm going to do everything in my power to win it. I expect you to do the same."

"You can be a hard man to get to know, Clint, and I can't say that I've been particularly fond of you on occasion, but I do respect you as a driver. I know you think I did you wrong last year in Florida and that you still owe me one. How do we address that issue?"

"You know how this game works, Glen. I'm still not over you stealing my crew chief out from under me either. That was a low blow, as well as you stuffing me into the wall in Florida. Alliances are built on trust and mutual support. We've got a lot of fence mending to do before we become teammates."

Glen extended his hand. "We understand each other. Again, my congratulations on your beautiful bride."

Clint shook his hand. "Thank you, Glen."

Chapter Thirty-Six

Leah answered the doorbell Thursday afternoon eagerly assuming Clint had returned early from the race shop after the two teams had partied until the wee-hours of the morning.

She stared in surprise. "Allay?"

"I am here on behalf of Council."

She stepped back. "Please come in."

Allay looked around appreciatively. "This is a beautiful home. You are very fortunate."

"Clint traded a sponsorship on his race team for it and the furnishings were a wedding gift. We were married last evening. It's all a dream come true. Please, sit down. I'll get us some tea."

Leah returned and handed Allay her glass as she sat down on the sofa across from her. "Why has Council sent you to me, Allay?"

Allay set her tea on a crystal coaster on the coffee table. "Council has decided with Aunt Bessie's passing to approach Clint and inform him of your child's lineage. They want to seek your advice on how best to do so without inadvertently offending him."

Leah set her tea down. “Aunt Bessie informed him of this prior to her passing on to the other side. He is trying to become more tolerant of my beliefs, but I can’t say he actually believes in our Craft yet.”

“We were not aware of this, and of course do not wish to act imprudently, but protecting his seed you carry is of utmost importance to us.”

“Allay, we were married only last night. This is the most wonderful phase of my life. I don’t want to disrupt our harmony over the issue of him meeting with Council so soon. Surely you can understand this?”

Allay sipped her tea and placed it back on the coaster. “Council does not wish to disrupt the harmony of your marriage, Leah. I’m sorry to ask this of you in such a time of personal happiness, but based on Council directive, I have little choice.”

Leah sighed. “I will talk to him, and ask him to meet with Council, if that is your wish.”

“I hate to burden you, but Council is most anxious to resolve this matter. Thank you for understanding.” Allay stood. “You have Council’s best wishes on your life union with this one.”

When Clint came in that evening he noted with approval the candles on the table as Leah placed his plate before him. “This looks great.”

She sat across from him nervously. “I grilled the steak out on the patio.”

“I missed you today,” he said as he cut his steak. “The guys at the shop missed you, too. They think of you as part of the team now. I told them your first priority is motherhood.”

"I miss being there with them and being a part of the team, too. I'd like to still spend time with them until I get too big to get around, if that's okay with you?"

"My Firebird would be too much for you to handle, so I'll get you a car with an automatic transmission and teach you to drive so you can come and go as you please."

"Clint … there's something else I need to talk to you about. I hope it doesn't upset you. Council has approached me again about you meeting with them."

His eyes narrowed. "I'm not sure how I feel about that, to be honest."

"They asked how to best approach you."

He set his knife and fork aside. "Leah, I'm not ready for that yet. I still don't understand your world. Why is it so urgent they talk to me?"

"I have advised them to give you more time, but they are fearful of losing contact with our child. I don't like upsetting you, but I'm trapped between your wishes and their needs."

He patted her hand. "If it's that important to you, we'll talk more about it after the race on Saturday. If you'll tell me what to expect, I'll make a decision then, but no promises, okay?"

Relief settled through her. "Thank you for hearing me out like this."

"We'll work this out together somehow," he reassured her as he resumed working on his steak. "Mmm, this is good. What's for dessert?"

She grinned seductively. "Me.

Chapter Thirty-Seven

When Clint's hauler pulled into the pits and they rolled his car out on Friday, eyebrows raised and a great deal of whispered speculation followed with the yellow and brown colors of Sunrise Sausage now sharpened by the logos of Glen's primary sponsor, American Tractor, on both rear quarter panels and the rear deck. Cameramen began filming the crew at work for future commercials with the logos of Mr. Roberts' tractor company prominently sewn on Clint's and his crew's uniforms and painted on the sides of their hauler.

The media quickly besieged Clint and Glen about the implications of their shared sponsorship, with each deftly deflecting questions concerning the future of Glen's number twenty-six team, and to what extent the two teams would work together for the remainder of the season. Clint remained positive throughout, pleased that both his primary sponsor and his new co-sponsor were receiving a surplus of welcome publicity. With the assertion that he and Glen were not teammates, the press immediately sparked controversy with speculation that American Tractor intended to replace Sunrise Sausage for the next season on the thirteen team and drop the twenty-six team altogether, creating a great deal of distraction as they ran their cars through the practice laps and prepared for qualifying. When Clint qualified on the pole and Glen qualified outside pole, the controversy heated up.

Glen and Sheila joined Clint and Leah for dinner afterwards in a tense atmosphere with members of the media watching from a distance. Clint stood politely as Glen seated Sheila.

"Mrs. Long," Glen acknowledged courteously to Leah. "Good run today, Clint," he offered cordially as he seated himself across the table.

"Mrs. Johnson, glad you could join us," Clint greeted Sheila before settling back at the table. "Your run wasn't too shabby itself, Glen. Two-hundredths off my time, wasn't it? That's razor thin."

Glen shrugged. "Close, but no cigar."

"Is the media driving you as crazy as they are me?"

Glen looked over his shoulder in annoyance to where several reporters sat at the bar watching them intently. "Should we stand up and start slugging each other or something? They seem to expect it."

Sheila smiled. "Or hugging?" She leaned towards Leah. "I had a marvelous time at your wedding."

Leah smiled. "It was supposed to be a small affair, but it turned out to be a big bash. We really appreciate you and your crew coming and making it so much fun."

Glen stared at Clint. "So what are our ground rules, Clint?"

Clint met his eyes. "What do you want them to be, Glen?"

Shelia grimaced at Leah. "I suspect you and I are going to have to sort this out. Our two macho male beasts will never figure it out for themselves."

Leah nodded. "I'd like for us to be friends. We think the world of the Roberts and don't want to do anything that would upset our friendship with them."

Glen scowled. "When another team goes after your sponsor, it's hard to just grin and bear it."

Clint bristled. "It wasn't that way, Glen. I don't steal sponsors ... or crew chiefs, as may be the case."

Glen glared at him. "I know what you *said*, Clint, but apparently that's not the way it *is*."

"Are you calling me a liar?"

Sheila sighed. "What's done is done. Are we going to eat or are you two going to ruin our evening? I thought you were going to discuss working together, not fight about who did what to whom. It's a long season. Either you're going to be teammates or not." Silence surrounded them as they studied their menus and placed their orders.

Clint leaned forward earnestly. "Glen, I'm going to say this just one more time—I never made a move on your sponsor. I did not approach the Roberts in any capacity about a sponsorship on any level. You can believe that or not, but in either case, I'd just as soon not hear about it again. As for working together, we can do that, or we can continue to go our separate ways. It's your call."

Glen pursed his lips. "What about Florida and my crew chief?"

"Florida and *my* crew chief will need to be history if we work together, it would seem."

"And if we don't choose to work together?"

Clint shrugged. "Then it is what it is."

Glen hunched forward intently. "I leaned on you on that last lap, I'll admit that. But I never meant to put you in the wall. My tires were used up. I slipped. You have my word on that."

Clint looked at him, his manner bland. "Okay."

"You don't believe me, do you?"

Clint shrugged. "It was a sixty thousand dollar slip, Glen, and it busted three of my ribs and my ankle in addition to tearing up my best car. That hurt almost as bad as when you stole my crew chief in mid-season."

"The crew chief was business, Clint, not personal."

"You stealing my crew chief damned near ended my career, Glen, because it cost me my season and ultimately my primary sponsor. That felt pretty personal at the time."

The waiter appeared and placed their meal before them as they glared at each other and the girls sat in quiet discomfort. When the waiter departed, they ate in strained silence while the girls traded inane small talk together. When they finished their meal, each paid their separate check and stood to pull the girls' chairs out without a word.

Clint nodded. "Mrs. Johnson, a pleasure."

Glen met his eyes. "Mrs. Long, likewise."

Sheila hugged Leah. "Let's you and I be friends in spite of these two hardheads."

"I appreciate that, Sheila. I don't understand all of this, but I'd like for us to be friends. Good luck to you tomorrow, Glen," she offered, holding out her hand. Her expression changed to alarm when he took it. "Sit back down!"

"Leah?" Clint warned.

"Everyone please sit back down," Leah ordered. "We can't end things like this!"

Glen cleared his throat. "My apologies, but Sheila and I have to go now. It's a long day tomorrow."

"If you and Clint don't work this out tonight, something bad is going to happen," Leah pleaded. "Please stay and talk to each other."

"Sorry, maybe some other time." Glen steered Sheila to the door.

Clint escorted Leah out behind them. "What the hell was that about?"

"Clint, please don't race tomorrow. Please!"

He drew up. "What? Of course I'm going to race tomorrow. What the hell are you talking about?"

"I just saw Glen's car involved in a wreck with yours. Cars were spinning everywhere and people were screaming. *Please* don't race tomorrow. It's not worth you getting hurt."

He opened the car door for her. "I don't want to hear any more of this foolishness, Leah. I can't just decide not to race. I'm the national point's leader, for Christ sakes. You're being silly."

"Take off your talisman, Clint," she begged. "Let me read your aura. Please!"

"Stop it, Leah!"

"You have the ability to change the future if you know what it holds. Please let me help you!"

He started the engine. "I don't want to hear another word. Not one word!"

"Please, please, be careful tomorrow, Clint."

He wiped the tears off her cheeks with his thumbs and kissed her. "Don't worry. Glen and I know how far to push and when to back off. These things have a way of working themselves out."

Her lips trembled. "Men are so stubborn. I'm so scared."

* * *

The morning flew by as the controversy continued with Mr. Roberts' and Mr. Hutchinson's interviews with the media.

Sam Hutchinson approached Clint afterwards. "Do we have a problem, Clint? Have I been replaced before I even get a chance to negotiate on next season?"

"No, Sam, everything is fine between us. American Tractor is a co-sponsor for this year only. There have been no discussions for next year. If and when they do occur, I'll keep you fully informed."

"Clint, I want your word that you will make no decisions on sponsorship for next year until I've had my chance to bid. With you leading the point's series and all the attention you're receiving, our national sales are skyrocketing and far exceeding our expectations."

"You have a good product, Sam. I'm glad I'm in a position to help you get some recognition for it."

"As a show of good faith, I'll add another hundred thousand to your budget for this year."

"That's mighty generous, Sam, and it would definitely help, but you don't have to do that. I'm willing to stay with our original deal."

"I insist. I don't want to lose the momentum we've gained and I want you to know I'm a fair man."

"I've always thought that to be the case, Sam, and it's greatly appreciated."

"Do you really think we have a shot at winning the championship?"

"Our chances just improved dramatically with the extra cash, but it's still a long season. If I start tearing up cars and blowing motors, we'll be in trouble."

"I'll see you in victory lane. Good luck."

"Thanks, Sam."

Leah leaned through the window to kiss him. "Please be careful out there, Clint. Don't do anything foolish. It's not worth it to Shelia or me. You both come back safe to us."

"We'll be fine. Glen and I have raced each other enough to know when to push and when to lay back."

After the command to start engines, the pace car led them out. He and Glen warmed their tires and locked in their positions at the head of the pack, side by side. At the drop of the green flag they roared down the front stretch and fell into turn one door to door as the field chased them in howling thunder. They swept out of turn two side by side. Clint pulled Glen down the back stretch and elbowed him high going into three. Glen slipped and then pulled his nose down hard left in an attempt to fall into second place behind him before the third place car closed the gap. His left front fender clipped the right rear of Clint's fender, sending him spinning into turn four in a cloud of boiling smoke as the crowd surged to their feet.

Clint saw the hood of the third place car coming at him full throttle as the right side of his car impacted against the cement wall with a resounding crash. He braced himself for the impact coming at him at over one hundred and fifty miles an hour as the driver frantically locked his brakes with nowhere to go in the tumbling melee of cars spinning in all directions.

Chapter Thirty-Eight

He could not find a seam of light as he floated, weightless but knowing, as a soft female voice chanted in a soothing rhythm. He could not comprehend why she spoke them in an endless cadence as he drifted in a river of cold darkness, spinning and turning, going nowhere. He was tired and wanted to sleep, but the voice kept calling to him insistently from far away. He wished it would let him rest, but it continued incessantly, pulling and tugging at his consciousness. His opened eyes saw nothing, but he sensed himself slipping deeper into the dark pit entombing him. He saw flashes of light, mere sparks in his mind, as he tried to tune in to the voice, the words indistinct and repetitive. He wished she would go away, let him rest, and slid deeper beneath the velvet blackness trying to escape the chanting voice, his numb body growing heavier as he spun slowly in the cold clutching at him, diving ever deeper into the silent darkness, eager to embrace it, to find warmth.

The soft voice called relentlessly. Instinctively, he tried to fight through the layers of blackness, but became exhausted and slid backwards into silence. The alluring voice returned to tug at him in words without meaning. He tried to focus on the voice, somehow familiar but unrecognizable, so distant, so far away, as the words began to make sense in a vague way.

" … don't go to the other side … my love … our baby … please hear me, my love, please hear me…open your eyes … I love you … I need you to fight … don't give up, my love … we need you so …"

The clinging blackness tugged at him, determined to suck him back down into silence, but the voice calling to him softly refused to let him go. He became annoyed, wanted the voice to go away, wanted to rest, wanted oblivion.

A yellow light in the blackness became a huge bonfire as he drifted near. Twelve robed figures stood before the flames, their faces hidden by hoods. One, dressed in a pure white robe, slipped the hood back to reveal a beautiful, golden haired woman. She smiled and lifted her hand out to him. With her touch, a strong current surged through his body. She leaned forward to kiss his forehead with a tenderness he had never known as the others, clothed in robes of many different colors, knelt around them in a circle, chanting softly, hypnotically. His mind filled with words even though no sound came from her lips.

"*Your child is of our flesh, and the chosen one to lead Council. The time has come for you to go to them.*"

His thoughts responded. "But I know nothing of this Council and I am not sure I want my daughter to lead them."

She smiled as her thoughts formed in his mind. "*It is time you joined our world and do battle with the evil ones who defile and betray our Craft. I have infused you with knowledge. Search it out within you. Trust in yourself. Use your new understanding to allow your child to give your fellow man knowledge and insight to find their way, to seek the truth and use it to help the meek and spiritually famished. Your child has powers to harness the vast forces of the universe and bring peace and harmony to mankind, for they are in need of newfound wisdom.*"

He shrank from her fearfully. "What wisdom have you given me?"

She placed her lips on his hand. "*I gave you the wisdom of love to guide and serve you. Love is the driving force for all good things. Love softens all sorrows and rights all wrongs. Love is often difficult to obtain and maintain. Love is whimsical and sometimes born in pain, but when found, love brings ecstasy to the body and passion to the spirit. Love fills the heart with the greatest pleasure and soothes the most troubled of souls. Seek love and you shall never stray from the path of righteousness onto the path of immorality. Give love and you shall never want for it. Find love and all of your days are blessed and your dreams gloriously fulfilled. Go now. Travel where you must and allow your child to lead others to where they thirst to go.*"

The chanting in the circle around them grew louder and they rose up together as the woman leaned forward to kiss his forehead, her warm, soft lips filling him with peace, removing all self-doubt from his consciousness. The beautiful golden haired woman dressed in the flowing white robe released his hands and turned and walked into the fire as the others followed her into the flames with their chanting voices growing dim. The fire vanished, leaving him alone in the now excruciatingly cold darkness.

He heard a male voice and felt a stab of pain. "It does appear to be a brain spike, but it could be a glitch. It's highly unlikely …"

He floated again, but no longer serenely, now uncomfortably bathed in the cold darkness. The soft female voice interrupted the weightlessness smothering him, pulling at him, tugging him somewhere, but he could not discern where. He fought to obey its tempting call, eager to do as the voice commanded, impatient for the warmth it promised. He concentrated on the distant voice in the vast nothingness encasing him.

"… my love … come back to me … help him find his way, Aunt Bessie … find him and lead him home from the other side … love you so … love you so … love you so… love you … love … love … love …"

He sank lower into the dreadful silence again, attempting to resist its determined pull. The soothing voice gradually penetrated to him there and he was elated it had not gone away. He wanted it to pull him up, to stay with him, apprehensive it would leave him alone in the darkness. He was so tired, so heavy, but knew he must try to follow the voice. He fought the temptation to let go, to slip downward, to relax. It would be so easy to let go … but the voice urged him softly demanding his attention, demanding he come to it. But try as he might, the darkness only grew colder, heavier, making him more uncomfortable than before. As the voice faded away, the silence became overpowering. He longed for sound. He longed to hear the soothing voice, the rhythm of the chant she was uttering so softly, so very far away. When the faint voice came to him again, he knew he did not have the strength to follow. He no longer had the power to resist. He slowly spiraled downward into nothingness.

Out of the strangling darkness, an old black woman emerged with white, scraggly hair in a soft glow of blue light surrounding her in the velvet gloom. She stared at him with unseeing, cloudy eyes as she floated silently towards him. The glowing light around her washed over him, bathing him in welcoming warmth. He felt strength returning to his numb limbs and an eagerness seeping into his depleted soul. She held out her hand.

"… youngster … come now … you must follow me … come with me … to your Leah and your child, youngster … I will lead you back … follow me, youngster … come with me …"

The old woman drifted back from him, hesitated when he did not, could not, follow, and then moved to him again surrounding him in her warm, blue light.

"…youngster … follow me … you must trust me … I have come for you … Leah has sent me to lead you back to her … you must come with me … follow me, youngster …"

Her frail, hypnotic voice commanded him to obey. He fought the weightlessness, willed his body to propel itself after her as she floated away beckoning to him. He slid silently through the darkness, willing himself to move, fearful of her leaving him behind as she continued to coax him from her funnel of soft blue light as he drifted after her in the endless void.

"… stay with me, youngster … follow me … don't be afraid … come, youngster … Leah is waiting …"

He urged his body through the space separating them, following the old woman encased in blue light.

Beyond her, he saw a speck of white light. He focused on the white light, forcing himself to increase speed as he zoomed past the old woman towards the white light growing larger and larger. Unable to control his plunging speed, he grew dizzy and spun out of control.

Everything stopped abruptly. He stared at a blonde headed, blue-eyed woman holding his hand, chanting. She stopped in mid-sentence, her eyes widening.

"*Clint*!"

Who the hell was Clint? And who the hell was she?

Chapter Thirty-Nine

"*Who … are … you*?" he gasped in a raspy, coarse whisper around the obstruction in his mouth as the blonde woman hugged him in joy.

The woman collapsed onto his chest sobbing as he looked around in bewilderment. He was in a white room on a bed with white sheets. His head and chest were strapped with wires and there were tubes in his mouth and nose. He had an IV in his right arm and a white plaster cast on his left leg and left arm. His back, left side, leg, and head hurt. Why was this woman crying and hugging him?

He worked his lips to generate moisture, trying not to gag in the process. "Are you … Leah?"

"*Yes*, *oh*, *yes*! *Oh*, *Clint*!" She pulled away from him, laughing through her tears. "I was so scared."

"An old woman … made me follow her here. Where am I?"

"You're in a hospital, my love. You've been here for three weeks."

She placed her lips on his cheek, soft and warm against his cold skin as he blinked at the harsh light streaming through the window. “What happened? What’s wrong with my … arm and leg?”

“You were in a wreck. Your leg is fractured and your arm broken,” she answered as a loud beeping came from the machine with the wires leading to his head and chest.

“He’s awake, Mrs. Chambers!” she sobbed as a heavy set woman in a white uniform rushed into the room. “He’s awake and talking! I told you he would come back to me!”

The heavyset woman with red hair peered down at him apprehensively. “Can you hear me, Mr. Long?”

Mr. Long? “Yes,” he replied, puzzled as to why she would assume he couldn’t hear her.

Her mouth flew open and she rushed back out into the hall as he stared after her in confusion.

The Leah girl appeared back over him. “Oh, Clint! I’ve prayed so hard for you and invoked every spirit I could contact. The doctors said you would never regain consciousness. But I knew better. I knew you would come back. I sent Aunt Bessie to find you. I was so terrified I had lost you to the other side.”

“Is that … the old black woman … with white hair?”

“Don’t you remember her?”

“No.”

“Do you remember me?”

“No … the old woman said … she was leading me to someone … called Leah.”

“I’m Leah, my love. I’m your wife. We were married three days before you had your accident. I’m pregnant with our first child. Oh, I love you so much, Clint! I knew you would come back to me!”

"A beautiful lady … in a white gown … said I was to let our child … lead others …"

The woman in the white uniform rushed back into the room with two men in white jackets following close behind her. They moved around his bed and stared down at him in wonder as they elbowed the blonde woman called Leah aside.

The older of the two leaned down to him. "Can-you-understand-me?" he asked, pronouncing each word with distinction.

He frowned in agitation. "Of course."

The nurse exhaled. "It's a *miracle*!"

"It defies science!" the younger doctor agreed.

He grimaced. "I'm hungry. Can you … take these wires and tubes off… so I can change positions? My back hurts."

The older man straightened up. "Incredible! Mrs. Chambers, summon Doctor Hensley. I want him to witness this. I want a full range of diagnostics run and an immediate CAT scan and complete series of blood tests. I want to document this event in every aspect."

He frowned. "Can I … have something … to eat first?"

"No, no, young man. You've been in a coma for weeks now and fed intravenously. You'll need some time before you can handle solid foods."

"But I'm hungry," he argued as two other women in white uniforms paused in awe to stare at him from the doorway. "Can you … crank this bed up or something? My back aches."

"You're lucky to be alive, young man," the older doctor replied as the nurse cranked up his bed to relieve the strain on his back.

"I won't be for much longer … if somebody doesn't … feed me."

Everyone laughed and the Leah girl brushed through them to hug him again, still crying. "He doesn't remember me," she said tenderly.

The older doctor pushed her aside and opened Clint's eyes with his thumb and forefinger to shine a light in them. "It's not unusual to experience memory loss, both short term and permanent, after being in a coma. We won't know how much brain damage he has incurred until we run extensive tests. The mere fact that he has regained consciousness is hard to explain. But he seems to have an unimpaired vocabulary, which is an excellent sign. It's just *amazing*! Mrs. Chambers, get this room cleared and get those tests started immediately."

Leah lingered at the door. "I'll call the Roberts, and Mr. Hutchinson, and Glen and Sheila. They've all been so worried about you. Jeff and Walt and Wild Bill have been here every day." She turned to one of the men in the white coats. "When can he have visitors?"

"Tomorrow or the next day, perhaps," the older doctor snapped without looking at her.

Clint spent the rest of the day undergoing endless neurological tests from a variety of specialists, with each treating him as an oddity. Leah was allowed to visit him that night and he went to sleep with her holding his hand. Late the next day somebody called the Roberts came in first, and then a Mr. Hutchinson, and finally three men called Walt, Jeff, and Wild Bill, but he recognized none of them. The next day he awoke to find Leah sitting beside his bed and a faint memory found its way into his mind.

"I remember you now. We got married by a pool of blue water and you wore a white lace dress. You were beautiful. We've got an ugly old black dog. I can't remember his name."

Tears of joy slid down her cheeks. "His name is Old Blue, and he loves you as much as I do."

"Do we live in a shack near a swimming hole? I remember you naked on a rock in the moonlight. I thought you were a goddess."

"That was my old home on the bayou in Louisiana. We live in a beautiful home here in Charlotte, North Carolina, now. The Roberts gave it to us for a sponsorship on your racecar just before your wreck."

"My racecar?"

A flood of memories began to slip back into his mind, and he suddenly remembered who Walt, Jeff, and Wild Bill were, and then recalled Mr. and Mrs. Roberts, but still couldn't place Mr. Hutchinson or recognize the names of Glen and Sheila.

When he awoke the next morning he had total memory recall, to include the brief image of the third place car coming at his window as he hit the wall. He had no memory of anything after that other than the troubling images in the darkness around the bonfire with the golden haired woman in the white robe before waking up in the hospital after following the old black woman and chasing after the white light.

He learned the doctors declared him brain dead and that Leah refused to allow them to turn off his life support, and that everyone had grieved for her as she sat by his bed day and night chanting softly and pleading with him. And he learned the doctors had no explanation as to how he had made such a miraculous recovery.

But he knew the reason.

Chapter Forty

When Clint was released from the hospital five days later, Leah wheeled him into their condo in a wheelchair as he looked around, having forgotten how luxurious it was. That afternoon Mr. and Mrs. Roberts flew in from Shreveport to visit him as he sat with his leg and arm propped up in their casts.

Mr. Roberts seated himself on the sofa in front of him while Mrs. Roberts and Leah went into the kitchen together. "It's good to see you out of the hospital, Clint. There for awhile we didn't think you were going to make it."

"Sorry to give everyone such a scare. Fortunately, I slept through it."

"The important thing is to get you healthy again."

"Mr. Roberts, I obviously can't fulfill my race obligations now. They tell me I may never drive a racecar again. It all depends on how much of my motor skills I've lost, which they can't predict for several more months. Based on that, I'm prepared to reverse our deal and return this place to you."

"Are you trying to fire me as your team's co-sponsor, Clint? We have a contract, remember?"

"Yes, Sir, but I can't fulfill my part of the deal. Legally, you have the right to void the contract, and it's the right thing to do under the circumstances."

"Apparently you didn't read the fine print. Your being unable to drive wasn't part of the deal. The deal was for you to run my logo on your car for the rest of the season. The last time I looked, my logo was still there."

"But my car is not on the track, Mr. Roberts, and hasn't been for three races now. I'd have to get a substitute driver to fill in for me, which means no chance of winning the championship for you now."

"I didn't realize you didn't know. Walt took charge of the team while you were in the hospital and put Wild Bill Moyer in as the driver. He's finished in fifth place, third place, and came in second last week. With all the media coverage about your horrible accident and miraculous recovery, and Wild Bill replacing you as the temporary driver, coupled with the impressive results he has achieved in the three races he has run, we've received more exposure than if we had *won* the championship. Currently he is in tenth place in points and Glen is in first place. I couldn't be happier on that end. I've already got more than my money's worth of publicity. My only regret is that you're not out there with us enjoying the show. Our deal stands, unless you want me to sue your pants off."

"I didn't know any of that, Mr. Roberts, but I'm relieved to hear it. I always knew Wild Bill had a lot of potential as a driver. I'm glad Walt stepped in and kept the team going for me. It eases my mind considerably."

"You've surrounded yourself with good people, Clint. That's the first mark of a good businessman. I respect you for that. For the rest of this year, since you can't drive, I have a proposition for you. I've spoken with Sam Hutchinson over at Sunrise Sausage and he's in agreement if you will agree. We want to combine our two teams into one two-car team, and we want you to run the whole show. We'll give you total control over budget and personnel."

Clint sat in surprise. "How … will Glen Johnson feel about that, Mr. Roberts?"

Mr. Roberts pulled a video cassette from his briefcase and handed it to him. "Watch this. It's the wreck where you were injured. Then meet with Glen and talk to him about it yourself. I'll have him stop by later this evening. I'll expect your answer by the end of the week. Now if you'll excuse me, Mary and I've got to get back to Shreveport. Good to have you home."

"I don't know what to say, Mr. Roberts."

"Say you're going to give me my championship, Clint, with Wild Bill and your team, or with Glen and his team. That'll make my day."

Leah saw them out and came back to sit in front of him. "Mrs. Roberts told me what Mr. Roberts was offering you. How do you feel about it?"

He sighed. "I'd rather be driving, but since I can't do that right now, I'd like to keep my finger in things by running a team, or in this case, two teams. A lot will depend on how Glen feels about it. Why didn't you tell me Walt was running my team with Wild Bill as the driver, especially with them doing such a good job?"

She smiled. "Walt's real nervous about you being upset with him about him taking charge. He wanted to tell you himself in case you wanted to fire him over it. I insisted he wait until I got you home."

He spent the afternoon watching the video of his wreck and napping. In late afternoon the doorbell rang and Leah escorted Glen and Sheila in to him. Leah seated Glen on the couch in front of him before escorting Sheila into the kitchen for refreshments.

"Glen, good to see you. I understand you're in the point's lead now. Congratulations."

"You're looking good. I wanted to come by and apologize to you personally. I wanted to tell you it was not intentional on my part. You hung me out and I thought I had room to dive in behind you. I made a bad mistake. I needed you to know that."

Clint smiled. "Mr. Roberts brought me a video of the wreck. I've played it a number of times. You didn't do anything I wouldn't have done. It wouldn't have been so bad if we hadn't been bunched up on the start like that. I counted twelve cars wrecked after the smoke cleared. I got pinned to the wall by the third place car. That's the breaks. By the way, congratulations on your win afterwards."

"It's the hardest race I've ever run after watching them cut you out of your car and put you in the helicopter on a stretcher. I'm so sorry for the way it happened, Clint. I feel personally responsible."

"Put it behind you, Glen. Concentrate on winning the championship now, since I can't. Next to me, you're the best driver out there."

Glen grinned. "It would've been an interesting season racing you for the trophy. I'm going to miss contending against you. You always brought out the best competitive fires in me. When are you going to be able to race again?"

"It looks like I'll be laid up a few months before the doctors will know for sure. It will depend on my reflexes and such after I've healed. I understand Walt's got Wild Bill running my car for me, and from what I hear, he's doing a pretty good job."

Glen laughed. "He gives me almost as much trouble on the track as you did. What do you think of Mr. Roberts' offer to combine the two teams?"

"What do you think of it, Glen?"

"I'd rather have you on my side than against me. I think we would be a tough combination to beat. I'd like for you to give it serious consideration. You're smart and you're tough. With a great driver like me around to make you look good, we could win us a championship or two and maybe move right on up to the Cup."

Clint held out his hand. "I agree, Glen. Let's do it!"

After Glen and Shelia left, Clint again napped, and was awakened by Leah leading Walt, Jeff, and Wild Bill in together.

"Clint," Walt nodded as they sat in a row on the sofa before him. "I understand you already know I've been running the team with Wild Bill as the temporary driver. I was just trying to keep the team together and not lose our sponsors until you got back."

"Walt, you're fired. And Jeff, Wild Bill, you both are fired as well," Clint replied coldly. The three of them hung their heads. "Now that I've got that out of the way, do you want to apply for positions in a new team I'm putting together as part of a two car package? One team is complete, but I need a team manager, a crew chief, a driver, and a full crew for the second team."

They looked at each other and then back to him. "What are you saying, Clint?" Walt asked.

"I'm going to combine my team and sponsors with the twenty-six team and their sponsors and become the general manager of both teams. I'd like you to manage and run team two, Walt. Jeff, I'd like you to become the crew chief of the thirteen car in team two. Wild Bill, I need a driver on a permanent basis. Just for the record, I plan to move up to the Cup within two years with one of those teams. Do you boys want to tag along with me and have some fun along the way?"

For a stunned moment the three of them sat with their mouths open, and then jumped up and started cheering as they shook hands and slapped each other on the back. Leah came in carrying a tray of refreshments and watched them with quiet joy.

Later the entire race team came over and wheeled Clint out to the pool. Walt dispatched one of the crew members to buy beer, and they sat around visiting with him until Leah ran them off late that evening so he could get some rest. Leah helped him into bed that night and settled in beside him.

He drew her into his arms and held her close. "There's some things I need to iron out and some deep thinking I need to do while I'm recuperating, Leah."

Tears glistened in her eyes. "I love you so much, Clint. I hope you do win the championship with your new team if that's what you really want."

He grinned. "Right now, I'm going to be a little selfish and take time to enjoy what I've already won. Getting my brain scrambled made me realize I've spent my whole life searching for you. Winning your heart is, and will always be, my greatest triumph. I want to savor that victory for a while." He pulled her close and kissed her. "After I've heal up a bit, it's time for me to get to know your world, and there are a dozen or so people somewhere I need to meet with to discuss their intentions concerning my daughter. Do you think you can help arrange that?"

"*Oh, yes, Clint*! *Oh*, yes! *Yes*! *Yes*!"